Prince

of the

Fallen Kingdom

Prince

of the

Fallen Kingdom

By

C. A. Doehrmann

(Arc Legends of Ellunon: Book 2)

Published by C. A. Doehrmann
Print Edition

ISBN: 979-8-8324-3173-4

www.arclegends.com

Chapter 1

The swordsman looked so much like Kyen of Avanna that when Adeya saw him she stopped. She peered across the street, catching only glimpses through the passing crowd.

He leaned against the corner of a brick house with his arms crossed over a burnished breastplate. Tall, black-haired, and armed with a longsword, everything about his bearing echoed Kyen. His eyes—the gray eyes of Avanna but as dark as twilight—surveyed the thronged street and found Adeya staring. They narrowed.

"Kyen—" she reached out— "Kyen, look!" Her hand groped empty air. Looking over she found the spot beside her vacant.

Thunder rumbled. The first patter of drops fell from the dark clouds wheeling overhead. The crowd hastened its pace and began to disperse, clearing around another swordsman ambling further down the street. The real Kyen of Avanna—a man also with black hair and gray eyes but gangling in figure—hadn't noticed the absence of his traveling companion. He walked with his head bowed, his unfocused eyes on the road, oblivious to the rain that was sending others running for shelter.

Adeya huffed when she spotted him. Flinging her golden ponytail over her shoulder, she trotted after him.

"Kyen!"

He didn't respond when she arrived at his side.

"Kyen? ...Kyen!" She grabbed his arm.

"Hm? What?" He looked at her, blinking.

"Look!" She pointed up the street.

The corner stood empty; the townspeople passed it by, all of them hooded and cloaked against the oncoming storm.

"Look at what?" he asked.

"I saw a swordsman. He looked just like you. Like..." Her voice trailed off for a moment. "Like he was from Avanna."

"So?"

"What do you mean 'so'? What if he's from Avanna!"

"Why do you sound surprised?"

"But—but, aren't you the last?" she said. "When Avanna fell..."

"Did you think I was the only survivor of Avanna?" He smiled a little.

"But he carried a sword!"

"Everyone of Avanna carries a blade, Adeya." He rubbed the back of his neck.

She pursed her lips. "I think he might have been staring at you."

"I would have stared at him, too, if I'd seen him." His smile faded. "It's not everyday I meet with my own people."

Thunder rumbled again, loud enough to tremble the

ground. Wind rushed in over the red-tiled roofs, whistled between the chimneys, and whipped at their cloaks. The last stragglers in the street cleared away, hunkering down and leaving the two standing alone in the quickening rain.

"Let's get under cover." Kyen pulled up his hood and hitched the pack up his shoulder. As he set off down the street, Adeya hung back to give one last look at the empty corner. The cobblestones began to darken as a gray curtain of rain descended. Throwing up her hood, she hurried away.

While the two made for the shelter of an inn, a shape moved on the roof above where the swordsman had been standing. A bird, blacker than the night, emerged from a shadow cast by a chimney. Its long, swan-like neck curled as it watched Kyen and Adeya run underneath the inn's porch. Without beak, eyes, or feathery crest, the bird's neck ended on an empty nub—empty but for a mouth crowded with pointed teeth. A hideous grin split the nub-head from end to end as the rain began pounding down in force. The bird sank back into the shadows as Kyen and Adeya shook water off their cloaks and looked out from beneath the porch.

"You won't be giving me my swordsmanship lesson tonight, I'm guessing?" Adeya, fingering the longsword strapped to her hip, looked to Kyen. He was staring out at the rain, frowning. When his silence stretched on, she spoke up again, "Kyen?"

His frown vanished as he looked at her. "Sorry. What?"

She leaned in to whisper. "Was *he* talking to you again?"

"It's—it's nothing." He edged away from her, coloring and shifting beneath his cloak.

"What was he saying?"

"Nothing. I'm hungry. Let's find something to eat." Turning on his heel, he entered the inn. Adeya huffed a sigh and followed him.

Inside, the square tables—all empty but two at the afternoon's early hour—crowded the room. A brick hearth stood cold on one wall. Savory smells wafted from an open door at the other. The rain streamed down behind them when they walked in, hiding the world beyond the doorway in a haze. An aproned man with a patchy beard approached.

"Welcome," he said. "Will you be staying?"

"Two for tonight, if you will. And a meal." Kyen pushed back his hood.

"It's three coin."

Both Adeya and Kyen looked at each other.

"I don't have any coin," he said.

"Oh… I forgot my purse back at Isea Palace," she said. "But, no matter…" She drew herself up, folded her hands on her skirts, and addressed the innkeeper. "I am Adeya, Princess and Sole Heiress to the Throne of Isea. You may send all expenses to my parents, the King and Queen of Isea."

The innkeeper stared for a moment then threw back his head and laughed. "I'm sure you are, dearie, but I don't run tabs. Coin before food and bed, that's my policy. Even for King Veleda himself."

Adeya glared and opened her mouth, but the innkeeper

spoke first.

"I'm not above bartering, dearie, if you've other valuables. Such a necklace fetches a high price up north." He eyed the aquamarine pendant at her neck. "Pass me that, and I'll give you room, board, and then some for your journey onward."

Her hand leapt to the pendant. "My summoner's amulet? How dare you! My nana gave me this! I'd never —"

"Could we barter a service for room and board instead?" Kyen cut in.

The innkeeper rubbed a bare patch on his chin until his fingers found a whisker to pluck at. "Well…my cook's short a scullery maid. Keep up on evening dishes, and you can help yourself to leftovers and kip the night in a bed, if there's one spare."

"I—don't—wash—dishes!" Adeya swelled.

"Pardon us a moment." Kyen grabbed her elbow and, after a few tugs, pulled her aside.

She made little "Ah!"s of indignation in her throat and cast a black look at the innkeeper. Kyen opened his mouth to speak, but she ran him over with a furious undertone.

"How dare he! How can he be so rude? Doesn't he know who I am? My parents are going to hear of this."

Kyen waved her down with both hands until she stood, huffing and glaring at him, but silent.

"Adeya, most innkeepers wouldn't offer half so much."

"Why don't you have—" She stopped and leaned forward to whisper. "Have *him* make us some? Just enough coin for tonight."

He shook his head.

"Why not? I know arcangels can," she said. "Creation is one of their three powers. Will you at least ask him?"

Kyen looked up at the ceiling as if for help then, with a sigh, he returned his attention to Adeya. "You should've remembered to pack your purse."

"But—"

"He said it, not me!" Kyen held up his hands. "Besides, he can't. Well, he can, but he won't. He can only do so much on his own power. He prefers to save himself for when he's needed. Fiends could find us at any time, remember?"

"He'd just let us sleep outside? In the rain?"

"It wouldn't be the first time," he said. "A little damp doesn't hurt."

"Damp and cold! We could get sick!"

"Dishes here for a bed and a meal. Or a stable loft elsewhere—maybe. And if not that, then…" He cast a look out the window at the pouring rain. She followed his gaze and slumped.

"I'm in favor of a bed and a meal," he said. "But what do you want to do?"

"Oh, very well." Adeya sighed. "But I don't know how to wash dishes."

Chapter 2

Kyen and Adeya stood together in the steamy kitchen. Behind them, the cook and her two maids shouted and clattered around pots bubbling over a long hearth. Before them, a table supported stacks of batter-crusted bowls, greasy kettles, and food-smeared ladles that nearly buried a couple empty tubs. One of the maids added a tottering pile of plates to the collection.

"I've never washed a dish in my life," said Adeya.

"I usually lick my plates clean."

"You what?"

"What?" He shrank under her look. "Water's for drinking in the wilds, not washing."

"Well, they'd better give us water here. I'm not licking all these. Ah!" A smile melted away Adeya's disgust as the cook approached carrying a steaming kettle. She shuffled them both aside to dump hot water into the tubs.

"You'd better hurry up. We need them dishes!" She pointed at a couple pails beneath the table before hurrying back to the hearth.

The two exchanged glances. Kyen picked up one of the pails; fine gray powder filled it to the brim. "What's this, do you think?"

"It looks like ash. What's this one? Sand?" She peered into the second pail. "Where's the soap? The sponges?"

Kyen looked bemused.

"Why are you looking at me like that?"

"You are a princess, through and through."

"And I will figure out how to wash dishes. Don't you dare think I can't!" She snatched the pail of ashes from him and stuck her nose in the air.

He smiled and winced away, putting his hands up as if in surrender, and edged around her to the tub. They plunged in: he washed, scrubbing with sand and rubbing ash for the grease. She dried and stacked plates, cutlery, and kettles on the counter beside them. The maids visited to leave dirty plates and to carry away what they'd cleaned.

Adeya, wiping perspiration from her forehead, grimaced at the sweat on the back of her hand. "I sure hope we get a bath out of this."

Kyen dabbled his hands in the water as he waited for the next dirty stack to arrive.

Lightning flashed through the windows followed by a loud bang of thunder that shook the walls.

Adeya jumped, clutching the amulet at her neck. As the rumble faded, she stared wide-eyed out the window. "Goodness! How is it so loud? We don't have lightning like this in Isea." She looked at him; he was trying to grab a bubble in the water between two fingers and failing.

"It—it can't hurt people, can it?" she asked.

"Only if it strikes you, but you'd be more likely run over by a wagon. Well, unless..." His face fell.

"Unless what?"

"He could…" Kyen shrugged a little, glanced at the cook and maids. "You know."

Adeya dropped her voice to a whisper. "Arcangels can use lightning?"

He nodded.

She watched a flicker through the window with wide eyes. Thunder rumbled in its wake. "Did he…?"

"No." Kyen smiled a little. A maid dropped off a pile of pots, and he sunk the first into the dishwater with a sigh.

Adeya watched him scrub, looking thoughtful. Her stare grew intense, and she edged up next Kyen. "So, when are you going to tell me?"

"Tell you what?" He leaned away from her, frowning as color rose to his cheeks.

"Nana said you'd tell me. About what she wrote in her letter, remember?" She sidled closer to him, dropping her voice to a whisper as she watched the maids hang up their aprons and leave. "All the arcangels vanished on the Feast of Restoration. Nobody has seen or heard of an arcangel in years. Until him. With you."

"Your grandmother wrote about me?"

"Look, see." She dried off her hands, pulled a paper from her pocket, unfolded it and held it out to him. Kyen, up to his elbows in greasy dishwater, leaned in to read. She waited while his eyes scanned through the lines. His eyebrows drew together.

"'Thin?' 'Battered?' 'Half-crazed?'" he repeated. "She says I'm half-crazed! Are you sure this is me?"

"Look, there's your name. Right there." She prodded

the bottom of the page. "Kyen of Avanna. Don't tell me you don't remember meeting my nana?"

"I don't know. Maybe? It was years ago."

"My nana said you know what happened to the other arcangels. When are you going to tell me? She said you would!" Adeya stuffed the letter away and put her hands on her hips.

"Not so loud!" he whispered. "You're not even supposed to know about him. After his big display with the Kingmaster, every fiend from here to Nalayni is going to be on my tail—like marauders after a peasant on a midnight road. We need to get somewhere safe, lose ourselves for a while."

"Where do you plan to do that?"

"I don't know. Maybe Eope. Prince Hepilaeus is good at hiding things."

"Well, you might be intent on hiding, but I'm here to find the other arcangels. They're hunting you, not me, after all," she said. "Tell me what happened!"

"Sh!"

They both fell silent as the cook deposited the last dirty pots. Kyen eyed her until she walked away.

"This isn't the best place to talk about this," he said, dunking a kettle into the rinse water.

"All you ever do is put me off, Kyen. Every summoner who left to search for the arcangels has disappeared, and I want to know why." Adeya grabbed the kettle from him and wiped it with such force, her towel squeaked against the metal. "My nana said in her letter that you know—that 'he has the answers!'"

"It's really… I don't know what words to even use…" He sighed as he laid hold of the next encrusted pot. "He thinks it best to show you."

"He—*He* wants to show me?" she repeated. "How?"

"'Words are too slow. I've not the patience for them,' he says." Kyen smiled but then turned his serious, stormy gray eyes on Adeya. "He will, if it's alright with you?"

"Really? You mean it this time?" She handed him the towel. "What do I need to do?"

"Nothing." He wiped his hands and held up his palm. "But, uh, you're sure?"

Adeya grabbed his hand and stared him in the face. "I'm ready!"

"No, no, not that." Kyen tugged his hand free. He wiped it on his tunic, looking uncomfortable, then after a moment of seeming to steel himself, he raised his palm to her forehead. "Here."

Adeya clasped the amulet at her neck, waiting.

He cast one cautious glance at the cook, the last one in the kitchen besides them; she stood at the far end, untying her apron. He pressed his palm against Adeya's forehead.

Her eyes widened. With a gasp, she clasped both hands over her mouth.

Chapter 3

A cosmos of light and darkness flowed through Kade.

Six fluxes of aura—like rivers bright, deep, and tingling with energy—splayed out in different directions and divided his world. They flowed from the Nadir, a blazing orb at the heart of Ellunon; it emanated a relentless stream of power that filled the universe, coursing out as the fluxes, flowing to the edges of existence, and dissipating. Each flux spread a fan of smaller tributaries, many feeding into little orbs or fading into a whirl of eddies tinged with pinks, yellows, or periwinkle blues. From Kade's vantage point, it seemed a vast net, studded with stars, breathing with color, light, and potential.

He hung afar and above the Sixth Flux, clear of the strong currents and most of the eddies. A pinkish one washed over him. It made him itch to plunge into it, to do something, anything. As the eddy drifted away, the itch faded. It left behind a thinness, and Kade shuddered in it.

In the distance across the Fifth Flux (mortals considered it Varkest), a gloom marred the cosmos. It swirled slowly, a dark maelstrom amidst the stars and rivers. The flux nearest to it, the Fourth, bent off its course to drift into the maelstrom's eye where it was sucked down. Its aura vanished from Kade's awareness as the maelstrom absorbed it, draining the light, pulling in the eddies.

Those nearest Kade shuddered again.

A little ping of light flared below, and he grabbed the distraction gladly. It carried the call of a summoner. As he caught it up, the mortal's thoughts burst into him: blood, hot water, a dim bedroom; a mother with a heavy belly screaming in bed; a midwife mopping her brow; the tight eyes of a scar-faced man and the little boy hiding behind his knees. The scenes tugged at him, but he resisted.

He'd help soon.

Stretching out his senses, he searched. Surely, they must be coming? He felt the pull of the gloom at the edge of his consciousness, but he tugged his attention away and focused on mortals instead.

Creatures so feeble, so… separated. Kade wondered at the Great Keeper—what could he have been thinking when designing them? They could not see for any great distance at all and felt even less. Small wonder Kade and his brethren had been sent to look after them. Mortals needed the help. Especially against such an enemy.

The pull of the distant gloom crept into his mind again, ever rotating, ever drinking. Even from so far, he could sense its subtle draw in the eddies around him.

The summoner's call flared below again. Kade snatched it. He let the thoughts slide through him: the mother laying pale and weak on the pillow; the midwife looking to him helplessly. The desperation wrapped in the summoner's call tugged at him harder.

A ripple spread out through the energies around him. Childbirth—speaking of the strange and incomprehensible! Why didn't the Great Keeper create enough mortals from the beginning? Why do they need to procreate? Why did they die so young? So easily? Not for the first time, Kade settled in himself: how glad to be an Arkian and not a mortal!

Kade let the summoner's call fade into the eddies.

What was keeping them?

A handful of sparks swirled up from the Nadir as if in response to his thoughts. As he saw them, he felt the jolt: "We come!"

The sparks cut through the eddies and plunged through the rivers before soaring up to join him. Maer the Gentle; Lode the Steady; Liel the Eager; Miel the Mighty; Fael the Quiet: their greetings all buzzed through him as they neared.

"Kade the Questioner."

"Always thinking."

"What's he thinking of now?"

"You've called us, and we've answered."

"Share with us your thoughts."

If his summoner were near, he'd be demanding Kade to painstakingly parse out who said what. Why did it matter so much? Such boundaries were a hindrance. All Arkians heard, all often spoke, together as one. Individual thoughts blended into a collage of images and ideas. Kade, not for the first time, wondered if his summoner thought him incomprehensible, just like he found mortals incomprehensible.

"You did not call us here to contemplate mortals,

Kade."

"Speak to us."

"You said it was a matter of great concern."

"We cannot spare long from our duties.

"You are troubled."

He answered them, the thoughts of the other Arkians whirling in between his own:

"Sair the Young no longer answers. I am concerned for him—"

"He is too young for such a charge."

"It was not wise to put him over the Fourth Flux."

"—he has been too long near the Consuming Dark, I fear. I sought him out. He will not let me draw close nor find him out—"

"The Consuming Dark's hold is too strong."

"—I am concerned he is taken—"

"We should bring this before the Great Council."

This last thought echoed from several of his brethren at once, even as he himself thought it. Everyone's mind quieted to a soft hum; none of the thoughts or ideas Kade heeded as they digested this information together. Fael the Quiet, who'd not yet struck out strongly, filled the space.

"I saw Sair the Young. He was coming as I joined the others at the Nadir. Perhaps he is already repenting as we are here now speaking of him?"

Kade doubted this. Sair had out-stripped him when he'd given him pursuit; but he couldn't hide the flickers of his thoughts. Dark weavings. Unsteady conversations with shadows. A breaking. And strongest of all—pulsing through Sair—the Consuming Darkness' hatred for the Arkians.

Hatred and hungry shadows closing their grip.

A wave of ripples cascaded through the others as they caught the flow of his thinking. Liel the Eager and Miel the Mighty shot away as one, speeding back for the Nadir, winged by their united thoughts of haste and care. They carved through the cosmos, eddies curling in their wake.

Below, another summoner's flare materialized: the birthing mother dying; please; soon. The visage rattled him, but he shook it off.

Before his aura settled, the thud of a distant impact trembled through them all and drew their attention to the Nadir. A huge pulse exploded out of the glowing orb. It roiled out as a giant shock wave, spreading like a ripple in the universe, the fluxes bucking and twisting, the eddies disappearing into seething whorls. Shock drew Kade tight together with Maer, Lode, and Fael. They watched Miel the Eager and Liel the Mighty near the shock wave. Neither arcangel balked, but fixing their course for the Nadir, the two dove into the shock wave head-on. They vanished for a moment into the brightness of its power. When they reappeared out the other side, both plunged into a spiral and dissolved from Kade's awareness.

His aura shuddered with Maer and Lode, but Fael the Quiet darted away. The sharp tingle of her concern radiated against Maer's shiver of warning in her wake.

The tidal wave of power bore down on them, spreading and roaring as it neared, until it filled all their awareness with blazing energy. Kade hunkered together with the other two. They braced each other as the wave struck.

A vicious mind burst through Kade's consciousness. With a jolt, his body of aura responded and began working without his bidding. He struggled against it, but he couldn't regain control. He felt the invading willpower surge through Maer and Lode beside him, locking them together, forcing them down. The three of them plummeted.

Kade wrestled against his rebelling aura, bending all of his willpower toward it, but his fall accelerated. The harder he tried, the more of his body burned away. The efforts of Maer and Lode beside him fizzled against the strength of the mind. He felt it working his aura, weaving through unfamiliar patterns, burning through him hot and fast.

Alarm flashed first from Maer, then inside himself.

Whoever's mind had a hold of them could drain them to death.

Lode gathered Maer and Kade to himself.

The world around them dimmed as they hurtled down. The cosmos began fading into shadows that were rising up on every side. The darkness was swallowing them.

Lode shared a thought with Maer; they both exploded into action before Kade could cry back.

They angled what little aura they could still grip towards Kade. Their desperate purpose swept him along—"Guide it, don't fight it!"

Kade sensed them weakening. The darkness smothered him, yawning up overhead. His senses grew numb. He was falling away from Maer and Lode.

Maer winked out.

The fading light swirled far overhead, the darkness closing over it faster and faster.

With a flash, Lode vanished. Kade caught his dying intent and threw every last ounce of himself behind it. Block it! Block the darkness! Block it! Block! He launched the last of his aura at the shrinking circle of light.

The darkness slammed in complete around him.

Kade reeled.

Emptiness and stillness filled everything.

Trembling, he re-gathered what he could find of himself. His body was his own again, the little left of it.

Kade reached out and met—

Nothing.

He grasped for Maer, for Lode. His reach floundered through the void. Their minds had vanished.

Grief turned him cold inside. He could feel nothing but himself, his own form and aura shivering.

Everything else was gone. Is this what it's like for mortals?

Oh, how he hated it.

He'd never felt such cold.

He'd failed. Had the Consuming Shadow won? Was Ellunon destroyed by the surge from the Nadir?

He'd never known an Arkian to die from cold. But if it could kill him, he felt he might be dying of it now.

The shivers refused to stop.

Then, the tiniest speck of warmth touched him, made him itch. Whirling around, he launched himself towards it. He searched where the last of the light had disappeared and found—the shadow hadn't swallowed it all.

The tiniest pinprick punctured his dark surroundings. A little eddy of light—a bare trickle—flowed through the hole.

Kade drank it in. He tried to press himself through, but he stuck fast.

Shimmying up close though he could feel—abnormal sensations. As if echoing from a great distance, they carried faint and difficult to make out. Only the strongest he caught when he focused hard.

Another mind. A young one—so young.

He called out and reached to touch it, but it did not answer him. The mind's thoughts drifted over him from a distance.

Death.

Stinging eyes.

A keening wail, frail, gasping.

A heavy hand in his hair.

Relentless sobs raw in his throat.

Mama's gone.

Kade shuddered away. It couldn't be. He knew something of mortals secondhand through his summoner. He knew of things like eyes, wails, hands, tears, and hair. But he'd never—he'd never—*felt them.*

A mortal's mind. He'd become trapped inside a mortal's mind.

Kade tried to quell a rise of alarm before he lost his grip on himself. Body-sharing, much less mind-linking, was absolutely forbidden. Trapped though, isolated, he couldn't do anything about it. Not yet. Whatever had trapped him hadn't completed its work.

He, Maer, and Lode had wedged the collapsing darkness. Through that wedge came the mere trickle of aura, but enough to sustain, enough to strengthen, given time. He may yet gain the strength to open the wedge further. Maybe escape. Though how long that could take, Kade trembled to guess.

Pressing himself to the hole, Kade reached out again. He stretched towards the mortal's mind. The grief that poured over made him flutter, but he steeled himself. He searched. If he could discover the name of this mortal, it may come in helpful; especially if he could break out enough to share his thoughts.

Sifting and riding the waves of grief, Kade tried to find it. What was the mortal called? He could sense something (Is this what mortals call sound?) coming to him over and over again. Speaking? Hearing? Is this it? This must be it. He could feel the mortal's mind—just a boy!—associating itself with this sound. It must be the mortal's name. Kade tried to make it out.

Kyen.

They called him Kyen.

Chapter 4

Kyen lifted his palm from Adeya's hair.

The cook hung her apron on a peg. The door creaked open and clacked shut behind her as she left the kitchen.

"Oh…" Adeya stared with unfocused eyes, looking pale. She grabbed out at Kyen as her knees unhinged. He caught her by the elbows and helped her to a chair.

"I'm sorry," he said. "Maybe I should have warned you. It's a little jarring."

Adeya sat down, gripping his arm with a shaking hand. "I've never… That was incredible!" She looked up at him. "Kade was trapped…in you?"

He nodded.

"Did you know?"

"Not until years later," he said. "Kade started breaking out. I thought I was going crazy at first."

"Then the others? Maer, Lode, and Fael?"

His face fell. "Kade says it's hard to know. Whatever befell the arcangels never finished its work on Kade because of Maer and Lode. He has no hope that either of them survived. We've looked for Fael and the others."

"Is he free now? Kade?" she asked. "Or is he..."

"He broke out completely just before the fall of Avanna."

"Yet he's still with you? After all this time?"

"Mortal bodies somehow mask him, particularly against fiends. He asked for my help. To hide him while we searched for the other arcangels. I agreed."

"And that's all you know?"

He nodded.

"Finding the other arcangels is going to be harder than I expected." She rubbed her forehead where Kyen's palm had lain.

Both of them fell silent until a growl from Kyen's stomach interrupted.

"Do you think we can eat yet?" He looked at the last couple of dirty pots.

"We'd better finish, I suppose." She rose with a sigh.

Lightning flashed through the window, and thunder cracked. Adeya jumped in fright onto Kyen's arm, staring wide-eyed out the window.

"It can't hurt you in here." He laughed a little and, wiggling out of her grip, draped the damp towel on her head. "Come on. We're almost done, and I'm starving!"

* * *

At one of the common room tables, Kyen perched on the edge of his seat while Adeya examined her pruney fingers. Patrons lingered over mugs of ale, their conversation a low mumble in the stuffy atmosphere. The innkeeper, watched eagerly by Kyen, carried a platter to their table. On it sat two heels of bread and a tureen of cold peas porridge lumpy with burnt scrapings from the pan. Kyen pulled the platter over as the innkeeper walked away.

"I'm so hungry." He sliced one of the heels in two and spooned on porridge.

Adeya laid her hands in her lap with a sigh. "When I'm home, I will summon the scullery maids to my chamber every night to thank them personally. I never knew eating created such a mess!"

Kyen balanced his second slice of bread atop the first. He held up the peas porridge sandwich to admire it. She shook her head at him and pulled the platter over. As she spooned porridge into a bowl, the door to the outside opened, catching her eye. Her spoon halted mid-scoop.

The swordsman who looked like Kyen had entered the common room. Dripping and leaving wet boot prints behind, he approached the innkeeper and spoke, his low tones indistinguishable through the murmur of the room's conversation.

"Kyen. It's him."

"Him who?" Kyen, about to take a bite of his sandwich, followed her gaze. When he saw the other swordsman, his eyes grew wide. The color drained from his face, and he wilted in his seat. "Oh no."

"What is it?" She whispered, watching the innkeeper lead the swordsman to table a span away from them. "That's the man I told you about in the street—" She looked over; Kyen's chair was empty, his sandwich abandoned. "Kyen? Where—what are you—?"

"Sh!" He said from where he crouched beneath the table.

"What are you doing?"

"Don't give me away!"

Adeya straightened. She pretended to stir the tureen.

"I'm going to retire. Excuse me." His whisper floated up. He crawled away, slinking from under one empty table to another. Darting out, he hid behind a couple patrons headed towards the stairs, walking with them until they stopped to give him irritated looks. Then, he dashed the last stretch to vanish up the steps.

Adeya, glancing to see him gone, shook her head at the tureen. She swirled the porridge around and fixed her attention on her bowl, watching the swordsman from the corner of her eye.

He took off his sopping cloak, hung it on an empty chair, and settled down to his table. When a servant girl placed a tankard in front of him, he thanked her without warmth. He took a deep drink. Resting a hand on the pommel of his sword, he looked around the common room but offered no conversation to any of the nearby patrons.

Letting him be, Adeya finished her meal by herself and without incident. She tied up Kyen's untouched sandwich in a napkin for him. As she rose, she stole one last glance at the swordsman. She tensed.

His dark gaze watched her, a gaze callous, calculating. She locked eyes with him for a long moment. Shaking herself, she whirled away and hurried towards the stairs. She collided with the innkeeper at the bottom in her haste.

"Oh! I'm so sorry!"

"Where be you off to?"

"Will you show me where I can sleep?"

"Aye that, follow me." He led her up upstairs.

The swordsman's eyes followed her out of the room. He set down his tankard and rose to leave.

Chapter 5

"Here you are." The innkeeper opened the door, then moved back to let Adeya enter. She took one step in and stopped.

Six enormous beds flanked the walls of the room. A fire crackled in its hearth on the far wall, casting deep shadows in flickering orange. A half dozen men, all in various states of undress, some even down to their smallclothes, stood about the room. Several already snored underneath sheets, two or three to a bed. The two nearest, both unshaven and dark, eyed her.

"You can't be—" Adeya turned, but the door clicked shut in her face. She swallowed and looked back at the room while her hand crept up to her amulet.

The two men nodded to her.

She pointedly ignored them as her eyes searched the room. In a dim corner, next to the only empty bed, Kyen sat on the floor underneath one of the windows. She hurried over to him.

"Kyen!"

He lifted his face to her.

"Where's our room?"

"Room?"

"I thought the innkeeper said we'd get a room for washing the dishes!"

He looked confused.

"I always get my own room when I travel. My own bed."

Kyen's confusion grew into wonder.

"You've not actually slept like this, have you?" Adeya lowered her voice. "Slept in the same bed as—as strangers! They don't even look like they've washed."

"You've never been to the north, have you?" He smiled a little.

With a huff, she plopped down on the bed and held out the napkin-tied sandwich. "Here."

His face lit up. "Thank you!" He unfolded it and stuffed it into his face.

While he ate, Adeya took off her longsword, her healer's pouch, and her cloak to pile them on the bed. She began unlatching her linen armor vest, but her fingers slowed to a stop halfway. Her eyes lingered on Kyen, still in his own vest, cloak, and sword. She stroked the aquamarine amulet at her neck and watched him finish his sandwich in silence. The low voices in the room quieted as more of the travelers took to sleep.

As Kyen neared the crust, she said, "We're not staying, are we?"

He paused mid-bite.

"That swordsman. Who is he?" she asked

"He didn't see me, did he?"

"I don't know. But he saw me. He saw me in the street,

too. He's the one I asked you about."

Kyen lowered his sandwich, staring off into space.

"So who is he?" she repeated.

"Ennyen, son of Madiryen, of the House of Dearthart," he replied. When his silence stretched long, Adeya frowned.

"And?" she said. "Why did you run when you saw him?"

"He nearly killed me once. If he sees me, he'll probably try to kill me again."

"But he's from Avanna."

"Exactly." He stuffed the last bite in his mouth.

"I don't understand."

Kyen rubbed the back of his neck while he chewed and swallowed, then said, "Eh, how do I explain? You're not of Avanna. It's—It's like this." He edged forward. "In Isea, if two people have a disagreement, they sit down and talk, right?"

"Or have my father, the king, judge the matter."

"In Avanna, the two would talk with their swords instead." He fell grim. "The one still alive is the one who's right."

"Whatever did you and Ennyen fight about?"

"I did about the worst thing anyone could do to a swordsman of Avanna," said Kyen. "Short of crippling him."

Adeya's eyes grew wide.

"I refused to kill him after I defeated him."

"How is that bad?" she cried. "Did he want to die?"

"I shamed him in front of all our people," he said. "And that with the worst of shames, returning alive from a lost battle."

Adeya stroked her necklace in thought.

"Killing me now would restore both his victory and his honor," he said.

"Even though Avanna is gone?"

"I'm of Avanna, and I don't really understand it, either." Kyen laughed and winced at the same time. He dusted crumbs from his pants, stood, and shouldered their pack.

"I'd rather not risk staying here because he might see me. It'd be an ugly fight." Kyen opened the window. "If I refuse to kill him again, the shame would probably drive him to kill himself."

"But the rain."

"Look, it's just about stopped." He put his hand outside; his palm caught a drip or two.

"After all those dishes? And it's still damp. And we're two floors up. Are you really going to climb down?"

He put a foot on the window sill. "I'd trade a damp night of sleep for a man's life any day."

"Well, I'm taking the stairs, at least." Adeya tossed her hair over her shoulder. "I didn't want to sleep in a room full of grubby strangers anyway. I'll meet you on the ground." She latched her vest back up, collected her sword, cloak and pouch.

Kyen clambered out the window, clinging to the frame. A two-story drop into a narrow alley waited below him. The rough wall—stone slabs and mortar—offered few grips or handholds, but he still lowered himself down, moving with care from one handhold to the next. Drips from the eaves splatted on his head and arms as he descended.

Silent lightning flickered through clouds hanging heavy overhead. He leapt the last stretch and landed hard on all fours in the alley. A few empty stable stalls blocked the end, so Kyen, lifting his hood against the drops, hurried towards the street.

As he did, Ennyen stepped around the corner.

Chapter 6

Kyen froze, riveted in place by Ennyen's glare as he blocked the exit.

Neither swordsman moved as they faced each other: Ennyen, built of taut muscle and sinew, put a hand on his hilt; Kyen, looking scrawny and underfed in comparison, shifted one foot back. Lightning flashed overhead. It gleamed off of Ennyen's burnished breastplate and illuminated all the patches on Kyen's linen armor vest.

"Kyen, son of Odyen, of the House of Crossblade," he said. "So you did survive."

"Ennyen. Ennyen, wait!" Kyen backed deeper into the alley.

Stepping forward, Ennyen drew his blade—a longsword—but it lacked the glint of metal; its length was a dull black as if made from obsidian.

"Where did you get that?" Kyen's eyes widened. "You shouldn't use that. That's a black w—"

Ennyen rushed him. Like lightning, his sword flashed out, and Kyen ducked. He scrambled back, dodging up, down, back and forth as the blade whipped and stabbed the air around him. Black sparks flew as the blade clipped the walls of the alley on either side.

Kyen jumped backwards out of range, but Ennyen walked after him. Behind, a darkness began spreading like ink on the sides of the ally. It covered the bricks that'd been scraped, swallowing them whole out of the mortar before vanishing.

The back of the ally neared as Ennyen raised his blade, pushing Kyen towards the dead end.

"Draw your sword," he said in a voice as cold as his eyes. "Kyen, son of Odyen."

"I'm not going to fight you." Kyen's back hit a pole holding up the stable's roof.

Ennyen struck, slashing out, but Kyen ducked, the sword whistling over his head. He dodged away as the blade cleaved through the pole behind him. The stable roof caved with a crash and billow of dust at Ennyen's feet. Unperturbed, he turned to meet Kyen lunging at him. He swiped at Kyen's face with the pommel of his hilt, but the blow just grazed him as he leaned out of the way. Kyen threw himself into the opening, seizing Ennyen's hilt with both hands.

The two swordsmen grappled for control of the blade. Ennyen slung Kyen sideways and slammed his back into the wall. Kyen grunted, but clung to the hilt, wrenched at it. Ennyen held on with a grip like iron. He jerked Kyen forwards only to slam him back into the wall harder, knocking a gasp of breath out of him and banging the back of his head against the stone. Kyen's footing slipped, and he slid down the wall as Ennyen pressed him down, down, until he was nearly sitting on the ground.

With a great wrench backwards, Ennyen freed his sword and stabbed. Kyen leaned sideways, the blade plunging into the ground beside him. Bracing himself against the wall, Kyen kicked up with both feet into Ennyen's midsection. His hands slipped off the hilt of the black blade as he stumbled backwards and caught himself.

Kyen launched himself up and tried to tackle him, but Ennyen grabbed him by the tunic and slung him past— straight into the opposite wall. Kyen smacked up against the brick, catching himself with his hands. Before he could turn, Ennyen was upon him. He seized his collar in one hand and pummeled him in the face with his fist. Kyen sagged under the blow. He struggled to recover, only to meet Ennyen's fist smacking him across the face again. Ennyen drove his knee into Kyen's stomach then slung him into the ground. He hit the dirt in a heap. Coughing and clutching his guts, he curled up on himself.

Ennyen turned away. He grasped his sword and pulled it free.

Kyen struggled to his hands and knees.

"Kyen!" A call rang out. Adeya had appeared at the mouth of the alley.

"Don't—" he croaked.

Steel sang as she drew her sword and charged in.

Ennyen turned towards her and eyed her as she lashed out. He leaned out of the way, grabbed her sword wrist, and stepped behind her, wrenching her arm inwards as he went. She gasped, arching in pain. Ennyen twisted harder until she stood, immobilized, on tiptoes, back arced, her shoulder on the brink of dislocation. Her sword hung useless in her hand behind her back.

Lightning flickered overhead.

Ennyen surveyed Adeya for a moment then smiled. He flipped his blade backhand and raised the point to her throat. His dark eyes shifted to Kyen.

"Draw your sword."

Adeya whimpered in pain as he tightened his hold even more.

Kyen rose to a crouch, holding to the wall with one hand. He glared at Ennyen. For the briefest moment, his eyes flickered a blazing gold.

With an explosive flash, lightning struck the rooftop, spraying down stones and roof debris, as a bang of thunder jolted through them.

Ennyen released Adeya to press himself to the wall under the cover of the eaves.

Adeya staggered away from him, covering her head.

"Run!" Kyen yelled.

"But—"

"Go!"

Adeya bolted from the alley and vanished around the corner.

Ennyen hefted his sword as Kyen straightened, but instead of drawing his own, Kyen lunged past him. He covered his head and threw himself into one of the inn's windows. Glass crashed as he burst into the empty kitchen. Scrambling to his feet, he fled towards the common room. Ennyen jumped in after him.

The few patrons left in the common room looked up in surprise as the two swordsmen banged out the kitchen door. Seeing the black blade in Ennyen's hand, those nearest abandoned their mugs and fled. The innkeeper ducked behind his bar. Two others edged around the room to escape upstairs.

Kyen, turning to face Ennyen, moved to keep several tables between them. But the other swordsman circled in, throwing chairs out of his way, moving to block the exit.

"You were always a spineless throwback, Kyen," he said. "When did you become a coward, also? Draw your sword and fight."

"I won't fight you, Ennyen," said Kyen. "Can't we talk about this?"

"Speak with your blade!" He lunged with a swing of his sword. Kyen upturned the table to block him. The black sword cleaved through the wood like butter, the blade nearly catching Kyen's nose before he jumped back.

Snatching up first one tankard then another, Kyen hurled them. Ennyen cut the first out of the air only to get sprayed with ale. With a look of disgust, he leaned out of the way of the second. Kyen seized a chair and slung it at him. Ennyen cut it down, but he missed the third tankard Kyen chucked right behind it. It shattered on his knee. He faltered a step.

Kyen flung a last table out of his way and sped out the door.

Cursing, jerking his sword free of the chair, and shoving aside a table, Ennyen walked after him. He watched, not even out of breath, as the retreating shape of Kyen fled down the street.

The innkeeper inched his head up to peek above the

bar but ducked back quick when Ennyen looked at him.

A pouch of coin plunked onto the counter.

"My apologies for the damages," said Ennyen.

The innkeeper only dared raise his head again as Ennyen's footsteps thudded out the door.

Striding out into the muddy street, Ennyen caught the last glimpse of Kyen, meeting Adeya, before they both disappeared down an alley.

The black, faceless bird fluttered down, alighting on the hitching post next to him. He glanced at it, and the bird cocked its head at him. Distant lightning flickered; the flash illuminated the bird's gaping, toothy grin.

Ennyen nodded.

The bird chortled—three sinking tones—and flapped into the air. Ennyen sheathed his sword as he watched it soar into the clouds over the alley where Kyen had vanished.

Chapter 7

Mountain peaks, black against the stormy dusk, dwarfed the figures of Kyen and Adeya running through the foothills. They jogged to a crest on the slope and stopped. Breathing hard, Kyen looked back while Adeya put her hands on her knees and hunched over.

The boulder-studded mountainside sank into the flatlands where a miniature collection of red roofs and chimneys lifted smoky threads. A dwindling forest patched the slope in young pines, many hardly taller than Kyen. Above him loomed the mountains, their valleys veined black in shadow, their tips bathed in orange where the light touched. The Arc—a blazing line of light that arched across the sky—burned yellow in a gap between the mountains for a moment before sinking out of sight.

As Kyen's eyes searched the slope, Adeya opened the pack on his shoulder. He stood unmoving as she dug around inside and pulled out a small shaded lantern.

"Is he chasing us?" She knelt to light it with flint and tinder.

He pulled his gaze from the flatlands and turned to walk away as if he hadn't heard.

"Wait! Wait for me!" She hurried to crack flint and blow on the tinder.

Kyen glanced back. "We should keep moving."

After hurrying to put the lantern to flame, she stamped out the tinder, pulled the shade down, and swung it aloft as she trotted after him. With its pool of light at their feet, Kyen set a swift pace. Night was setting in. They jogged and ran by stretches over uneven ground that climbed steadily upwards. Neither looked back as the town disappeared into the failing dusk.

Deep night had blackened their surroundings to pitch when Kyen slowed. Leading them to a stand of pines larger and denser than the others, he pushed apart the wet branches for Adeya. She ducked inside. He squeezed his way through after her. Hunched together, they clambered over and under the prickly limbs. The bed of pine needles on the ground felt dry despite the occasional drip from above.

Kyen dropped down against a tree trunk, propping his arms up on his knees. Adeya, sitting down next to him, held up the lantern to shed its light over him: blood smeared the cuts on his forearms from breaking the window; one eye had swelled shut; more blood encrusted a split lip. Her face pinched in concern to see his wounds.

Setting the lantern down, Adeya opened the healer's pouch at her hip. She took out a length of bandage, ripped off a square and then, drawing a bottle of tincture out, dampened it. She handed it to him.

"Clean up with that."

Kyen took the cloth to wipe at his arms.

Taking out a little tin, Adeya unscrewed the top and dipped her finger into the salve inside. She dabbed at his lip. "I didn't realize how serious you were when you said Ennyen wanted to kill you."

"Death feuds are a part of life where I come from. It's nothing new." He peered down his forearm then wiped a smear he had missed.

"Did he—his sword. That wasn't a...?"

"A black weapon," he said. "No mistaking it."

"First Galveston. Now Ennyen. I thought the Great Alliance locked all the black weapons away. Here, hold this to your eye." She handed him a bandage wad soaked in pink tincture.

"They are. Or they should be," he said. "Arc help him..." Kyen's gray eyes looked tired as he watched the lantern flicker. Adeya, stealing a glance at him, began daubing the salve on his arms. When she'd finished, he roused himself. "We should be safe here for the night. I want to make an early start for Bargston in the morning."

"So much for sleeping out of the damp." Adeya huffed as she replaced her bandages, bottles, and salves.

"I'm sorry."

"It's not your fault." She smiled, a look that brightened her face like dawn in the night sky. "It really isn't."

Kyen quickly looked away, but she missed it, busy tying the healer's pouch back to her waist. Wrapping her cloak around herself, she nestled into the bed of pine needles and pillowed her head on an arm before looking back at him.

"Does Ennyen hate you enough to come after you, do you think?"

"I hope not." He pulled his cloak about himself, settling back against the trunk. "If we can make Bargston, we can hire a boat down the River Bounding and lose ourselves in Eope."

"At least the fiends after you haven't shown up yet." She favored him with a reassuring smile. He returned it half-heartedly, his face still averted.

"Hopefully, that's the last encounter I ever have with Ennyen," he said. "He should get on with his life and forget about me."

Adeya's smile faded as she watched him staring at the lantern. A despondence hung in his expression, in his shoulders, in the hang of his head. The light in his gray eyes seemed dimmed.

"Goodnight," she said.

Kyen started out of his thoughts.

She smiled again, tentatively, but he turned his face away, leaning forward to blow out the lantern.

"Goodnight."

* * *

With drawn cloaks and fogging breath, Kyen and Adeya walked in the pre-dawn light. She hugged her arms to herself, her teeth chattering, while Kyen—silent, withdrawn, untouched by the chill—picked their path between the frosted rocks.

The mountains loomed to their left. The foremost range marched under a green verdure broken by gray rocks and jutting precipices. The range behind, rising taller, peered with snow-capped heads over their shoulders. Furthest back and off to the north, the highest peaks of all hid their heights in halos of cloud and mist. The rising Arc, though still below the horizon opposite the mountains, touched the halos and turned them gold with its first beams. Slowly, the light began to touch the mountainsides and crept down in a pale dawn. When the Arc broke over the horizon as a white blaze, it spread morning over the two travelers and warmed them.

Kyen and Adeya, finding a large boulder half-buried in the ground, climbed it to sit in the warmth and breakfast. Taking a map from his pocket, he spread it out on his lap as he ate the journey bread and dried apricots.

The map lay folded to show the rounded top of Ellunon. Little triangle mountains filled the west around the label: "Denmont." Beside it ran a line—"The Great Highway"— which disappeared into Norgard, the peninsula above Denmont. The line cut across a thicker squiggle which flowed south towards Veleda and east towards Eope, a circular kingdom perched on the lip of the continent. None of this caught Kyen's eye as it waited on his lap.

His gaze lingered on the distant sky. After a while, his food lay forgotten next to him as he stared unseeing at the rising Arc.

Adeya leaned over his shoulder to survey the map. She glanced at him.

He didn't show any signs of noticing.

She edged closer, nibbling an apricot.

The Arc's fiery arch lifted free of the horizon, beginning its long ascent to the midday zenith.

Adeya slipped the map away from him and held it up. "Are you sure going to Eope is a good idea?"

Kyen took a deep breath, yawned, and stretched. He looked at her mildly. "What's that? Did you say something?"

"Galveston was from Eope, and he tried to kill us," she said. "Papa said that kingdom is full of wizards and sky-gazers who never give a plain answer."

Kyen frowned at the map in her hands. He looked at his empty lap, then back to the map, and pawed after his journey cake.

"Well?" She looked at him.

"Well, what?" Kyen, taking a huge bite, leaned in towards the map.

"Are you even listening?" She flicked her hair out of her face.

"'Issening 'oo wha?" He said with his mouth full.

"Exactly!"

Kyen chewed, looking confounded.

"You're never paying attention."

He swallowed. "I'm sorry."

"Oh, never mind." She huffed. "You said something about Eope, yesterday."

"Yeah, I'm hoping we can make the River Bounding within the week and hire a boat to Eope at Bargston." He pointed at the squiggly line.

"And that's the Great Highway, right?" Adeya lowered the map to point at the roadway weaving through flatlands below them.

He nodded.

"If I'm going to search Ellunon for the arcangels, I need to learn its geography. Too bad I never paid attention to my tutor when he tried to teach me…" She shook the map out and folded it up as Kyen sat back, gnawing the last chunk of his bread. She rubbed the parchment between her fingers, before looking up at him. "Can I keep this?"

"Sure. You'd probably make more use of it than me." Hopping off the boulder, he dusted crumbs from his tunic.

With a smile, Adeya put the map in her pocket. She rose to follow him as he set off.

"What about morning training?" She laid a hand on her hilt. "You said you'd show me how to disarm last time."

"Maybe tonight," he said. "I want to put Ennyen as far behind us as possible today."

"Wouldn't we make better time on the road?"

"If he's looking for me, that's where he'll be," said Kyen. "We'll circle down once Bargston is in sight."

Together, they climbed across the mountain's foothills as they followed the road from a distance, two tiny figures half-hidden between the boulders and the trees. Neither of them noticed the dark shape wheeling in the sky overhead.

Chapter 8

Steel flashed underneath the afternoon arclight; the tip of Adeya's sword clipped Kyen's arm, slicing flesh, flinging out a drop of blood.

"Ow!" He leapt back.

Adeya stood opposite him, mouth agape, gripping her longsword at the end of its slash.

Shifting his hilt to one hand, he looked at the cut; it leaked a rivulet of red down his arm.

Her eyes grew wide with alarm. "Oh no! I'm so sorry!"

"It's just a scratch."

"Let me get my salve."

"Don't bother."

"But you're bleeding!"

"I'm alright. Really." He shook out his arm, Adeya watching with bright eyes as he slung the blood off.

The two stood in a clearing on the mountain slope. Bushes rimmed one side and a half-buried boulder on the other seated the only spectators: their pack and two cloaks.

Kyen reset his stance and lifted his sword, impassive to the blood that ran down his arm and dripped off his elbow.

"Let's continue."

As Adeya looked at him, a frown rose to her face. "How did that even happen?"

He blinked in surprise.

"You're the greatest swordsman in all Ellunon," she continued. He started to say, "I'm really not—" but she ran right over him with: "How did I, a novice, cut you? How did I even come close?"

He looked bewildered.

"Are you going easy on me?" She shook her sword at him like a long condemning finger.

"I—uh, I…"

"You're letting me win, aren't you?"

"Not… not—"

"Kyen of Avanna!" She swelled, clenching her fist. "What am I supposed to do against a fiend? Tell me that! A fiend isn't going to go easy on me."

"I know." He shrank under her glare.

"Then stop going easy on me!"

"Why are you mad?"

"I'm NOT mad!"

He shifted, looking at his toes, while he waited for her to huff through a few breaths.

"I'm not mad," she repeated. "I'm serious. I want to learn properly. So fight me like it's serious, Kyen!"

"Alright."

"Good."

Straightening out of his stance, Kyen flipped his sword backhand. She stared as he slipped the blade back into the sheath at his hip; the hilt hit the scabbard with a clank. He fixed his attention on her. "Ready."

A lock of hair slid out from behind her ear as both her face and mouth worked for some sort of understanding. Neither found any.

"What?" Kyen asked.

She swept the hair away with a flick and a huff. "You're *sure* you're ready?"

"Yup."

"But your sword."

"What? You can come at me."

"Oh, never mind…" She took up her blade with both hands; its edge glinted in the late afternoon light "You're sure?"

"Absolutely."

Adeya gripped her hilt with both hands. All at once she charged him. He stood at ease until she slashed out. He flashed forward, a loud smack rang through the clearing, and Adeya stumbled back to find the point of her own sword at her throat.

Kyen, holding the hilt high next to his cheek, looked concerned as he pointed the blade at her. "Sorry."

She stared back, wide-eyed.

"Do you want to try again?" he asked, lowering the sword a little.

"How did you—oh, ow…" Adeya winced and cradled her hand. "Ow!"

"Are you alright?" He hurried over. "Did I break anything? I'm so sorry!"

"Fine! It's—fine!" She blinked back tears, and with an effort shook her hand out. "Let me try again."

"Are you sure?"

"Yes, again. Like a real sword fight." She snatched her sword back and brandished it at him.

He held his hands up as if in surrender. "Okay."

Walking back to her starting position, Adeya tossed her hair out of her face. She dug in her toes then charged Kyen again. This time she stabbed, but Kyen sidestepped. She whirled around to slash but he'd already vanished, darting behind her. There he lingered. Adeya whipped first one side, then the other, looking for him, but he leaned this way and that to stay out of her line of vision. Suddenly, she frowned. Whipping around, she slashed out at him, but he side-stepped it with ease. A smile crept onto his face.

"Stop laughing at me! Be serious!"

"I'm trying." Kyen danced out of range as she came slashing after him.

Yelling, she lobbed at him, but he ducked under her guard and grabbed her hilt.

"You're swinging wide."

"Give! It! Back!" She wrenched her sword back and forth, but he hung on.

"You'd do better if you calmed down."

"I am—CALM!" Adeya threw herself into jerking her sword free—and Kyen let go. She staggered backwards and fell, landing with a crash into the bushes. She whimpered. "Ow…"

"I'm sorry! Are you alright?" He trotted after her.

Adeya stirred as he neared, struggling to sit up. He stopped, about to offer her a hand up, when she sat up with a "Ha!" and smacked the flat of her blade on his shin.

His jaw tightened, but otherwise he remained unmoved by the blow. "That wasn't fair."

"I win!" She popped out of the bushes with her arms in the air. "It's over."

"A real battle is only over when one of us is dead, Adeya."

She poked the blade at his throat, glaring at him.

Kyen sighed and shook his head.

"Being a fair damsel has its advantages, you know." Beaming, Adeya sheathed her sword. "It's easy to lure honorable swordsmen into a false sense of security." She walked with Kyen, chin held high, a hand on her hilt, and, together, they returned to the boulder where they'd left their things.

"Nobody will believe that I defeated the legendary Kyen of Avanna," she said. "Does that make me the greatest swordswoman in Ellunon now?"

"Can you get a fire going?" he asked.

"Don't be a sore loser." She plopped to her knees and dragged the pack over. Digging out the flint and tinder, she shot him a glance.

At the edge of the camp, Kyen bent to collect fallen branches and brush with a forlorn expression. His gray eyes gazed unseeing at the wood he piled in his arms.

"I never thought I'd miss roads. But after three days in the foothills..." Adeya shook her head. "What I wouldn't give for a bath!"

He deposited the pile of wood next to her.

"Your black eye is looking better," she said to his back as he walked away. Without an answer, he began to collect twigs and pine cones, so Adeya formed a nest in the tinder.

"I don't know how you expect me to be trekking mountains all day, then training all evening." She struck several sparks into the tinder and blew into the nest. It smoked then flared to flame. She set the nest down while Kyen brought over a mess of sticks.

He broke one and fed it to the growing flame.

"I bet you never had to train so hard." Adeya, folding her hands in her lap, looked at him archly.

A smile quirked the side of his mouth.

"What? What are you smiling about?"

"Nothing."

"Don't lie, Kyen of Avanna." She fixed him with an intense stare.

He picked up a pine cone. Crunching it in his hand, he scattered the bits into the fire. The flame licked at them eagerly. "Our blademasters would drive us into the Five Frowning Men—"

"The what?"

He looked up and nodded at the mountains. "The furthest peaks that ridge Norgard. Blades all the morning, then run the mountains—when we weren't climbing—sometimes until full dark, before another session with blades."

Adeya gaped at him. "Run?"

"Rather run than be flogged." The flame danced in Kyen's stormy eyes.

She grew pale.

"It's how children of Avanna trained for the test where they'd earn their sword," he said.

Her mouth fell open.

"At least, those that survived the mountains." Kyen turned his gray eyes on her. "Does it really seem strange to you?"

"It seems terrible!" She sat up straight, outraged, and repeated, "Children?"

"My people were warriors—trained to deal death and to die well. It's all they lived for," he said. "I'm sure Isea is unpleasant in ways, too?"

"Like fathers constantly arranging suitors for their daughters? Absolutely." Adeya snapped a branch and fed it to the growing campfire.

Kyen tumbled the rest of his sticks in.

Watching him gaze into the fire, she spoke up, "How come you never talk about Avanna?"

He prodded the fire, frowning.

"That's the first time I've ever heard you mention it," she said.

"It's… It's not... What's there to say?"

"I don't know. You had a family? Friends? A town you grew up in?"

"None of it seems worth mentioning." He kept prodding the fire.

"Don't you have any good memories?"

"I suppose so…" said Kyen. "Most everyone is dead now. Dwelling on memories doesn't do me any good."

Adeya's eyes grew bright as she watched him, but Kyen avoided looking at her. He sat back, his gaze wandering to the mountains' peaks.

The Arc had long disappeared behind them. The

clouds, spreading down from the Five Frowning Men, cascaded around the shoulders of the nearer peaks. Great thunderheads rose up behind them.

"We might need a more sheltered campsite tonight," said Kyen.

She followed his gaze up and moaned. "Not another storm?"

Chapter 9

Their boots squished as Kyen and Adeya walked along the mountain's shoulder. Mud slopped up on the hems of their cloaks with every step. Their hair clung to their faces under damp hoods, Adeya's in lank strings and Kyen's plastered to his brow. The misty drizzle fell from dark clouds that billowed over the mountainside and curtained the winding road below in haze. A settlement, a cluster atop a gray foothill, overlooked the highway and the lowlands.

"Kyen?" Adeya pulled at her soppy cloak; it slapped as she folded it against herself. "Can we please stop?"

He ducked around a dripping boulder.

"Please, Kyen? We haven't seen any sign of Ennyen."

He paused for a moment to survey the ground then picked his way across a stretch of tumbled rocks and scree.

When she didn't receive an answer, Adeya kept whining. "I just want a hot bath. A fresh meal. A soft bed with a pillow and piles of blankets. Eek!" Her foot slipped in the mud, and she dropped bottom-first to the ground with a *splat*.

Kyen looked back.

She pouted at him, and with a slump and a sigh, he

walked back to her. He extended a hand to help her to her feet, but she didn't take it. She sniffed, gazing up at him, her eyes brimming with tears.

"Alright. We'll stop." He sighed again.

"Oh, thank you!" She took his hand, and he lifted her upright.

He angled their course down the slope, heading for the settlement in the foothills.

The drizzle eased up as they neared, and the form of the village emerged from the mist. Roofs, broken in and patched, poked above the walls of a wooden stockade that bristled with a stakewall. A road split off from the Great Highway and, after passing between the stakes, ended at a wooden gateway flanked by a watchtower.

Seeing these defenses materialize, Kyen's face grew pensive. He slowed to a stop. "I don't think we'll be finding an inn here, Adeya."

"Look, though. Smoke! It's warm and dry, at the least," she said. "Nobody would refuse the honor of lodging a princess in their midst."

"I'd not mention your title, if I were you," he said. "This close to the Claimless Lands, it might be a thief hold as easily as a village."

"For a hot bath, I'd fight thieves," she said. "Can we see, at least?"

Kyen hesitated.

"Please? They might have sandwiches."

"Alright, alright," he said. "But if anyone finds out who we are—who I am—it'll be trouble."

Adeya mimed sealing her sweet smile with two fingers.

She started towards the gate, but when Kyen lingered behind, she stopped to wave him forward. He hung his head and picked up his step to join her.

Wooden spikes long enough to skewer a horse lined the road leading up to the gate. One spike, larger than the rest, pounded straight into the ground, stood like a column beside the watchtower. An array of rusty swords and knives pinned faded rags up and down its side. At its pinnacle hung a human skull, still wearing a bandit's headband, impaled in place by a broken spear.

When Adeya hurried up to the gate, her eyes traveled up the column and grew wide when they saw the skull. Kyen stopped beside her with a hand on his hilt.

He leaned in to whisper. "I'm not sure about this..."

"Well, they're not bandits." She whispered back, her eyes still on the grisly display. Craning her neck up towards the watchtower, she put a hand to her mouth. "Hail up there! Greetings?"

A sentry rose from the shadow underneath the tower's peak. He held a bow in one hand. With the other he drew an arrow from the quiver at his hip.

"What do you want?"

"To beg lodging for the night," she called up.

"We don't lodge strangers. Begone!"

"But we're travelers!"

"Thieves more like. Or fugitives. Troublemakers either way," said the sentry. "Nary an honest traveler in these parts."

"We really are travelers. Cold, wet, hungry travelers. We're from Isea—"

"Save your tale-spinning. Get gone!"

"Please?" Adeya clasped her hands under her chin. "I'm a healer from Isea. If there's someone sick or wounded, I'd care for them in exchange for lodging."

"No. Now get!" He notched the arrow on the bow string.

"Adeya." Kyen laid a hand on her arm, pulling at her.

She shrugged him off. "See here, you! I need a bath. And a dry bed. And a meal. I demand to speak with your leader!" She pointed at the ground.

"Adeya." Kyen whispered.

"I will not stand for such incivility," she continued. "No wonder you never see an honest traveler! You should be ashamed of yourself. I'm not leaving this spot until I speak to your leader, and I insist on being treated with respect."

The sentry's frown faded. He pursed his lips but it did nothing to hide the growing twinkle in his eye.

"Do you know who this is?" She pointed at Kyen.

Kyen stiffened. He whispered out the side of his mouth. "Adeya—Don't!"

"He's… He's my escort," she stammered. "And he's a very good man, too."

"Aren't you a genuine article?" The sentry chuckled. "You must be travelers, and lost. Very, very lost. Do you know where you are, little dame?"

"Don't you patronize me!" She swelled.

"Many apologies." He laughed. The sentry nodded back at the shadows behind him. The sound of feet descending within the wooden tower answered.

Adeya stood with her arms crossed, her nose in the air,

and said to herself, "I will get my bath."

Kyen buried his face in a hand.

Around them, a deluge of rain began pouring down through the mist. It soaked their already damp cloaks, streaked down the stockade, and gathered in puddles at their feet. Adeya deflated.

The sentry smiled at them from under the shelter of the watchtower.

She glared back, speaking to Kyen, "What kind of heathen place is this?"

"These are the highlands, Adeya," he said. "It's not like Isea, or Veleda, or Nalayni."

"Give me lumbergadders of Varkest rather than this!" She huffed. "Heathen."

Steps thudded up the inside of the tower. The sentry moved aside for a man with a large mustache. He threw back his hood and leaned at the railing.

"Who be you?"

"A brabbling hoddypeak and her escort, townsmaster," answered the sentry.

"I am not—!"

"Where you be from?" demanded the townsmaster.

"Isea. And I just want a bath." Adeya's voice broke over the last word as the rain continued to drench her.

The townsmaster's gaze found Kyen. "And your companion?"

"I'm not anyone worthy of note," he said. "Just her escort."

"Are you not Kyen of Avanna?" asked the townsmaster.

Kyen hung his head.

"Yes," Adeya answered. "Yes, he is." She shrugged an apology at him, but his stormy eyes stayed fixed on the ground.

"Let them in," the townsmaster said to the sentry. They both disappeared from the watchtower. A moment later, the gate gave a clunk. It hinged upward on ropes, lifting until Kyen and Adeya could duck under its edge.

The townsmaster, pulling up his hood, met them inside the stockade. A purple vest with brass buttons peaked out between the folds of his cloak. His thick, dark mustache covered his mouth. "My name is Theiho."

"Adeya of Isea," She nodded to him.

"And Kyen of Avanna." Theiho surveyed him up and down but couldn't catch his eye. "I thought you'd be a larger man."

"Most do." Kyen smiled weakly at his feet.

"You have the Avanna countenance. It's not easily forgotten," said Theiho.

"You've seen another from Avanna?" asked Adeya.

"A swordsman," replied Theiho. "Stopped at our gate a day back looking for you. Described you in detail."

Kyen stiffened, but he said nothing.

"Is he still here?" asked Adeya.

"No," replied Theiho. "He kept on up the highway when he learned we'd not seen you this way."

Kyen relaxed.

"He had your hair and eyes. Though, he stood a good deal higher. Come. It'd be an honor to have the Hero of Ellunon stay with me. Come out of the rain." Theiho led away.

Within the stockade's wall, a handful of houses hunched together with their garden patches full of puddles. Beside each garden sat a pyre with wood stacked dense against the rain. They flanked the road that ran up the middle of the village—this Theiho followed—and ended at a small dome of seamless rock. A heavy slab covered its entrance.

When Adeya saw it, her face lit up. "A Firstwold ruin!"

"We are attacked by fiends more often than bandits these days," said Theiho. "The ruin is our only refuge. At least against the smaller ones."

Kyen and Adeya exchanged glances. They followed Theiho through the muddy street to the door of the largest house: a log structure of two stories built between a couple river-stone chimneys. An oilcloth covered what looked like a bite that'd been taken out of the corner of the roof.

Theiho opened the door to let them into the entrance hall.

"Marhei?" He called up the hall before turning to them. "Here. Let me take your cloaks and boots."

A thin lady with gray-streaked hair and a somber dress hurried in from another room. She stopped short seeing them.

"Kyen and Adeya will be our guests, Marhei," said Theiho.

"Welcome," she said, unsmiling; then to Theiho. "Travelers off the great highway?"

"Will you house them comfortably?"

"Townsmaster!" A soaked lad ran up to the open doorway and leaned in. "You're wanted again at the watchtower, townsmaster. Fiends have been spotted!"

Kyen and Adeya paused to exchange a glance.

Theiho sighed. "Forgive me," he said to them. He laid a kiss on Marhei's forehead. "I'll be back by dark." He strode into the rain and followed the lad out of sight.

Thunder rumbled in the distance.

Marhei pursed her lips. She edged past them with cautious steps to shut the door. "I imagine you'd like to use the baths before dining?"

Adeya's "Very much so!" ran together with Kyen's "Actually, I'm pretty hungry." They looked at each other.

"Baths first," he said.

"A real bath?" asked Adeya. "With hot water?"

"What other kind is there?" said Marhei.

Chapter 10

Kyen and Adeya sat at the table with Marhei and her two children. Theiho's seat at the head stood empty. Behind it, rain dripped with a hiss into a fire that burned low in the hearth.

Marhei served rabbit stewed with turnips and peas into bowls. Her children—a boy and his younger sister—sat across from Kyen and Adeya. The two stared at the travelers with wide eyes.

"I can't thank you enough for your hospitality." Adeya fluffed out her damp hair with her fingers. "I can't remember the last time I had the luxury of a hot bath."

Marhei offered her a tight smile and a bowl.

"Are you really travelers from the Great Highway?" asked the boy.

"Manners, Kelleth," said Marhei. "Pass this to your sister." She placed a bowl at Theiho's empty spot and then sat down.

Kyen began shoveling food into his mouth.

"It feels so good to be dry!" said Adeya, taking up her spoon. "And clean. I'm never taking baths for granted again."

"Where have you come from?" asked Kelleth.

"We've traveled up from Isea."

"Isea." The boy's eyes grew wide with wonder. "The Kingdom of Summoners."

"Kelleth." Marhei shot him a warning glance.

"Are you a noblewoman run away with your lover?" asked the little girl.

Adeya flushed.

Kyen almost tipped his bowl into his lap and fumbled it back to the table.

"Sareth! Don't ask impertinent questions!" said Marhei.

"But that's what you said, mama," replied the little girl.

Marhei sat up straight as a rod, coloring. "Forgive my children."

"It's alright." Adeya fiddled with her napkin.

"May… may I have seconds?" Kyen asked in a quiet voice, red to his ears, and holding out his bowl without meeting anyone's eye.

Another drip hissed into the fire.

Spoons clinked on pottery.

Marhei poured one ladle of stew into Kyen's outstretched bowl.

"You're on a quest, aren't you?" Kelleth started again.

"Yes, I suppose you could say that," said Adeya.

"What kind of quest?"

"We're looking for the arcangels."

"Arcangels." Kelleth breathed it out like a sacred word. "You mean they're real?"

Adeya glanced at Kyen; he kept his eyes on his bowl,

but his spoon slowed to a halt.

"Of course," she said. "Isea used to be full of them, but they fell silent. We mean to find them."

"Wow…" said Kelleth. "So you're a summoner then?"

"No, not exactly. But if I find an arcangel, I will train to become one." Adeya tucked her hair out of her face.

"Wow…"

The sound of the front door opening caught all their attention.

"Thank the Arc!" Marhei threw her napkin to the table and rose from her seat. She stepped out into the hallway where Theiho's deep tones carried in to them.

Sareth watched her mother leave then looked back at Adeya. "Are you sure you're not lovers?"

* * *

"This will be your room for the night." Theiho, candle in hand, opened a door into the bedroom: a narrow bed with a side table, a fireplace with a mantle, a window dark with the swirling mists of night. "Wake me if you need anything." He passed the candle to Adeya.

"Thank you." She watched Theiho's back as he descended the stairs. She sighed contentedly and looked at Kyen, but seeing his serious face, her smile faltered.

"I'm sorry," she said.

He blinked and looked at her. "About what?"

"Did I say too much?"

"Too much about what?"

"The arcangels."

"Oh." He thought for a moment. "No, but I'd still be careful. The less people know about Kade the better."

"I'm sorry," she said again.

"It's alright. It really is."

A silence fell between them.

Kyen walked to the window to peer out into the blackness. The rain had died away into an infrequent drip. "We should be safe for the night with a Firstwold ruin so close. Safe from fiends, at least."

"Will you take Kade to the ruin tonight?" she asked.

"Maybe," he said. "He's short aura after our encounter with Ennyen."

"It'd be good to keep him strong," she said. "We don't know when we'll find the next ruin."

He nodded.

Silence fell between them again, but it lasted only a moment.

Seizing upon a chair, Kyen began dragging it towards the doorway.

"What are you doing?" she asked.

"Going to sleep."

"With a chair?"

Kyen stopped at the doorway. He didn't meet her eyes as he colored a little. "I'd rather you have the room."

"Oh, I didn't think of that." Adeya fiddled with her sleeve, casting the single bed an uncomfortable glance and coloring also. "You could ask Theiho for another room?"

"It's late. I don't sleep well in beds anyway. I'll be more comfortable with this." Kyen gave her a reassuring smile as he nudged the chair. She looked unconvinced.

"If you say so," she said. "Good night."

"Good night." Kyen closed the door behind him.

Adeya, shaking her head, heaved a sigh. She set the candle on the bedside table and gazed out the window. Taking her amulet, she placed it beside the candle and climbed under the covers.

Outside her door, in the dimness of the hall, Kyen slumped into the chair. Crossing his arms over his chest, he reclined back to bobble the chair on its two hind legs.

* * *

The fire had burned low in Adeya's room. She slept under its faint glow with the cold candle and her amulet laying on the table beside her. The occasional drip still hit the window with a *plick*.

Out of the night, a shape blacker than darkness swooped to the windowsill. It alighted, feathers whispering against the glass as its wings flapped to a stop. Sharp teeth glinted in the firelight as the fiend pressed its empty face to the pane. Seeing Adeya fast asleep, it grinned.

The outline of the fiend swelled and disappeared into an inky cloud that emitted from its body. It stained the glass, obscuring the pane and eating it away, until all at once it vanished.

Stepping out of the cloud, the fiend slipped through the opening in the window and entered the room. Its claws clicked softly on the sill as it stalked towards Adeya's bed. The long plumes of its tail snaked in behind it as it hopped onto the bedside table.

The wicked mouth spread wider. Dark, cloud-like miasma began to drift off its body again, forming tendrils that thickened and slithered into the room.

The amulet at the fiend's feet glowed blue, but the fiend paid it no attention. It took another step toward Adeya, its miasma crawling through the air towards her and alighting first on the candlestick. Where it touched the windows, the walls, the floor, the table, it began spreading—like ink spilling over the surfaces and oozing up the walls. The candle, completely blackened next to the fiend, disintegrated. Only the amulet remained untouched in the midst of the miasma, growing brighter and brighter as the room darkened. Adeya groaned and shifted as the blue light touched her face.

The tendrils crept along the bedclothes, inching their way towards her.

A sudden flash exploded from the amulet. It swept the room, burning the air clean of miasma, wiping it from the furniture, the bedclothes, the walls. The fiend hissed and stumbled away. Adeya started upright with a gasp. Her eyes found the fiend, and all of her tensed as she drew in one great breath. The fiend lowered its head to chortle at her, and she leapt from bed.

"KYEN!" She screamed. She flung open the door, only to leap back with a cry as a shape tumbled into her room. Kyen, chair and all, fell over backwards and crashed to the ground. His head made a loud thunk as it hit the floorboards.

"Ow..." He struggled to lift himself to his elbows, holding his head. He gave Adeya a confused and groggy look as she stared back with wide eyes, clutching her collar.

"Fiend!" she squeaked out, pointing.

Kyen looked back and, seeing the dark shape, scrambled to get to his feet and draw his sword.

The fiend backed out of the window and wailed at them: three spine-tingling notes. It leapt from the sill as Kyen reached it. He threw open the sash.

The fiend winged a wide circle to settle on the roof across the street. It shook itself, puffed out its feathers, and shrieked at them.

Kyen's brows drew down, his jaw took on a grim set, and his face darkened the longer he stared at it.

The fiend shrieked at him again.

Adeya, having lit a spare candle from the mantle, joined him.

"We need to go. Now," he said, without taking his eyes from the fiend.

"I've never seen a fiend like that before."

"It *was* a caladrius." A muscle worked in Kyen's jaw.

"A bird of healing? But I thought those were a myth from the Firstwold!"

The caladrius fiend purred out a strange growling chortle. With a flap of its broad wings, it shot into the sky, trailing its tail plumage like black ribbons, and vanished into the night.

"We really need to leave now?" repeated Adeya. One look at his face sent her hurrying after her amulet, sword, and pack.

A bell began clanging wildly outside, catching Kyen's attention and bringing Adeya to a halt. It rang out over the rooftops from the direction of the gate. A signal fire lit up the watchtower as the tolling rose to a frantic pace. A loud crunch jolted the tower askew, silencing the bell. The tower sank below the rooftops, crumpling, and disappeared with a crashing thud that trembled through their room. Several other warning bells began ringing into the silence left by the first.

Kyen whirled away, and he dashed with Adeya out of the bedroom.

Chapter 11

Kyen and Adeya ran out of the house and stopped on the doorstep.

Shouts and screams had joined the clanging of bells. Up and down the street, orange blazes sprang to life, wet wood hissing and smoking, as the villagers lit the pyres. Families fled for the Firstwold ruin, away from the roof-capped wreckage of the watchtower that lay blocking the gateway.

A clamor of footsteps inside the house made Kyen and Adeya turn.

Theiho and his family crowded to the doorway. They wore their shifts, and Theiho had his nightshirt tucked into his breeches. Marhei looked the color of paper while she clutched Kelleth and Sareth to her sides.

"The Firstwold ruin," said Theiho. "Quickly!"

Adeya scooped up Sareth and hurried with Marhei after the others. Theiho ran behind them, but Kyen stopped in the middle of the street. The fleeing villagers jostled past him, unnoticed, as his eyes searched the wreckage.

The fearful murmur of the families crowding around the dome filled the air. Theiho pushed through them to get to the stone slab that served as a door to the ruin. He threw his weight against it, sliding it open. Beyond, a pillar of crystal filled with light waited, illuminating the bare interior with a soft glow. Theiho stepped back to usher the women and children inside. Adeya handed Sareth off to Marhei, but didn't join them as they entered. She stepped aside, looking back for Kyen.

He stood alone on the street, his eyes still on the wreckage of the watchtower. His brows drew together. Near the top, almost invisible in the dark, a man's hand waved frantically from underneath the roof. Kyen dashed forward. Sprinting to the pile of broken beams and splintered slats, he began climbing. He reached the man's hand, shoveled away broken bits of board from around it, and thrust aside a beam. Wood clattered down the pile as he ripped an opening in the rubble. He grabbed the man's hand and, bracing a foot against the roof, pulled. The watchman slid free.

"Are you alright?" Kyen helped him stand.

He nodded even as he grimaced, favoring one foot. "My leg."

The wreckage jolted beneath them. They both wobbled, the man grabbing Kyen to keep his balance. The warning bell gave a muffled clank as something deep in the pile shifted. They looked at each other in alarm.

"Down! Down!" Kyen shoved the man forward.

They both scrambled away as the pile of splintered beams shifted again. It swelled underneath them, cracking, rising, and shedding the rubble. They leapt, hitting the road on hands and knees.

"Go!" Kyen pulled the watchman to his feet and tried to

run, but the man's leg buckled and he fell sprawling. Dragging him back up, Kyen drew his arm over his shoulder, and they hobbled down the street together. Boards clattered to the ground behind them, and wood cracked as a dark mass the size of Theiho's house pushed out from underneath the watchtower.

Theiho and Adeya ran out to meet them. Together, they grabbed the watchman from Kyen and carried him towards the dome, but Kyen turned back.

His eyes grew wide.

The tower's peak lifted out of the debris. A huge head, jaws gripping the base of the roof, emerged. The timbers and beams fell away from a fiend shaped like a giant mountain cat. It jerked its head back once, twice. The tower sank into its throat as teeth like cave spikes closed over it with a crunch. The fiend swallowed, then turned its faceless grin towards Kyen.

He whirled around and fled.

The fiend leapt from the wreckage. In two bounds it caught up to him. Kyen dodged left and right as massive paws thundered around him, passed him. The fiend spun, blocking his path to the dome, its grin widening, its tail swishing through the air.

He backed away, a grim clench to his jaw.

The fiend lunged, swiping at him, and he jumped to one side only to meet giant jaws snapping down. He stumbled backwards. Teeth cracked a hand's breadth from his chest. Kyen tried to run. Left, right, backwards, forward, claws slammed down and teeth breezed by, driving him like a mouse between a cat's paws. One final stamp snagged him by the cloak. The cloth ripped. The jerk sent him off balance, stumbling and falling.

Adeya, after passing the watchman into the dome, looked back. Her eyes widened as she saw him hit the ground. He rolled, looked up as the fiend's jaws opened wide. He started to scramble backward, but the giant mouth came down, closed in around him, and snapped shut.

"Kyen!" Adeya screamed. She started forward, but Theiho grabbed her arm.

Dirt dribbling from its jaws, the fiend lifted its head. It left a hole in the road where Kyen had been. The fiend slung back its head once. And swallowed.

Adeya paled.

The giant fiend turned its grin towards her. It took one thunderous step when a flash of light slit out of the fiend's neck. Its grin fell. The fiend's head slid from its shoulders, hitting the ground with a thud. Its body crumpled behind with another thud that trembled through the street. Its fallen form disintegrated into smoke, leaving Kyen facedown on the road.

Adeya slung off Theiho's grip and ran to him. He was already struggling back to his feet when she reached him. He grabbed onto her as she helped him up.

"Are you alright?"

He lifted his face, his gray eyes steely, as he shouted, "Inside! Get them inside, Theiho!"

Beside them, the giant head moved.

Adeya gasped, and Kyen pushed her behind him as they both backed away.

With the corner of its mouth, the head gnawed at the

dirt. Rock crunched as its teeth worked, the fiend eating itself into a hollow. From the base of its severed neck, a black nub began to swell out.

"Run!" Kyen grabbed her hand, and they turned to flee for the dome.

Theiho was ushering the villagers inside. Men tried to press after their families, crowding around the entrance, but the dome would hold no more.

"Go!" Kyen slung Adeya onward towards the entrance. He stopped and turned.

She reached the crowd of bodies and looked back.

Kyen faced the fiend as it rose again. A new body swelled out from its neck, and fresh limbs stretched to the ground. It stood, thin and knobby, but back to its full height. It rounded on Kyen.

With a chortle so deep that it vibrated the ground, the fiend stalked forward. The grinning teeth split its face in half. Every footfall shuddered up the buildings, trembled beneath their feet, and pushed Kyen backwards up the road. The villagers, whimpering and crying, cowered together while Adeya watched with bright eyes. Her hand crept towards her amulet.

The fiend lowered its head, wiggling it back and forth. It blew a hiss through its teeth that breezed through Kyen's hair, grabbed at his cloak, and kicked up dust around his feet.

Within the space of a blink, Kyen's eyes transformed in color, from gray to gold. His expression hardened.

The pillar inside the dome surged with light.

A hundred white ribbons exploded to life in the air

around him. Shooting forward, they lashed around the fiend, wrapping its legs, its torso, its head. The fiend balked. It strained and pulled against them, but finding itself unable to break free, it plunged forward instead. With a roar, it lashed out.

Its massive claws swiped into Kyen. The impact knocked him off his feet and slung him across the street. He tumbled over the cobblestones and, hitting the front of Theiho's house, he fell in a heap across the doorstep. The ribbons dissolved into a haze.

"Kyen!" Adeya dashed after him. Falling to her knees next to him, she put her hands on his shoulders. "Kyen!"

He writhed on the doorstep, clutching his side and coughing. His arm lay on the ground at an awkward angle. Broken.

"Are you alright?"

Bone cracked.

"Ah!" Kyen gasped and jolted as his arm snapped straight. He curled up on himself, hissing through his teeth.

"Kyen!"

Grimacing, he pulled the healed arm underneath him and looked up, his eyes still golden, his face still grim. Adeya followed his gaze.

The fiend stepped up to the dome. The villagers trapped outside shrieked and scrambled to flee, but the fiend ignored them. It sank its teeth into the dome's roof with a crunch. Cries from the women and children inside rang out. Bracing a claw on either side, the fiend began to pull. Cracks splintered around the perimeter of the dome.

The cries grew into screams.

The roof of the dome gave way all at once, splitting away from the base, ripped free by the massive jaws. The fiend lifted the roof into the air. The women and children inside the dome covered their heads as rocks and dust rained down. In their midst the glass pillar glowed.

The giant fiend crushed the roof in its jaws with another crunch and a shower of debris. It gulped the whole mass with a toss of its head. Its limbs swelled larger. With stone still crumbing from its teeth, the fiend grinned down at the sobbing, huddling villagers.

Throwing off Adeya's grip, Kyen jumped back to his feet. He sprinted hard for the dome as the villagers shrieked and cowered.

The fiend drew back on itself, opened its mouth, and plunged its head into the dome. Kyen leapt in front of it, throwing his hand upwards. Light burst from the pillar with a blaze like the Arc. A thousand ribbons exploded out around Kyen like a geyser of spears. They blasted into the fiend's chest—its snapping jaws missed the pillar by a hand's breadth, pushed back by the onslaught. The spears of aura shredded the fiend's body, shearing through the pieces left behind, and disintegrating the darkness in a blaze that swallowed up Kyen and the dome. With a thud, the light went out, dispersing as a shock wave of white mist that curled across the road and faded.

In its wake stood Kyen, hands still upraised, chest heaving from breathlessness. Nothing remained of the fiend.

The pillar stood as it had before. Its soft, gentle glow touched the women and children as they raised their heads; on the faces of the villagers who peered out between the houses; on Adeya at Theiho's doorstep; on Kyen. He stood before the dome's threshold, his gold eyes so brilliant, it was as if they were lit from behind. He lowered his arms. In the space of a blink, the color flickered out, the sternness emptied out of his face, and his stormy gray eyes returned.

Chapter 12

Kyen swayed where he stood, staring into space.

In the ruins behind him, the women and children rose to their feet. The men approached from between the houses. Murmurs and whispers joined the crackle of the pyres and the soft whimpers of the babies. As the villagers gathered together at what used to be the dome's entrance, Adeya joined them.

Slowly, Kyen turned. His gaze trailed over the stunned faces—over Theiho, his family, and the villagers—as if not really seeing them. Finding Adeya, his eyes suddenly sharpened back into focus, and he paled.

"Oh."

"That wasn't... It couldn't be...." Theiho stepped forward.

Whispers and little gasps of "arcangel" ran through the crowd.

Kelleth gripped his father's hand and stared with eyes as round as marbles.

"Are you alright?" Adeya came up to Kyen.

"I-I need to go. We need to go." He started towards

the dome, the crowd parting around him.

"How did you do that?" Kelleth's question cut above the murmurs.

"We really should go. The fiends'll be back. And with stronger numbers. Probably tonight. I need to leave." Kyen scanned the ring of rubble, all that remained of the dome. "Where's our pack?"

"It's on my shoulder, Kyen," said Adeya.

"We're attacked by fiends all the time." Theiho glanced at the watchtower's ruins. "They're not usually so big, however."

Kyen walked back to Adeya, looking left and right as if searching. "There's not enough aura left in the pillar to hold them off. I will draw them away as best I can. Where's the pack, Adeya?"

"I have it, Kyen." She lifted the strap off her shoulder for emphasis.

He looked at her hard for a long moment, brows drawn together.

"Are you sure you're alright, Kyen? Did you hit your head?" She touched his elbow.

"Do you really have an arcangel?" Kelleth asked more loudly. Theiho put a hand on his shoulder.

"We need to go—"

"Kyen." Adeya's grip on his elbow tightened. She was staring down the street, her aquamarine eyes bright, her face afraid. Theiho and villagers followed her gaze.

Kyen, seeing her expression, whirled around on the spot.

In the middle of the street stood Ennyen. The black

blade gripped in his hand absorbed the flickers of the pyres, looking like a shadow extending from his hilt.

Kyen tensed.

Ennyen shifted his stance to brandish the sword, and began to approach.

"Who is...?" Theiho looked to them.

Without taking his eyes off of Ennyen, Kyen said, "Tell the other villagers to keep away, Theiho."

"He's only one swordsman. He's outnumb—"

"A hundred men would not save you from him. Don't engage him." Kyen looked at Adeya. "Don't."

Her eyes glanced at him with alarm.

Putting a hand on his hilt, he took a couple steps towards Ennyen and separated himself from the others. The glow of the pillar behind him haloed his outline.

"Draw your blade, Kyen of Crossblade!" Ennyen pointed his sword at him.

"I don't want to fight you," he replied.

For an answer, Ennyen rushed him.

Kyen watched, gold flickering briefly through his gray eyes. The pillar flared. Several ribbons of light burst out of the air, shot out, and and seized Ennyen. Wrapping around his arms and legs and enveloping the black blade, they pushed him to a stop a stone's throw away. Ennyen strained against them, but when they tightened, his dark eyes narrowed on Kyen. He let his sword-point dip.

"I will not fight you," said Kyen.

"Hiding behind an arcangel?" Ennyen smiled, both pleased and disgusted. "Coward."

The ribbons holding Ennyen suddenly quivered

upwards. A sinking chime rang out as a dark body dive-bombed out of the night. Swirled in dark miasma, the fiend caladrius dropped straight into the ribbons and broke them: those gripping Ennyen dissolved; the rest snapped taut, snagged by the miasma as it spun into a vortex.

Kyen's eyes grew wide. He jolted as the ribbons anchored in the air around him began to strain thin. He tried to take a step back, but his feet slid forward through the dirt. He dug in his heels, leaning away, sheltering his face with an arm.

Adeya went pale, gripping the amulet at her neck with both hands.

The pillar of light behind them grew brighter and brighter; the hum of its power filled the air, rising in pitch higher and higher. The villagers backed away from it.

The ribbons began to shimmer like water flowing under sunlight, flowing into the vortex. The pillar's glow began to wane in and out as the hum of power faltered.

Kyen yelled and flung out his arms. A flash cracked through the air. The ribbons burst in the middle, their ends whipping into the vortex and vanishing. The ends nearest Kyen disintegrated into a haze. In the wake of the flash, the pillar faded out, leaving only the flickering of the pyres for light. A dozen cracks laced up and down its surface.

Panting, Kyen stared hard at the fiend caladrius.

A sinking cry issued from its toothy maw as the miasma evaporated. With a heavy flap, the bird shot upwards.

In its wake, Ennyen charged.

Chapter 13

Kyen barely had time to draw his sword before Ennyen struck like black lightning. They collided with a clash of steel. Their swords—flashing, singing blurs—whipped around them. An unrelenting clamor rang out, steel clanging steel. Within seconds, Kyen cowed under the onslaught. He struggled sideways, reaching for space, drawing Ennyen away from the others, as Ennyen bludgeoned him with a speed born of ferocity. They crossed the street in a matter of moments.

Ennyen's blade suddenly flashed out underneath Kyen's guard. The blade slit him across the stomach, its sharp edge digging across his linen armor vest. Kyen staggered backwards but caught his balance in time to leap sideways. The black blade cleaved apart a pyre behind him, slinging sparks, as it just missed him.

Running a stone's throw away, Kyen turned with his sword upraised. The slice to his armor had left a black stain. From it spread inky tentacles that grabbed at the material. Without taking his eyes from Ennyen, Kyen ripped open the latches, shrugged off the vest, and threw it aside. It hit the ground, crumpling into the dark tentacles and vanishing.

Ennyen turned on him and flourished his blade. With a casual step, he walked over the flaming debris of the pyre, his dark eyes hard and focused. The two swordsmen traveled up the street, Kyen walking backwards, Ennyen closing in.

Breathing hard, Kyen held a defensive stance. The tip of his sword was trembling. Up and down its edge, black pockmarks were spreading, eating gaping chunks into the steel.

Ennyen launched himself forward, and Kyen dove to meet him. When their swords connected, Ennyen slung Kyen's sword aside and stabbed. Kyen bent; the sword-point grazed his side. He swung his hilt down at Ennyen's head with both hands. Ennyen caught it with one. Staring him in the face, he held the hilt firm even as Kyen's arms shook from the strain, trying to press down on him and failing. Ennyen's one-handed grip on the black blade clenched.

Kyen's eyes widened. He jerked his sword free as Ennyen attacked at close range, striking with one lightning blow after another. Kyen parried the first two, but at the third, an odd metal snap resounded. The top half of Kyen's sword flew off as the impact from Ennyen's blade snapped the steel in half. The point skittered away between a couple pyres. Kyen tried to lean out of the way as the black blade flashed out again.

Adeya covered her eyes with a cry.

Blood splattered the cobblestones.

The force of Ennyen's sword catching across his chest

slung Kyen to the ground. He hit the dirt at a roll. Coming up in a crouch out of range, he steadied himself with a hand on the ground. He panted, his broken sword still clutched in a fist, the other hand holding a gash across his chest. Red oozed into his tunic.

Ennyen advanced. Firelight glistened off Kyen's blood along the edge of his black blade.

"No, stop!" Adeya drew her sword and ran after them.

Ennyen turned at the sound of her voice.

"Don't!" Kyen made to stand, but Adeya reached him first.

She lashed out.

Ennyen blocked and disarmed her with an easy flick, and her sword clattered to the ground. He pointed his blade at her neck. She backed away, drawing out her dagger and brandishing it at him.

Ennyen smiled—a black look that didn't touch his eyes. He said over his shoulder where Kyen struggled to his feet. "You'd let a half-trained maiden break in on our battle? She's not even a swordsister." Then to Adeya, he said, "There's no honor in killing you, maiden. But if you break in again, I will not hesitate."

"Adeya. Don't!" Kyen said through gritted teeth, finally reaching his feet, bloody and unsteady.

Her gaze jumped between them.

With a yell, Kyen charged with his broken sword. Ennyen whirled to meet him, slamming him back with rapid blows too fast for the eye to follow. Kyen dodged to the left, again and again, to get out of range, Ennyen's blade a black wind nicking him. They cut a diagonal across the street.

With a crack of metal, the rest of Kyen's sword snapped off at the base, leaving him with only a stub and a hilt. He caught an overhead slash on the crossguard. Ennyen threw his weight to bear down on him. Kyen gritted his teeth, bending deeper and deeper under Ennyen's strength. The black blade dug into his shoulder, drawing blood as Ennyen pressed closer. He suddenly slipped his blade from Kyen's hold to smack him hard across the face with the pommel.

Kyen went down. He landed face-first, sprawled out between a couple of pyres. He groaned and pulled his hand underneath him.

Adeya gripped her dagger with white fingers. Tears bubbled up in her eyes as she watched Kyen shift painfully in the dirt.

Ennyen straightened out of his sword stance. Hefting his blade, he stepped over and stood above Kyen.

Cradling one arm to his chest, Kyen struggled to his hands and knees. The other arm holding him up trembled. Blood dripped to the ground as his breath came in hard, shuddering gasps.

"That look suits you." Ennyen flipped his blade underhand. "I know only one better." He drove his blade down at Kyen's exposed back.

Adeya shrieked.

Kyen dropped into a roll—the black blade driving into the dirt behind him—and came up on his knees at Ennyen's feet, underneath his guard. His hands, clapped over glint of steel, flashed towards the inside of the other swordsman's hip. Ennyen's eyes widened. He tried to shift back, out of the way but not far enough. Kyen's hands slammed into his thigh.

For a fraction of a second they stood. Ennyen stared down, wide-eyed, bent awkwardly over Kyen who crouched beneath him. He glared up, blood oozing over his fingers where he held the base of his broken blade; the bloodied tip protruded out the other side of Ennyen's leg.

The swordsmen snapped apart: Ennyen stumbled away and Kyen lunged backwards to his feet.

Kyen sprinted for Adeya. She opened her mouth, but he yelled "Go!", grabbed her arm and dragged her after him. They ran hard down the street.

Ennyen, limping up, watched them clamber over the ruins of the watchtower and vanish into the night beyond the firelight. He looked disgusted. The villagers edged away from him, crowding close to the dome. He ignored their stares and their frightened murmurs as he wiped his sword off on his cloak.

The fiend caladrius fluttered to the ground beside him. The grinning face bent up, cocked sideways. He eyed it.

"Quit smirking." He slammed his sword back into its sheath. "You do your job."

The fiend chortled—it sounded like a laugh—and took to the sky.

Ennyen limped down the road after Kyen, ignoring the broken blade sticking through his leg.

Chapter 14

The pines and boulders of the foothills—mounds of shadow in the morning twilight—crowded Kyen and Adeya. He strode between them at a feverish pace. Blood soaked the front of his tunic, spread a damp patch around his shoulder, and dripped from where he'd gripped the naked shard of his sword. Besides a tight clench to his jaw, he showed no signs of being slowed by the pain.

Neither spoke as he dragged Adeya behind him. She clung to his hand with both of hers. In the dimness she tripped on a jutting rock, but Kyen hauled her back up before she could fall.

Growing dawn gave shape to the trees and texture to the rocks. It illuminated the cold puffs of their breath.

Kyen clambered to the top of a stone outcrop with Adeya struggling behind him. One hand braced against a rock, he heaved her up the last stretch and turned to continue. Adeya's eyes caught on a smear of blood he'd left on the rock as they passed.

"Kyen, you have to stop," she said, her gaze on the dark wet streak that had spread down his back

He trudged towards a copse of trees.

"Kyen? Kyen, please. You'll kill yourself if you keep going."

He said nothing.

"Kyen!" Adeya jerked back on his arm, forcing him to a halt.

He turned his hard gray eyes on her and stared, uncomprehending and dazed. Slowly, his face softened.

"Please," she repeated. "You're wounded."

His face pinched as if it took an effort to understand her.

"We should find somewhere to stop," she repeated.

"You're right." He turned, letting go of her hand, and kept going.

Adeya watched him with concern, but he walked to some young pines that squatted together in a cluster. She followed as he pushed his way through their branches. In the center, a pocket between the branches sheltered from wind and offered a soft carpet of pine needles.

With a soft grunt, Kyen lowered himself to sit against a trunk. He looked at his cut hand in confusion as if just noticing it.

Adeya slung open her healer's pouch and dug the water skin from their pack. "Take off your tunic. I need to get at those wounds."

He unclasped his cloak and shrugged it off. It fell in a blood-smeared heap to the side. She took it and spread it over the ground.

"Tunic off, too," she added, when he made to sit back again. She set out a jar of salve, bandages, a needle and thread.

With an odd, pinched frown, Kyen loosened the laces of his tunic. He pulled it over his head.

"Come over here. I can't sew you up if you're sitting all scrunched up." She glanced at him as he shuffled over and stared.

Ennyen's sword had cut a nasty gash that crossed his bare chest from shoulder to waist. Another gouge bled beside his neck. But what held Adeya's eyes was an old scar. A starburst of rough, gray skin puckered the center of his chest. He scooted onto the cloak, revealing its twin on his back for an instant, before he laid down with a wince.

Adeya gave herself a little shake then threaded her needle. Sitting with her legs tucked under her, she put the needle in her teeth, poured water onto a cloth, and began cleaning the gash on his chest.

"Ennyen would have split you in half if you hadn't leaned out of the way," she said as she dabbed. "The blade nicked your ribs as it is."

Kyen stared tiredly up at the patch of gray sky visible between the pine-tops.

"Wounds this bad are going to slow you down. Can't Kade help with any of this?"

"He would have mended it already if he could. He used everything he had against the caladrius fiend."

"What would you do if I wasn't a healer of Isea?"

Kyen didn't answer.

"You'll need to keep still for two or three days at least." Adeya took the needle from her teeth and began to stitch him up.

"I want to make Bargston by tomorrow."

"I just said you needed to keep still. Do you want to heal or not?"

"I'll rest on the boat to Eope," he said. "If we don't make Bargston tomorrow, we may not make it at all."

"But you wounded Ennyen. He's not getting very far, very fast on that leg."

"You've not met with a fully trained Blade of Avanna, have you?"

"Why? Are they all as inconsiderate of their health as you?" Adeya shot him a glare.

He said nothing.

"Why can't we just hide in the foothills for a few days?" She tugged at the thread and bent for another stitch.

"Ennyen has a caladrius fiend."

"So? Your body should hide Kade's aura, like it does from the rest of the fiends."

"It's not a normal fiend," said Kyen. "Most fiends are birthed when the Consuming Dark gets a hold of an animal, but caladrius aren't like squirrels or cougars. They are creatures left over from the Firstwold. They live half on the mortal plain and half on the plain of the arcangels."

"What are you saying?" Adeya, having sewed Kyen's chest up most of the way, shifted around to sit at his shoulder to finish the rest.

"In the foothills, under the mountains, in me, Kade can't hide from it. It can see him in his world, even though other fiends can't see him in ours," he said. "Eope is the only place where we might be able to shield Kade from its sight."

"The wizards?" She bit off the end of her thread. "You

talk like you've met with a caladrius fiend before. Sit up."

Clenching his jaw, he eased himself upright.

Adeya started dabbing the gouge beside his neck.

For a few deep breaths, Kyen stared hard at the tree trunk across from him with his brows drawn together. "Illeth of Norgard kept a caladrius fiend."

Adeya, poking a fresh thread through her needle, paused. "Illeth of Norgard?" She bent to seam up the gouge. "All the stories say you died when you fought Illeth of Norgard in the Black Wars, but you're still here. Illeth of Norgard isn't—she's not still alive, too, is she?"

"I beheaded her."

"Could it be her fiend is still alive?"

"And working with Ennyen now," he said.

She bent to finish the last few stitches.

"I'm not sure how the Consuming Dark has twisted the caladrius' original abilities, but it's the only fiend that can eat aura," said Kyen. "It nearly ate Kade. He had to burn up the pillar and everything else he had just to break off its hold. Without Kade, I may not have any choice but to fight Ennyen."

"Not in this condition, you won't!"

In the silence that fell between them, Adeya tied off the final stitch and bit the thread off. She wiped off her needle and curled up the thread without looking at them. Her eyes took in the nasty scar on the center of Kyen's back.

"Did Illeth of Norgard do this to you?" She touched it.

Kyen arched his back away from her fingers, flushing. "Can I put my tunic back on, please?"

"I've to bandage you first. Hold on."

He tried to edge away from her.

Adeya, gathering up her salve and bandages, scooched after him. "Hold still!"

He slouched as she spread the salve over the stitches then began wrapping his shoulder. He fixed his eyes on a pine cone, looking nettled, growing redder in the face.

"There's no need to be embarrassed."

"Kade normally—" He hesitated.

"Heals you?" she offered.

"He'd like you to know. He's very pleased with your skills."

"Praise from an arcangel." Adeya blushed and smiled. "I'm flattered."

"It was a lot less painful when Kade—" A flinch and a breath through clenched teeth finished his sentence as Adeya tied a bandage tight at his shoulder.

"You're a warrior. Aren't you used to pain by now?" She reached around to wrap several layers of bandage around the gash on his chest. She gave the ends a firm tug.

"Ah!" He tensed.

"There. You can put your tunic back on now."

"Thank you," Kyen said in a taut voice.

"But not this one. Use a new one." Adeya arose, dug a fresh tunic from the pack and tossed it to him.

He tugged it over his head, slowing to be ginger with his injured shoulder. As he laced up the neck, he said, "We should keep moving."

She sat back down with a huff, sweeping bits of hair out of her face. "Maybe you don't need to rest, but I do. I'm exhausted! I didn't hardly sleep at all."

He frowned.

"Can't we rest a little bit? We'd make better time in the long run, don't you think?"

"Alright, but only until noon." Kyen settled himself back against the tree trunk. "I'll get you up."

"You know, you're so difficult sometimes." Adeya, curling up in her cloak, leaned back and shot him a frown, but he didn't hear. He stared into the space in front of him with unseeing eyes, a troubled look on his face.

Adeya sighed and laid her head down to rest.

Chapter 15

The orange arclight of evening was streaming through the branches when Adeya opened her eyes. She looked up at the tree tops, brushing a lock of hair out of her face. She frowned.

Bolting upright, she looked at Kyen.

He lay limp against the tree trunk, head lolled on his chest, his face pale in the shadows.

Adeya crawled over to him.

"Kyen?" She shook his good shoulder. "Kyen!"

With a groan, he lifted his head and opened tired eyes.

She sat back with a sigh of relief.

He lifted his face to the light and, seeing it already dimming, he came fully awake. "What time is it?"

"You scared me."

"We should've been gone two arcquarters ago." With a tight clench to his jaw, he rose to his feet, gripping the tree trunk with one hand.

Adeya put out her hands as if to catch him. "Are you sure you can?"

Kyen nodded. He straightened and after a moment

steadied. In a taut voice, he said, "We'll need the lantern."

She grabbed the pack and dug out her shaded lantern. She set the wick alight with a bit of flint and tinder while he gingerly pushed his way out of the copse of trees. Latching up her pack, she picked it and the lantern up and hurried after him.

"We need to make it down to the highway. Hope we can outrun Ennyen. I won't stand a chance up in the foothills." He looked at her as she emerged out of the trees behind him.

They both turned to head downhill but a few steps brought Kyen to a stop. Adeya, fiddling with the shades on her lantern, almost bumped into his back. She looked up.

Hidden in the shadows of the trees, a black outline perched. White teeth glinted as the fiend caladrius grinned at them.

Kyen backed away, pushing Adeya behind him.

The fiend's mouth widened.

They turned and hurried the opposite direction.

"Don't stop." He glanced over his shoulder.

The fiend kept its perch, still grinning, even as the copse of trees they passed hid it from view.

They fled. Kyen held the arm with the wounded shoulder close to his side, using the other to help himself up rocky slants or push aside piney branches. Adeya kept close, lantern in one hand, her other hand outstretched to support or catch him in case he fell. They both kept looking over their shoulders, but the fiend caladrius didn't reappear.

"Your sword, Kyen. And mine. I never picked it up after Ennyen disarmed me. What are we going to do if it catches us?" Adeya asked.

"What do we have left for weapons?"

"I don't know. I've the knife on my belt. You should take it."

Kyen paused a moment to catch his breath. "You keep it."

"But—" She began but cut off when Kyen faced her. He looked troubled, his stormy eyes bright with uncertainty.

"You might need it." He turned away and kept walking.

"But…" Her face sank.

"This way."

Adeya hurried after him.

Kyen, having made a wide sweep around the caladrius fiend, angled their path downhill again. The twilight died around them, leaving the glow under the lantern as their only light. The round clumps of pines and the lumpy boulder mounds materialized out of the darkness to meet them, then disappeared into it again as they passed. The descent of the slope offered the only guide to the highway below in their pitch black surroundings.

Reaching the crest of a half-buried boulder, they stopped. An unearthly wail screeched from the outline of some pines ahead. Adeya clapped her hand to her ears and Kyen winced; he ducked them both low. As the sound echoed away, shadows slid into the edge of the lantern light —two cougar-like fiends stalking towards them.

Adeya sucked in a breath.

"Run," Kyen said, putting himself between her and the fiends.

Together they turned and fled.

A skin-tingling wail followed them.

Skirting outcrops of stone and weaving between trees, they ran. Kyen lagged, and Adeya slowed long enough to take his good hand. She pulled him along, holding her lantern aloft in the night. They both started panting hard as the ground steepened under their feet. Another wail, this one more distant, rose into the darkness of the night. Adeya glanced over her shoulder. The forest lay empty behind them.

As they dashed away, Kyen's knees gave out, and he dropped to the ground. His weight yanked on Adeya's arm, pulling her down with him, and she landed with a thump on her backside, barely saving herself from smashing the lantern. It bobbled back and forth in her upraised hand.

"Kyen! Are you alright?" She clambered back to her feet. Gripping him under his good arm, she tried to pull him upright, but his knees unhinged beneath him. He collapsed back to the ground. He remained on his hands and knees, breathing hard, head hung.

Adeya set the lantern down, drew her dagger and stood at the ready. Her eyes scanned the dark trees on one side and the steep slant of rocks on the other.

Below them another wail screamed out, but nothing appeared from the trees.

Her breathing slowed.

Kyen shifted himself to sit down. He looked pale.

"Where are they?" she asked him. "We couldn't have outrun them."

Another wail answered the first, this one to the left. A third joined in, but rising in the distance on the right.

"They... they aren't coming for us?" Adeya glanced at Kyen.

He frowned. Clenching his jaw, he struggled to regain his feet. "We need to keep moving."

Adeya pursed her lips and, with bright eyes, watched him wobble, but she said nothing. She gripped him under his good arm. Sheathing her knife, she bent to take up the lantern.

"Keep moving," Kyen whispered as if to himself.

Deep night set in as they pressed on. The air grew chill. A black sky yawned over their exposed backs as they met with a steep slope of rock and began climbing. The lantern alone held back the darkness. Beyond, it swallowed up all else. Only the sounds of their heavy breathing—Adeya's panting and Kyen's ragged—disturbed the silence. Clambering to a stretch where the slope relented, she set the lantern down to help Kyen to the top. He staggered a little.

"We should stop. You need rest," she said.

Kyen only nodded. He lowered himself to the ground next to a pumpkin-sized boulder.

Kneeling next to him, Adeya set aside the lantern to dig the waterskin from their pack. She offered it to him. He accepted it, but when he lifted it to his mouth, he didn't drink much.

She pulled up his tunic to check the bandages. He made no protest. Fresh red splotches marred the undersides of the white strips.

"You're still bleeding." Adeya tugged his tunic back in place. "If you keep going like this, you're going to kill yourself."

Kyen upended the waterskin, but again, took only a mouthful. He handed it back. Their hands touched as Adeya took the waterskin. She frowned. Snatching his hand in both of hers, she felt it and then rubbed it between her palms.

"You're going cold. You're losing too much blood."

"It's cold out here." Kyen sounded weary.

"My hands are cold, but yours are freezing!"

"We need to keep moving." Holding onto the boulder, he climbed to his feet. Adeya hurried up in time to catch him as his knees buckled.

"Let me help you." She pulled his arm over her shoulder. Propping him up, she bent to pick up the lantern. "Hold onto me."

Kyen gripped her without a word.

"We've got to get to the highway." She angled them downwards, but they didn't get more than a few steps.

The cougar fiends rose out of the rocks.

Adeya stopped. She turned her back on them and staggered back up the slope, walking as quickly as Kyen could go and biting her lip.

A chortle sounded behind them, but she didn't dare glance back, not until they'd made it a stone's throw away. Then she looked over her shoulder.

The fiends had vanished.

Kyen dragged on her as they inched their way up the mountain. He walked with his head hung, gray eyes fixed on his next step, saying nothing. Adeya broke a sweat from supporting him; he began to shiver with chills, and his feet slowed to the pace of a crawl.

They struggled together up a slope so steep and rocky, they both bent to hands and knees, scrambling for the top. Almost falling twice as Kyen lost his balance and nearly dropping the lantern altogether, they topped the precipice. They both collapsed, Kyen to his back and Adeya to all fours.

"No more!" She panted. "We can't go farther."

Kyen stared at the black sky as he struggled to breathe.

Shoving herself to her feet, Adeya held the lantern aloft. In front of them, a mound of boulders lay half-buried in the mountainside. Young pines clustered around two or three towering elders in the shelter of the outcrop.

"We can rest there." Adeya bent to help him up. He struggled to rise as she lifted him by his good arm. Without warning, he dropped, but she clung to him and strained with all her strength to keep him from falling. She half-carried him, stooped under his weight, and they staggered together into the cove between the boulders and the trees.

Beneath the largest pine, Adeya lowered him to the ground. He rested back against the tree trunk. She placed her lantern beside him and set about gathering pine cones and sticks. Kyen watched her with tired gray eyes, shivering uncontrollably. Arranging the needles, cones, and branches in a hollow, she lit a stick from the lantern.

"I don't care if the fiends see us. If they wanted to kill us, they'd have done it already." Adeya thrust the burning twig into the wood and blew on it until tongues of fire crackled up. Hopping to her feet, she seized on a heavy log twice as long as she stood tall. Her first tug failed to budge it. She puffed out her cheeks and threw her weight against it. The log shifted, and she dragged it over to drop its fat end in the fire.

Kyen, with slow hands, fumbled with his empty scabbard until he got it untied from his belt. He set it aside. Shivers continued to wrack through him.

"Here." Adeya unlatched her cloak. She dropped it around his shoulders.

"You can't. It's cold," he said as she tucked the folds around him.

"Don't tell me what I can and can't do, Kyen of Avanna." She shifted to sit beside him, holding out her hands to the fire but not quite repressing her own shiver. The blaze crackled and cast off waves of heat as it licked up the hefty log.

"You've got to keep up your strength." Adeya dug out the waterskin and a journey bread. "Eat something."

"I'm not hungry."

She broke off a piece and held it out under his nose. "Eat it."

His hand emerged from the cloaks to take the piece, only to withdraw into the folds with the bit uneaten.

Adeya glowered at him.

"I'll take some water," he said.

She handed him the bottle; he drank a couple mouthfuls, no more.

"Rest!" she said. "I'll stay up and keep watch."

Gingerly, Kyen lowered himself to the ground, curled up under the cloaks.

Adeya, breaking a big stick, added it to the fire and

chomped on the rest of the journey bread. She searched the surrounding woods, watching the firelight dance off the trunks and play over the boulders. It reflected in Kyen's dark, tired eyes as he watched it.

"We should have made Bargston already," he said.

Adeya stopped chewing, swallowed with difficulty.

"If we go much higher into the mountains," he said. "We'll be nearing the borders of Norgard."

Adeya frowned, setting aside her bread.

Kyen, still shivering, nestled deeper underneath the cloaks and edged closer to the fire. His eyelids sank. His mussy, black hair stood in sharp contrast to the paleness of his skin. "If he comes... don't fight him."

"You're in no state to defend yourself," she said.

"Promise me. Don't fight him."

"But he'll kill you!"

Kyen opened his eyes to look at her, but she wouldn't meet his weary gaze. He waited until she finally looked at him.

"He's not after you. Don't give him a reason to be," he said.

Adeya sulked, turning her face away from him.

He sighed, closing his eyes. "Take Kade, if it comes to it. Find the other arcangels."

She drooped as her stubbornness dissolved. Tears bubbled into her eyes. "By myself? But—"

"Promise me." He murmured, half-conscious. Adeya watched as his face relaxed and his breathing deepened into sleep. She drew up her knees and hugged them to herself.

"I promise," she whispered. "Just promise me you

won't die."

The fire snapped and crackled.

Adeya, her gaze flitting over the shadows beyond the firelight, wiped away an escaping tear. "Don't leave me by myself."

Chapter 16

The fire burned hot as the first streaks of morning hit the rocks overhead.

Adeya, bleary-eyed and wilted, sat hugging herself and watching flames dance. They licked at the stub of the log, half-burned away through the night, and reached for more, flaring up the sticks and branches that'd been freshly piled on. Beside her, Kyen groaned. Shifting under the cloaks, he muttered something unintelligible. Adeya brightened as he opened his eyes.

"Good morning." She leaned over him. "How are you feeling?"

Kyen's brows pinched together as he looked up at her. He shifted as if to rise only to lie back again with a groan. His dark hair, damp with sweat, stuck to his head as he shivered, and his face looked gray.

She put a hand to his forehead, her smile fading. Pulling away the cloaks, she checked the bandages under his tunic. The stitched gash across his chest glared raw; little red veins were spreading from the wound towards his heart. She drew a sharp breath. Fumbling with her healer's pouch, she cast it open, dug around, and pulled out the salve. She spread the last of it over the wound, smearing it thin in order to cover its length. Violent shivers wracked him up and down as she worked, and he said nothing. He struggled to focus on her face when she tugged his tunic back in place and covered him again with the cloaks.

"Is it s-s-nowing?" he asked, teeth chattering, a strange haze in his gray eyes. "It's s-so cold…"

"No. Let me build up the fire for you." She reached for a stick.

"W-where's Kilyenne?"

"Kilyenne?"

"My s-s-sister."

Adeya's hand froze in midair. She looked back at him.

"Kilyenne s-s-said she'd be back before the s-snow. She promised me s-s-she'd never go marauding."

As the words stumbled from his mouth, Adeya's eyes grew wide. Her hand crept up to the amulet at her neck and gripped it till her fingers turned white.

"She promised." Kyen stared up at her, his face concerned, his gray eyes looking at her without seeing her.

Adeya swallowed hard. Taking Kyen's hand in both of hers, she struggled to find her voice for a moment then said, "Kilyenne isn't here, Kyen."

He suddenly squinted hard at her. "Wuh-why are we talking about K-Kilyenne? We have to k-keep moving." He made as if to sit up.

She held him down. "You're not well, Kyen. You've been badly hurt. You need to rest."

Unable to resist her gentle hand, he laid back and closed his eyes. "T-tell her not to go. Tell her…"

"I will." Adeya drew in a shaky breath. "Kyen, is Kade there?"

He looked at her, his eyes unfocused, uncomprehending.

"Can I talk to Kade?"

"...s-s-sure." In the space of a blink, his gray eyes changed to gold. Despite the chills wracking him, his body relaxed back, and a strange, serious expression overtook his face.

Adeya flinched when the golden eyes shifted to her. "Kade?"

"Yes, Adeya of Isea?" he said; though he used Kyen's voice, Kade spoke flatly with a different tenor and without much feeling.

"Kade, Kyen's losing too much blood." Tears bubbled into her eyes; she swallowed hard and continued. "Fever is taking hold. He's not going to make it if we don't help him. Isn't there anything you can do?"

"I'm sorry, Adeya of Isea. Had I the strength, I'd have used it already. I need more aura—an arcstone or an auramere—before I can do any more."

"You wouldn't know of any Firstwold ruins nearby? Anywhere we could find aura?"

"Yes, deeper in the mountains," said the arcangel. "But I do not know your landscapes. I cannot tell you where or how far in mortal steps."

"What if you go to the ruins and bring the aura back?"

"I can't leave the shelter of Kyen's flesh. If I do, every fiend on the mountain will see me and come down on us."

"But my medicines are out! What are we going to do?"

A tear escaped down her cheek, and she put her face in her hands.

"Are you not a healer of Isea, trained in herbal lore?"

"Yes." She lifted her head a little.

His golden gaze shifted to the trees sheltering them. "Do not herbs grow on this mountain? Is there any you might find if you hunt?"

"Yes. I'll try. Maybe I can look for any signs of ruins nearby also. Will you keep watch over Kyen?"

"He cannot go far on his own power, but I will hold him down if he tries."

"Thank you."

The golden color flickered out, leaving Kyen gazing at the space between their faces.

"I'll be right back," she said.

He didn't respond, looking exhausted.

"Stay here."

"Is it s-snowing...?" He mumbled as he settled back. His hand reached out from under the cloaks, groping around. Adeya shifted his empty scabbard into his reach, and his fingers gripped it. He drew it near, drifting into semi-consciousness again.

Adeya rose, loaded branches on the fire, and gave Kyen a last worried look. Then, she faced the rising mountain. Walking out of their cove, she stepped atop a half-buried boulder to gaze up at the heights where the trees thinned away into rocky, barren ground.

A dark shape winged out of the nearest copse.

Adeya bristled.

The caladrius fiend swooped down to alight in a nearby

tree. It cocked its toothy grin at her and swished its cascading tail.

"I've had enough of you!" Adeya drew her knife. "What do you want with us? Get out of here! Go!" Snatching up a rock, she chucked it at the fiend.

The fiend watched as the stone flew wide then turned its grinning nub back to her. It chortled.

A man's chuckle joined it, and Adeya tensed. She whirled around.

Ennyen stood at the fire beside Kyen; he gazed at her, amusement shining in his dark eyes, the faintest smile playing across his face.

Chapter 17

"You have the courage of a swordsister, though you lack the skill and the blood." Ennyen rested a hand on his hilt. "Not even I would challenge a caladrius fiend with nothing but a rock and a dagger."

At his feet, Kyen stirred. His eyes sharpened into a glare when he saw Ennyen. He struggled to sit up, clutching his empty scabbard.

Ennyen caught the movement. His smile fell as he eyed him for a moment. He kicked Kyen in the face hard enough to fling him onto his back.

With a cry, Adeya started forward but Kyen's hoarse "Don't!" stopped her.

He writhed on the ground, groaning, holding his head. He struggled to lift himself with his good arm again.

Stooping, Ennyen seized him by the collar and heaved him up out of the cloaks. He threw Kyen back-first against the tree. Before Kyen could sag to the ground, Ennyen drew his blade, seized him by the arm, and stretched him up against the trunk. He cried out in pain as he hung in Ennyen's grasp.

"Kyen!" Adeya stepped closer, but he shot her a hard

look.

"Don't," he croaked. His empty scabbard dangled in his hand.

"You'd do well to listen, maiden," said Ennyen. "I won't kill him. Not yet. He's wanted; him and his arcangel."

Kyen met Ennyen's gaze. His stormy gray eyes shone fierce and hard, and Ennyen met the look with some consideration. He dragged Kyen's arm up further, drawing from him a whimper and forcing him onto his tiptoes.

"I have a feeling you'll cause less trouble without a sword arm." He shifted the point of his blade to the crook of Kyen's outstretched elbow.

Kyen, his face stony, hung limp as a doll. His grip on the empty scabbard tightened.

Ennyen thrusted.

Adeya screamed and covered her eyes.

Kyen's hand shot up as Ennyen's sword stabbed down. The scabbard connected with Ennyen's chin moments before the sword thrust landed. The blade skived the tree bark next to Kyen's arm as a loud smack rang through the trees. Ennyen's head snapped backwards and he staggered, losing his grip on Kyen.

Kyen slipped down the tree trunk and dropped to his hands and knees.

Regaining his balance, Ennyen wiped at the blood from his split lip. His dark eyes burned with fury as he looked at it.

"You spineless throwback!" He lifted his sword to cut Kyen down, but a sudden screaming stopped him.

Three figures cloaked in gray burst out of the trees

behind Kyen. Yelling warcries and slinging longswords, they attacked as one. Steel flashed and clanged. Ennyen's lightning-fast sword slipped by the intruders' flurry, slicing across the breastplate of one and the shoulder pad of another. But the three drove him back anyway.

The caladrius fiend's grin fell. With a mighty wingbeat, it rose from its branch. It dove towards the fray, but a fourth swordsman leapt from the forest to meet it. He drew a blade that gleamed silver-white as he slashed out. The fiend veered aside with a squawk. Swooping back into the air, it winged away with a chortle.

Ennyen whirled around and fled.

The tallest and shortest of the attackers stopped, but the third gave chase.

"Oda! Get back here!" snapped the swordsman with the white blade.

Oda skidded to a halt. He shook his fist after Ennyen's retreating back and yelled, "MAGGOT!"

The three cloaked attackers turned on Kyen. Rising to his knees, he swayed and squinted at them for a moment then crumpled face-first into the ground.

"Don't touch him!" Adeya ran to stand between them. She lifted her dagger, but the swordsman with the white blade lunged forward. He seized the dagger and with a deft twist, wrenched it free. Adeya squeaked to find her own dagger at her throat. She stepped back.

The other three attackers closed in, swords in hand.

"Don't hurt him," she said. "Please."

"We didn't come to hurt him." The swordsman with the white blade threw back his hood. "We came to find him."

Adeya's eyes widened. She stared at the withered, old man before her. He wore a long white ponytail, and his mist gray eyes sized her up. She looked to the other three as they threw back their hoods. A bear of a man, all height and muscle with claw-like scars on his face, held up his sword. His companion, a sinewy man—the one who'd tried to chase Ennyen—shifted eagerly from foot to foot. The third, a petite woman fierce-eyed and handsome, wore a braid to her knees that bristled with iron spikes. All three turned gray eyes on her.

"You're—"

"Gennen," the old man interrupted, thumping his chest with a fist. "Inen." —he motioned to the giant. "Odallyan."—the man bouncing on his heels "Wynne."—the woman surveyed Adeya; she didn't look impressed.

"You're—" Adeya tried again.

"Of Avanna," Gennen finished for her. "You'd better get those off." He nodded at the cuts on Wynne's shoulder pad and Oda's breastplate. Ennyen's blade had left its dark poison behind, and it was spreading across their armor. The two began unbuckling the pieces and cast them off.

"He got your sword, too." Oda pointed at Inen's blade. The huge swordsman lifted it to see a vein of darkness that'd eaten almost half-way through the steel. His eyes narrowed, and with a grunt, he cast it on top of the other's discarded items. Dark tentacles splayed out and curled around the pieces, drawing them in. The dark mass grew as it swallowed them, and began groping for more.

Gennen strode over. The old man lifted the white blade high and stabbed the center of the blob. It flailed for a moment before disintegrating into smoke.

Adeya stood, watching with wide-eyes, as he jerked the white blade out of the ground.

"You'd better get your spare, Inen," he said.

With another grunt, Inen nodded and pulled off a second longsword that'd been strapped to his back.

Meanwhile, Wynne had walked over to Kyen. She nudged his body with her toe. "Ugh! I think he's dead, Gennen."

"No! He can't be!" Adeya whirled and dropped to her knees next to his prone form. She turned him over and brushed away the pine needles sticking to his sweaty face. His chest struggled to rise and fall as he lay limp in her arms.

Gennen walked up beside her.

"He's lost too much blood, and fever is taking hold. You have to help him! Please!" she cried.

Gennen surveyed Kyen for a moment then shrugged. "Just give him this. Block-headed boy..." Digging a pouch out of his pocket, he tossed it to her. He tucked Adeya's dagger in his belt with a fluid movement then turned to snap out orders. "Inen, get a litter put together. Oda, keep an eye out for those fiends. Wynne, get our packs."

"You go get the packs!" Wynne shoved Oda.

"Gennen told you to do it." Oda jabbed his blade at her.

"I'm better at killing fiends than you. You do it!"

"No, you're not!"

"Go get the packs, Wynne," said Inen, cutting through their argument with his deep voice.

Wynne shot him a murderous glare, shoved Oda out of

the way, and stomped into the trees.

Adeya, disbelief written on her face, stared after her for a moment before remembering the pouch in her hand. She opened it to find dried crimson flowers. Smelling it, she jerked her head away with a grimace. "Ugh! What is this?"

"Ihnasah flower," said Gennen. "From the slopes of Avanna and a remnant of the Firstwold. It'll cut just about anything that ails the body."

"How do you use it?"

"Poultice it! Make a tea! Stuff it down his throat! I don't care—Just get it inside of him!" Gennen stomped off after Inen. Together, they began to bring down branches for a litter.

Adeya hurried to pull a tin cup out of her pack, filled it from the water skin, and threw in a handful of flowers. She set it carefully in the hot coals.

Odallyan stood nearby. Rocking back and forth on his heels, he dawdled with his bare sword, flipping grips with a lazy flourish.

The tea grew steamy, and Adeya took it from the fire. She stirred it, blowing on it, when the sound of cracking branches drew her attention. A stone's throw away, Inen stood at the base of a small dead pine, watching it topple over, oblivious to Gennen trimming a branch beneath it. Gennen noticed the growing shadow and leapt out of the way in time to avoid being crushed. He rounded on Inen, cussing him out. Inen took it with a quiet and sour expression, but Adeya blushed at the furious words ringing through the trees.

She returned her attention to the tea. She tasted it,

gagged, and swallowed with a visible effort. "Ugh." She shuddered—twice. Gathering Kyen up, she propped him up in her lap, and after a deep, steadying breath, she poured a little into his mouth.

He immediately choked and spit it out, sloshing her cup over them both. He opened his eyes. Still coughing weakly, he looked up at her with a frown, confused.

"You've got to drink it," she said. "It will help you." She held the cup to his mouth again, and this time he took it with a grimace. "I know it tastes terrible. I'm sorry," she said as he struggled to get it down. Once he'd emptied the cup, he fell back limp, resting against her, his eyes closed again.

Adeya kept him in her arms as she watched Gennen and Inen lash their cloaks between two pole-like branches.

Wynne stomped out of the trees and threw three packs to the ground at Adeya's feet.

"Be careful!" She clutched Kyen's conscious form and shot Wynne a look of disapproval.

The swordswoman eyed her; she drew her sword and jabbed it at her. "Are you challenging me, mainlander?"

Adeya glared back.

"Peg it down, Wynne," said Odallyan.

"But she's giving me the dagger eye!"

"Wynne!" Gennen snapped. He and Inen carried over the stretcher.

With a growl, Wynne slammed her sword back in its sheath.

Gennen and Inen lowered the stretcher down. They grabbed Kyen's limp form from Adeya, dragged him over and dropped him onto the litter as if he were a piece of baggage. She opened her mouth to protest but couldn't get a word in.

"Wynne, you take the back," said Gennen.

She cast a disgusted look down at Kyen's prone form and crossed her arms. "I will not!"

"You will to," said Gennen. "Inen, take the front."

"I'm not carrying this spineless throwback for a bladebrother all the way back to the hold."

"Wynne." Gennen stared her down with a dangerous glint in his pale eyes.

"Fine!" She snapped. Bending, she snatched the poles and heaved them with a violence that jostled Kyen. Inen lifted his end with a steady strength.

"On your feet," Gennen said to Adeya. "We've to get to the hold before the fiends be on us again and thick."

Chapter 18

Once out of the shelter of their camp, the warriors set a brisk pace, jogging up the mountainside. Gennen led Inen and Wynne who were carrying the stretcher. Odallyan scampered hither and thither, leaping over boulders and dashing between the trees, always on the lookout. They bounded over rocky outcrops, plowed up the steepening slopes, and wove through the pines as if it were a merry jaunt. None of them so much as lost their breath as Adeya scrambled and panted and clawed after them, often going to her hands and knees because of the ascent. She lagged further and further behind until Inen shouted.

"Gennen! The mainlander!"

The warriors stopped.

Adeya dropped to the ground, fighting for breath and trembling.

With a scitter and leap, Gennen crossed the space to kneel next to her. "Are you well?"

"I'm sorry—I can't!" She panted, shaking her head.

"Climb on." Gennen offered his back to her.

She stared at the wry old man in disbelief.

"You're wasting arclight!" he snapped.

Adeya clambered on and looped her arms about his neck.

The old man lifted her as if she weighed no more than his pack and jogged back up the slope to rejoin the others. They set off together.

Higher up the mountains they climbed. Rounding the shoulder of the slope, they entered a valley covered in deep green verge. Pale curves of rock jutted through the evergreens that clothed the mountainsides. Above, peaks gleamed white with snow. A shimmering lake of cobalt water filled the floor of the valley. Along its banks they trotted, Adeya bouncing and clinging to the old man's neck; Kyen being jostled on the stretcher unnoticed by Wynne and Inen.

Near midday, one of the cougar fiends emerged out of the shadows of some tumbled boulders. Oda, seeing it first, charged it. He screamed a throaty war cry while he slung his sword in circles over his head. The fiend bolted, scrambling away over the rocks before he got close.

When he came trotting back, he grinned at Wynne. "That's how you deal with fiends."

"Shut it," she growled, jerking up on the litter as she jogged over the rocks.

By the time they skirted halfway along the lake, the arc had sunk behind twin peaks to the east. It blazed like a line connecting one mountainside to the other, shedding a failing wedge of light over the valley. As it sank deeper, it turned the heights of pines black, the verdure brown, and the pale rock faces gold.

Gennen stopped in a sandy clearing under the shade of some old pines. The water glittered like fire on black glass a stone's throw away.

"We stop here for the night." He let go of Adeya.

She squeaked and squeezed her grip on his neck to keep from falling, and Gennen choked.

"Gerrouff!"

"I'm sorry!" She lowered herself to the ground.

He shrugged his cloak on straight and swung his head back and forth as if to work out a crick in his neck. "Oda, fish. Wynne, firewood. Inen, scout a perimeter."

Odallyan gave a shout, a leap, and sped towards the lake. He stripped off his boots along the way, casting them haphazardly behind him. Water splashed high when he hit the shallows.

Inen lowered his end of Kyen's litter to the ground; Wynne all but dropped hers with a thud. She sulked into the trees muttering under her breath.

As Inen set off to scout, Adeya hobbled over and sank to her knees next to Kyen. She put a hand to his forehead. Still clammy and pale, he mumbled under his breath and shifted in unconsciousness. She pulled up his tunic to check his wounds. Old blood darkened the underside of the bandages, and his gashes glared an angry red, veined out into the skin of his chest and shoulder.

Gennen stepped up next to her. "Well?"

"He's not worse." She replaced the bandages. "But he's not better."

His white eyebrows drew down into one fuzzy line.

"Don't you know anything?" Wynne dumped a load of firewood down off to the side. "Ihnasah flower can heal everything."

"Unless he wants to die," said Oda from where he stalked in the shallows. "Nothing helps then."

"Heh! I'd want to die if I was him," she said.

He laughed as if it were a good joke.

Adeya frowned at them both, but before she could open her mouth, Gennen cut in.

"Quit squawking! The both of you," he said. "I want dinner!" Then to Adeya, he said, "Still have that pouch? Get more of that in him."

Adeya unslung the pack from her shoulder.

Wynne with two flint strikes and a puff had the fire crackling.

Adeya rose to fill her tin cup from the lake.

With a splash, Oda plucked a green pike from the water with his bare hands. He gave a loud whoop and charged back ashore with the wriggling fish, splattering water all over Adeya. She huffed and shook droplets off her sleeve. Scooping up a cupful, she took it to the fire. She refused Odallyan even a glance as he smacked the fish's head with a rock until hung limp. He bared a dagger and set to gutting and cleaning it. On the opposite side of the fire, Adeya set the water to heat. She snatched it back a moment later as Wynne dumped an armload of wood on the flames.

"Don't any of you have manners?" Adeya cried.

"What of it, mainlander?" Wynne squatted down next to her and thrust her face in close. When Adeya leaned away, she drew a knife from a sheath on her belt and wiggled it under her nose. Adeya lifted her chin, glaring back and gripping her skirts, but it didn't hide her trembling. Wynne smirked. She looked at the knife's edges glinting in the firelight then began picking dirt out from under her finger nails, all beneath Adeya's nose.

Adeya's jaw dropped open in a mixture of horror and outrage.

"Leave her alone, Wynne." Inen stepped out of the trees.

"She's just a chitling," said Oda.

"Keh!" Wynne made a noise of disgust in her throat and sprang to her feet.

Adeya gave Inen a grateful look, but he sprawled out next to the fire, saying, "She'd probably hurt herself on a sword before she'd give you a challenge."

Wynne and Oda chuckled; Gennen sat off to the side fixing himself a pipe.

"Kyen has been training me!" Adeya stuck her nose in the air.

Inen, Wynne, and Odallyan all stared at her for a long moment. They broke out in loud guffaws, laughing hysterically: Wynne doubled over clutching her belly; Inen fell over backwards; Odallyan paused scaling the pike.

Gennen puffed away at his pipe, ignoring them all.

"Kyen trained her! Kyen trained her!" Wynne wheezed.

"We should give her a sword," said Oda, wiping tears from his eyes. "See if she even knows which end to hold it from!"

"Kyen is the best swordsman in all the kingdoms of

Ellunon!" cried Adeya.

This sent Wynne laughing so hard she had to sit herself down.

"The kingdoms of Ellunon have some sad standards," said Inen.

Odallyan snorted and flung fish guts into the water. "I wonder what they'd do if they ever met with a real warrior of Avanna?"

"Soil themselves," said Inen.

"The mainland kingdoms know nothing." Wynne clenched her fist and flexed her bicep.

"You! All of you!" cried Adeya. "You're so—so—*mean!*"

The three looked at her: Odallyan grinned; Inen scoffed; Wynne leaned over.

"You're like all the mainlanders," said Wynne. "Soft!"

Adeya glared at them, but they all kept chuckling amongst themselves.

"My name is Adeya of Isea, Crown Princess and Heir to the Throne," she interrupted them. "Not mainlander." — she glared at Wynne— "Not chitling." —she glared at Oda. "And you—stop laughing!" She snapped at Inen.

Inen shut his mouth.

Wynne shrugged. "Whatever you say, mainlander."

"Will you get the fish on already?" snapped Gennen.

With angry tears shining in her eyes, Adeya put the cup on new coals and watched until the water heated.

Oda spit the fish and set it up to roast.

Turning her back on them, Adeya went to sit with Kyen, stir in the Ihnasah flowers, and blow off the steam. He lay unconscious on the stretcher, still and quiet for the moment, his dark hair damp on his pale skin. Biting her lip and with tears still in the corners of her eyes, she pulled up Kyen's tunic and parted the bandages. Night had closed in around them, and the cool evening air redoubled his shivers. Taking out a wad of bandage, she dampened it with part of the tea, saving aside the rest, and washed his gashes with it. He mumbled under his breath as he stirred. His hand grabbed weakly after something beside him that wasn't there.

"I'm here. I'm right here." Adeya took his wandering hand in hers and gripped it as she kept bathing his wounds.

"It's disgusting how she babies him," said Wynne, not bothering to keep her voice down. "I'd die of shame if anyone smothered me like that!"

Adeya ignored her. She put Kyen's tunic and bandages back in place then covered him up with the cloaks. As she did, his eyes opened. His stormy gray gazed wandered until it found her face.

"Can you drink this? It'll help." She lifted his head a little and held the cup to his lips. He choked on the first sip, convulsed once, but drained the whole thing down.

Adeya set the cup aside and lowered him back into the stretcher. "Are you warm enough? Do you want anything?"

"…you alright?" he asked, his voice hoarse and his eyes tired.

"Yes," she said. "We're safe."

Shouts erupted from the fireside. She glanced back. Wynne gripped Inen in a headlock with one arm while holding the spitted fish far over Oda's head with the other. Gennen, despite his slow pipe-puffs and his closed eyes, had a twitch working in the corner of his mouth.

"At least, I think we're safe," said Adeya.

When Kyen didn't answer, she looked back at him. He'd dropped back into sleep. His chest rising and falling with deep, even breathing. She lowered him back to the stretcher to rest.

Adeya sat at his side. Warm firelight and the nonstop arguments of the others washed over her back. She looked up when Gennen approached her. He set a plate at her side without a word then returned to the fireside. She left the roasted pike to grow cold, untouched.

After having eaten, the three young warriors calmed down. Wynne sprawled out by the fire, picking at her teeth with a fish bone. Odallyan stretched out on his belly. Inen and Gennen leaned against the same tree.

"Found tracks when I scouted," said Inen. "Two or three fiends at most. They seem to be tailing us."

Gennen grunted.

"I doubt they'll be a threat. They know we've got them outnumbered."

"Unless they bring others." The older swordsman growled around his pipe stem.

Adeya glanced over her shoulder when Inen mentioned fiends. She spoke up, "There's a caladrius fiend, too."

"Inen, take first watch tonight," said Gennen, ignoring her.

She scooched closer to him, pointing at Gennen's belt. "Can I have my knife back?"

His eyes narrowed on her.

"I want to help Kyen. You want to help Kyen. I'm not

stupid. I'm not going to make enemies of you," she said. "You—you do want to help Kyen, right?"

Gennen pulled out the knife and slapped the hilt into her outstretched palm.

"You told me you came for Kyen," said Adeya, returning it to its sheath on her belt. "How do you know him?"

Wynne snorted and flicked her bone into the fire.

Odallyan chuckled to himself.

"We grasped the hilt with Kyen. We are his bladebrothers and swordsister," said Inen.

Wynne made a noise of disgust in her throat. "Keh!"

Adeya looked to Gennen with confusion.

"Inen, Wynne, and Oda are Kyen's peers," said Gennen. "They grew up together, you might say."

"And you?"

Her question brought another round of chuckles from the three, and it only deepened Adeya's perplexed look.

"I am Kyen's blademaster." Gennen tapped out his pipe. "I've come to finish his training."

Chapter 19

"Blademaster?" repeated Adeya. "You taught Kyen swordsmanship?"

"Tried," said Gennen.

"Kyen never finished," said Wynne with a smirk.

"He quit," added Oda.

"We passed the initiation to become Blades of Avanna," said Inen. "Kyen did not."

"He's not even a real man, yet!" said Wynne.

A look from Gennen's pale eyes made her fall silent and poke the fire with a stick. He addressed Adeya, "I thought Kyen died in the Black War. But then I met with a procession of King Veleda escorting some criminal not long ago, and I learned Kyen had been involved. Seems all these years he's been in hiding."

"Coward," muttered Wynne.

"We've been tracking him all the way from Isea." Odallyan yawned out the words as he stretched.

A small smile rose on Gennen's face as he looked back to Adeya. "Before that, I found these three on the southern borders of Varkest. Playing bandits."

Wynne jolted as if stung, Inen avoided meeting anyone's gaze, and Odallyan's eyes grew wide.

"And some thrashing you gave us when you caught us!" he whined. "I still don't know what we did wrong."

"We only killed a few travelers," said Inen.

"We should have killed more!" said Wynne. "It's such a pain sparing them all the time!"

Adeya stared at the three; she'd gone pale in the firelight.

"Blades of Avanna get into trouble if you don't keep an eye on them," said Gennen.

"Are…" She began. "Are you sure you're of Avanna?"

Her question drew frowns from them all. Gennen raised an eyebrow in surprise.

"I've got my reasons to be wary of people not being where they say they're from," she said.

"Our looks aren't enough for you?" asked Gennen, his smile returning. "What proof can we offer you?"

"Kyen always said Avanna fell," said Adeya. "That there aren't many of Avanna left. How did you escape?"

"Oh, that?" said Wynne.

"We three left marauding that night in Denmont," said Oda.

"When we returned in the morning, all the bridges had been snapped," said Inen. "Avanna was just… gone."

"I don't think any of us know what happened." Wynne shot Gennen a sharp look.

"Don't look at me," he said. "I was snug at a Veleda Inn the night it fell. I've not been back to the bridges since."

"I've heard Kyen was there, that he saw it happen, but

he doesn't talk about it," said Adeya.

Wynne let loose a big yawn and rolled over. "It was probably his fault somehow."

"Knowing Kyen?" Odallyan ended his thought with a scoff.

"First watch, Inen," Gennen cut in. "Sleep, the rest of you. I want to reach the hold tomorrow."

* * *

The afternoon Arc shone down bright and clear on the little figures toiling up the mountainside.

Kyen lay in the stretcher, still and pale. Gennen carried its foot in Wynne's place while she and Odallyan scampered about the rocks on either side. Their strong, lithe figures stopped upright now and then to scan the surrounding terrain. Inen carried the head of Kyen's stretcher as well as Adeya on his back, bumping her about as they jogged along. The warriors kept up their steady dogtrot along a mountain path, puffing a little at the steepest parts, but slowing for none of it.

The path, after appearing at the lakeside, had left the trees behind and threaded between a pile of boulders the size of houses. It skirted alongside a wide talus slope—a spray of shale and boulders piled against a high cliff. A narrow shelf spanned the cliff's width, but rather than follow it, the path mounted straight up its face as a narrow stair-like zigzag. While they ascended it, Adeya tightened her grip on Inen's neck and squeezed her eyes shut against the drop-off to the sharp rocks below. The path kept rising after the cliff along the ridge of a ravine, heading towards a dark crack in the mountain's shoulder ahead of them.

While they traveled along the ridge, Oda trotted up. He opened the pack on Gennen's back and, without either of them slowing a step, he dug out the water skin. After taking a long swig, he trotted up to offer it to Inen.

Inen shook his head so Oda took another long swig.

Swiping his mouth, he looked up at Adeya. "Did you know King Isea is offering a reward for you? Said you'd been kidnapped."

"I am *not* kidnapped!"

He pulled a scroll from his belt and unrolled it. King Isea's seal stamped the bottom of the notice that he held up to Adeya's nose. "See how much he's offering for you? You're worth a pretty penny."

"I am NOT kidnapped. I left of my own accord!" She shot back. "Didn't they get my letter?"

"Too bad." He smirked. "Had me wondering if Kyen finally did something worth being proud of."

"Kyen did not kidnap me!" cried Adeya.

"Good luck explaining that to your father." Oda snickered. He tossed aside the scroll and waterskin on top of Kyen and bound away.

Adeya stared after him in open-mouthed outrage.

"Gennen!" Wynne's shout rang from ahead as she bound back to meet them. "Fiends!"

Without stopping, Gennen and Inen looked in the direction of her pointing finger.

Five feline shapes loped to the top of the staircase. They bound up the path behind them, gaining fast.

"Inen, get Kyen and Adeya to the hold," said Gennen. The two ground to a halt and lowered the stretcher. Adeya hung tight to his back as Inen stooped to pick up Kyen. She scrunched herself over with a cry as he slung Kyen's unconscious body over his shoulder like a sack of wheat. Inen took off at a full sprint up towards the crack in the mountain.

Adeya looked back.

Wynne, Oda, and Gennen drew their swords as the fiends spurred towards them. Two veered off, the shale flying from their paws as they skirted the warriors. With grinning mouths wide, they bolted after Inen.

"Inen! Behind us!" Adeya cried.

Inen pushed himself faster. He dashed up the last stretch of path to the mouth of the crack—an opening into a dim, narrow canyon. His pounding footsteps rang off the walls as they entered.

One cougar fiend skidded in behind them, outlined in the bright entrance.

"Where's the other one?" asked Adeya.

Inen suddenly slung them off his back. She cried out, landing in a heap on top of Kyen's limp body.

Inen leapt sideways as a dark shape dropped down from above. The second fiend landed where they'd just been standing. Drawing his sword, he charged the fiend with a roar. It dodged the whipping blade and swiped with its claws, forcing the warrior back.

The fiend at the entrance turned its faceless head from the battle to Adeya.

She scrambled to her feet and drew her knife.

Its toothy grin split wider; the fiend made a weird, purring chortle as it stalked forward.

Off to the side, Inen's whirling blade took out the second fiend's back leg. Its body buckled. He smashed down on it, slicing and hacking in a whirl of dark haze as the fiend disintegrated. Even as it fell in pieces to the blade, it shrieked at him and slashed again.

The other fiend cougar neared Adeya.

Drawing a deep breath, she tried screaming at it as loud as she could—as Oda had done—and brandished her knife. The fiend flinched for a moment; but only a moment. It crouched back on its hind legs to pounce.

Before it launched, a boulder flew out of the depths of the canyon. The fiend gave an awkward squawk as the rock smashed it flat.

Chapter 20

Adeya stared.

The sound of rocks grinding and cracking filled the dimness and drew her eyes deeper into the canyon.

Rays of light appeared, streaming and dancing, as boulders shifted and rose. Of their own accord, they gathered, combined, linked together until a man-shape stood haloed in the light. He stood three times higher than Inen—his head reaching the top of the canyon—his shoulder spanning its width. A sparkle from a single eye winked down at them.

Inen stopped hacking the small piece of fiend at his feet to look up. His eyes widened, and he backed away.

With a massive stride, the golem swung its leg forward. It stamped on the piece of fiend and ground it into the floor. Then, rocks cracking together, it bent its head all the way to the ground to eye Inen.

Adeya whimpered a little as she stepped back.

The golem swung its head towards the sound, neck-rocks grinding together. Its eye, as clear as diamond and full of light, neared her.

She backed away, tripped over Kyen's legs and fell on

her backside. She covered her head.

"Stand down!" Gennen's voice echoed through the canyon.

The golem paused, turned as Gennen strode over. He held up the white blade to display it.

"Stand down!"

The golem straightened, raining dust and pebbles on them. It took one massive thud of a step backward and stood still but for the steady crumble of dirt.

Wynne and Oda hurried into the canyon; their mouthes fell open a little when they saw the massive pile of rock standing on two feet like a giant.

"Come with me! And hurry! We'll be safe once we're through the entrance," said Gennen. He strode right by them with Wynne and Oda at his heels. Inen came and slung Kyen over his shoulder. Adeya hurried to her feet after them.

Without the body of the golem, the other end of the canyon had opened. Arclight streamed as a bright wedge through the exit. All of them shielded their eyes and squinted as they stepped into it.

Beyond, they arrived at the bottom of a bowl-shaped valley scooped from the mountainside. Three crescent-shaped terraces ringed the sides of the bowl as if a giant had carved a set of enormous steps. Jagged ruins of a Firstwold city lay scattered over the three terraces like broken teeth gleaming under the arclight. A broad set of stone stairs cut down through the center of the ruins, from the topmost terrace all the way down to the paved circle under their feet.

As Adeya gaped up the staircase, the golem's thudding footsteps shook the ground. It stopped behind them, towering over them all, despite being hunched and twisted from the mismatched boulders of its body.

"Not you!" Gennen snapped at it. "I wasn't telling you to come, too. Go back to your ward!"

The golem turned. With slow steps, it returned to the entrance of the canyon. It dropped to its knees and sank back into a pile of boulders blocking the entrance.

Without another word, Gennen set off up the stairs. Wynne, Oda, and Inen—who still carried Kyen—followed, and Adeya trailed behind.

"What was this place?" she asked, gazing around at the ruins.

"Who knows!" said Gennen. "It's the hold of Avanna, now."

As they climbed up the central stair, the descent of the bowl fell away behind them. The crevasse of the entrance stood out like a black thorn in the rock wall shrinking below. Gennen and his three warriors climbed the staircase at a casual walk, rather than the dogtrot, but Adeya still lagged, huffing and puffing. She was crawling on all fours when they reached the last few steps of the topmost terrace. Climbing to her feet, she stared around and regained her breath.

White ruins rimmed an open circle tiled in dirty, cracked stone. The flank of the mountain met the back of the circle, and there, carved into the rock, jutted a ruin of sprawling girth. Topped by a broad oval dome, decorated with a pillared portico, the ruin looked to have served as a common hall of the bygone city. Now goats in cobbled-together pens bleated beneath its empty windows. The doorway—long since rotted or broken open—allowed a traffic of rough-shaven men in patched breeches carrying dead game or burlap sacks. Along the right rim of the circle, women in stained aprons and fly-away hair worked slushing laundry cauldrons or tended flapping clotheslines strung between poles and ruins. Along the opposite rim, broken bits of block ringed two swordsmen in-training while others swung in unison, in formation, next to racks of wooden swords and old river reeds. Grimy, dark-haired children threaded through them all, running, play-fighting, or chasing a stray goat.

Gennen led them towards the common hall. They were crossing the pavement as a hush fell. Swordsmen left off their training, women looked up from their laundry, and children's play slowed to a stop. Every one of them had Kyen's black hair and gray eyes. Those who didn't—a pale beauty of Varkest, a flaming-redhead of Veleda, a willowy brunette from Nalayni—stood out next to the black-haired babies on their hips or the youngsters at their knees. Everyone of Avanna, from the washerwomen to the children, the young to the old, wore a longsword strapped to their waist. All eyes followed them. Adeya, edging closer to Kyen who was still-unconscious over Inen's shoulder, looked them over. Most met her glance with hard stares.

As they drew near the common hall, a short, stout, elderly woman in an apron appeared in the doorway. The flecks of red in her grayed hair and her hearty, pear-shaped figure all marked her of Veleda birth. She hurried out to meet them.

"Oh no! Is someone hurt?" She peered up at Kyen. When she saw his face, she gave a little gasp and covered her mouth. She turned her wide eyes on Gennen. "You found him?"

Chapter 21

"Have a room readied," said Gennen.

"Best have him in a private chamber, you think?" The stout woman didn't wait for a nod from Gennen before hurrying back into the common hall. Inside, a cluster of cook fires lit the expansive interior. A multitude of fire pits, each ringed by disheveled bedding and sleeping mats, filled the space and had long since blackened the vaulted ceiling.

Wynne and Oda wandered away while Gennen and Inen carried Kyen towards the back. A grass mat hung like a curtain from a stone door frame. As they neared, the Veleda marm emerged from inside.

She held open the mat while they carried Kyen inside. As Adeya passed through, she stopped her by taking her hands and pressing them warmly.

"I'm Nellalain, dear. Call me Nella, if you'd like." She said before smiling Adeya the rest of the way inside.

In the small stone chamber beyond, a stream of light beamed through a hole in the corner of the ceiling. Several grass mats lay piled on the floor. Nella hurried to spread a sheet over these and plumped a pillow at one end.

Inen, lifting Kyen from his shoulder, let his limp form

flop down onto the bed.

"Gently! Gently!" Nella cried, then muttered under her breath. "Ruffians."

Adeya sat on her knees next to Kyen and pulled up his tunic. "Can you bring wash water? Fresh bandages and any herbs for fever?"

"Right away," said Nella.

Gennen and Inen followed Nellalain out without another glance at them.

Adeya had begun to strip off the blood-encrusted bandages when Nella returned with a stack of bowls, a steaming kettle, and a pouch. Getting on her knees opposite Kyen, she poured out the steaming water, sprinkled in Ihnasah flowers from the pouch, and handed it to Adeya.

He lay quiet as she set to bathing the stitched-up wounds. His skin burned hot with fever and sweat soaked his hair, but delirium had exhausted him into stillness. He looked as gray as the floor stones next to his face.

Nella gazed on him. "Poor dear. Whatever happened?"

"Ennyen attacked him."

She clucked her disapproval. "That Ennyen! He's the only one Gennen hasn't been able to rein in. Almost took my Gennen's head off when he tried. What else do you need, dear? How can I help?"

"Can you hold him up? I can't dress the wound near his neck with him half-laying on it."

"Certainly."

Together, they cleaned and redressed Kyen's chest, shoulder and hand. As Adeya tugged the last knot tight, Nella rose to her feet.

"Let me go get some more blankets, and some broth, and more bandages, too. And I wonder where I put that other pouch of Ihnasah…" Nella's mumbling followed her out the door when she left.

Adeya covered Kyen with the blanket, not bothering to replace his tunic. She poured a fresh bowl of water. Dipping a clean length of bandage in it, she wrung it out, flapped it until it cooled, then folded it neatly on Kyen's forehead. She sat back on her heels with a sigh.

Nella hustled back with her arms laden anew, this time with blankets, more bandages and pouches, and a bowl of broth. Kneeling beside Adeya, she set all these items down.

"Are you unhurt?" She put a hand on Adeya's shoulder. "You look exhausted."

"I'll be fine." She managed a smile.

"Why don't you get some rest? I can look after him."

Adeya shook her head. "I'd rather stay. At least until the fever breaks. "

"You must take care of yourself, too, dear."

"I'll be alright. Really."

"Rest will put him right, you'll see. Sitting here won't hurry that along."

"I don't want to leave him."

"Really, wearing yourself out—"

"I won't!" Adeya's shout rang through the room, silencing her and making Nella draw back.

"I won't leave him," She repeated, her voice shaking despite her attempt to seem calm.

Nella said nothing, looking on with concern.

"I'm sorry." She rubbed her forehead with the palm of

her hand. "I didn't mean to raise my voice at you."

The Veleda marm patted her shoulder. "No need for it. Let me get you a blanket and a cup of tea in the least."

"Thank you," said Adeya, but Nella was already bustling out the doorway. A murmur of "poor dear" floated in her wake.

Adeya sighed to herself. When she turned back to Kyen, she started to find his eyes half-open. He was looking up at her out of a tired daze.

"I'm sorry. I shouldn't have been so loud." She tugged at his blanket. "You should drink something. It'll give you some strength back."

His eyes closed a fraction.

"You stay awake!" Adeya snapped at him. "Don't you drop out until you drink something!"

His opened his eyes all the way, staring at her, shock breaking through the weight of his exhaustion.

Adeya, all puffed up, glared back with hands clenched in her lap.

"Is it…" His voice was hoarse, soft. "…as bad … as the last two?"

She deflated, smiling a little. "No. This is food, not medicine."

He nodded.

Taking up the broth, she helped him hold up his head to drink it. Nella walked back in as Adeya laid him down. He closed his eyes again.

"I'll bring another bowl for when he wakes next. A bowl of broth can do a kingdom of good." Nella draped a blanket over Adeya's shoulders. "Is there anything else you need?"

Adeya shook her head. She tugged the blanket around her. "No, thank you, Nella."

"Men of Avanna are all steel and spitfire." Nella smiled down at Kyen's sleeping face. "It'll take more than this to undo him. You'll see."

A clamor of shouting broke out from beyond the doorway, echoing around the cavernous space outside. Wynne's high-pitched tones cut above all the rest.

"Arguing again." Nella sighed. "I better see to that. Get me if you need anything. I'll be by the cook fires." She hastened away.

Adeya stared as the grass mat flapped shut behind the Veleda marm. Clashing steel joined the shouting. Gripping the pendant at her neck, she edged a little closer to Kyen and looked down at him.

He was still so pale, the color of the sheets. It made his black, sweat-soaked hair stand out in sharp contrast against his forehead. His breathing came slow, shallow, weak in his sleep.

Tears brightened Adeya's eyes. She hunched into her blanket, whispering, "You've got to keep alive."

More angry voices joined the shouting and clamor beyond the mat.

Adeya buried her face in her hands as silent sobs shook her shoulders.

Chapter 22

Adeya slumped, bleary-eyed, at Kyen's side. An empty broth bowl sat next to her. The light coming from the hole in the ceiling streamed down strong and bright.

Kyen lay in a deep, easy sleep, sprawled out underneath his blankets.

Nella pushed open the mat with a fresh broth in hand.

"Good morning!" she said. "How's the invalid? Managed another bowl in the night, did he? Is that his third or fourth?"

Adeya drew in a deep breath, but it turned into a long yawn.

"Morning?" She blinked up at Nella. "It's morning?"

"And going on well towards noon, too," said the marm. She placed a hand on Kyen's forehead. "If I didn't know better, I'd say his fever's broken. He doesn't look quite so pasty either."

"Really?" Adeya felt his forehead, too.

"Surely now, won't you take a little rest? You've been up all night."

"I don't think I could sleep if I tried."

"Then how about a bath? A little something to refresh you?" Without waiting for an answer, Nella stuck her head out the doorway.

Outside, Wynne was striding by with a hand on her hilt.

"Wynne, will you please take Adeya to the bathing pool?" asked Nella.

"No." She passed by without even a glance.

"If you do, I'll bake you a loaf of bread," Nella called after her.

She stopped.

"The soft, white kind of Veleda that's your favorite."

Wynne glared back.

"A whole loaf." Nella smiled.

"You won't make me share?" She looked suspicious.

"All for you," said the Veleda marm. "But you have to take Adeya to the bathing pool and back, and see to all her needs like a good host."

Wynne growled to herself for a moment. "Fine! Come with me, mainlander!" She stomped off across the common hall.

Nella pulled Adeya to her feet. "You can come right back once you're cleaned up.

"But—" Adeya began.

"I can look after Kyen plenty fine for a span or two." Nella ushered her towards the doorway.

"But—"

"Refreshing yourself will help you nurse him back to health. Now go on!"

"But—"

"Go on with you!" Nella gave her a final nudge out the

mat. "Besides, you're filthy. You've not had a good bath in days. And I can't abide filth."

Adeya looked down at herself. Dried blood smeared her clothes; mud, pine needles and sweat tangled her hair that had long since fallen out of its tie. "Ugh! You're right…"

"Wynne?" Nella called.

"What?" She yelled back from across the common hall.

"Get her a fresh pair of clothes, too?"

"Fine! But I'm not sharing mine!"

* * *

"Hurry up, mainlander!"

Adeya, puffing, labored up the steep footpath. It wound from her heels down the mountainside to meet the valley of the city. Wynne stood on a crest above, hands on her hips, watching her. She staggered up next to Wynne. Doubling over with her hands on her knees, she panted to regain her breath.

"Soft!" Wynne sneered at her.

Adeya, straightening, opened her mouth as if to say something, but a massive yawn came out instead. She rubbed a hand in her eyes.

They'd arrived at a shelf in the mountainside that held a little pool. Cedars and evergreen bushes crowded around it, and moss fuzzed over the rocks at its edge. Clear water pattered down from a stream on high, filling the pool, before cascading over its lip and away down the mountainside.

"This is the bathing pool?" Adeya asked.

"Be quick about it." Wynne threw her a clothes bundle.

Adeya fumbled it, and it fell at her feet.

"But—but, we're in the open!" she cried. "Anybody could see!"

"So?"

"What do you mean 'So?' I don't want anybody looking at me in the bath!"

"Well, nobody's here right now. What's your problem?"

"At least," said Adeya. "Stand guard. Make sure nobody comes up."

"Fine, if it gets you moving."

Adeya snuck away to undress, hidden behind a thick patch of bushes. "You keep your back turned, too!"

"I should have asked for two loaves." Wynne sat down cross-legged on a rock. She'd just settled when a loud "Eek!" made her leap up and draw her sword.

"The water is so cold!" cried Adeya's voice from behind the bushes.

Growling, Wynne slammed her sword back into her scabbard. She plopped back down, shouting, "What did you expect in the mountains? An Eope hot spring? Mainlanders!" She took out her knife and began trimming the nail of her pinky finger.

The splish-splashing of water carried through the bushes.

"I sure hope Kyen is back on his feet soon," said Adeya.

"I hope he dies." Wynne held up her nails to examine them then trimmed the nail on her thumb.

"Why do you hate Kyen so much?" Anger bristled in Adeya's tone.

"I don't hate him," said Wynne. "He just makes me retch."

"What's he ever done to you?"

"Nothing." The swordswoman laughed. "He shames Avanna, just being what he is—a dull, cowardly throwback. As soft as a mainlander—no, softer!"

"Kyen's not a coward."

"You think so, do you?" Wynne grinned and sat back. "Since we wore swaddling clothes, he's never spoken a single word to me. Not one—to me—and we're betrothed!"

Droplets pattered off the mountainside into the pool; not a ripple came from Adeya's hiding spot.

"I even tried to beat it out of him once. Couldn't get a single word out of him no matter how much I bloodied him," said Wynne. "Heh! And I bloodied him good!"

"You're Kyen's... fiancée?"

"I kept trying to talk Father out of it," said Wynne. "I nearly had him convinced to change my marriage oaths to Ennyen, but 'Be patient,' he always said. 'Kyen will harden up.' Keh! Blind old fool. I'm glad he went down with Avanna, so I can do what I want."

"An arranged marriage?"

"Is it not so on the mainland?"

"No. Well, I suppose. My father is always trying to find me a suitor," said Adeya. "But he's never bound me to someone by oaths."

"Does he try to marry you to idiots, too?" asked Wynne.

"Not idiots. Just no one I felt I could love as I should,"

said Adeya. "I'm to be a summoner anyway. Summoners never marry."

"I'd never do that," said Wynne. "Women of Avanna gain great honor by marrying before their thirtieth year and bearing new warriors for our people. Mother always said raising Avanna children is harder than besting any enemy in swords!"

"Why do you want honor, even though Avanna is gone?"

"Avanna still lives because we live, mainlander. Why do you understand so little?"

"Then," Adeya's voice sank, "you'll marry Kyen?"

"Please! I'd kill myself before I'd marry Kyen!" Wynne looked disgusted. She tapped her chin with the dagger point as she thought for a moment. "Inen's not a bad choice, but he doesn't look at me sideways. Odallyan is strong, but he's also an idiot. He's not smart like Inen. I don't know what's got into Ennyen's head. He's too unpredictable nowadays, and I won't marry a man I can't beat in a fight. I could never marry a mainlander. I hate soft men worse than fiends. And I hate fiends a whole lot!" She brandished her dagger and bared her teeth at the very thought. "Are you done yet?"

"Yes, can you hand me the clothes? I forgot them."

Wynne took up the bundle and chucked it at the bushes.

Adeya squeaked as it crashed atop the leaves. Her hand dragged it inside while she muttered under her breath.

"Are you saying something, mainlander?" Wynne glared at the bushes.

"Nothing." A long yawn punctuated the word.

"Hurry up! Or I'm going to leave you here."

Chapter 23

Light, streaming in through the hole in the ceiling, inched over Kyen's eyes. He winced and blocked out the beam with a hand. He stared at it for a long moment, blinking slowly.

"Oh, look, he's awake."

Kyen turned his head.

Nellalain sat next to him. Behind her, Gennen glared down, arms crossed, with his pipe puffing like a smokestack.

Kyen's gray gaze fixed on the old man. "Blademaster Gennen?"

"Kyen." He nodded.

Carefully and with a clench to his jaw, he sat up.

"You should drink this." Nella handed him a bowl of broth.

He accepted it, but rubbing a hand through his hair, he muttered to himself. "I'm not dead..." Then, louder, he said to Gennen, "You're not dead?"

"Care to try me?" The blademaster growled around the stem of his pipe.

"No. Thanks." Kyen laughed a little and raised the bowl to drink.

As he drained it, Gennen spoke, "If you please, Nella."

She rose without a word and disappeared outside the mat.

"Ennyen give you those wounds?" asked Gennen.

Kyen set the bowl aside; he nodded.

"Why did you let him win?"

"I didn't let him w—" He began, but the blademaster cut him short.

"Don't lie to me!"

Kyen frowned up at him, his stormy gray eyes hard, but Gennen returned the look evenly.

"You defeated Ennyen before," he said. "When he was twice your height, three times your strength, and fully trained. Why did you let him win, Kyen?"

"He's gotten better, blademaster."

"When goats fly! Ennyen's been as good as he can get since before his bladeday. You've not even reached your bladeday."

Kyen looked away. "I... I've been slack with my drills."

Gennen's frown twisted into a full scowl. "Come with me." He growled. Turning, he strode out through the grass mat.

Kyen, rising slowly, hobbled after him.

* * *

Wood smacked against wood like the sound of bones

cracking. Outside in the training area, pairs of Avanna warriors faced off with practice swords. Gennen led Kyen through the chaos of sweating, yelling, heaving bodies towards a stack of river reeds leaning against the wall. As they passed, the battles stilled. Every eye followed the two towards the edge of the ruins, but Kyen kept his head down, avoiding them all. With swords long since cast aside, Inen and Oda wrestled on the ground; they stopped and rose as Gennen and Kyen passed.

The blademaster picked up three of the river reed poles, each as tall as himself, and threw them at Oda and Inen. "Set up the Councilman's Test."

They hurried to grab three stands which, when they planted the poles in them, held the river reeds upright. They stood as thick as a man's arm and as hard as bone. Oda arranged them a stretch apart from one another. As he stepped back, Gennen drew Oda's blade from his hip and stepped forward. Oda opened his mouth as if to protest, but the blademaster moved first.

He slashed the first pole.

Its top half clattered to the ground.

Bending to pick up the piece, Gennen thrust it under Oda's nose. He ran a finger along the straight, even, diagonal cut.

"Slice the pole, Odallyan."

"Right!" He grinned, took his sword back, and hacked away: once, twice, thrice.

"Enough, Oda," said Gennen as the pole clattered to the ground in pieces. He stooped to pick up one. "Look at that!" He thrust up the slice into Oda's face. "Look at it!"

The diagonal edge wobbled unevenly across the cut. Casting it away with a clatter, Gennen said, "Give Kyen your sword."

"But—"

"Don't argue with me! Just do it."

Oda handed Kyen his hilt, looking wistfully at his gleaming blade.

"Thank you," said Kyen. He hefted it in his hand and glanced at Gennen.

The blademaster nodded at the third pole.

Gripping the hilt with both hands, Kyen poised. He swung. The longsword flashed in the arclight. The blade's tip halted, pointing toward the ground at the end of its swing, but the pole remained standing upright, whole.

Kyen straightened and looked back at Gennen.

"Heh! He missed!" said Oda.

The other Blades watching repeated Oda's words in murmurs.

Gennen strode up to the pole. He snatched it, and as he did, the top half of it came away with his hand. A cut in a perfect mirror of Gennen's strike had severed it. He walked back to Kyen. Holding up the pole, he put the straighter-than-a-ruler edge underneath Kyen's eyes.

"Slack with your drills, huh?" Gennen brandished it at him.

Kyen swayed a little where he stood, gazing unfocused over Gennen's shoulder. He looked faint. "Can I have something to eat?"

Gennen grunted and walked by him.

He started to follow, but when he noticed Oda's blade

still in his hand, Kyen paused long enough to hand it back. The whispers of the other swordsmen followed them as they headed towards the common hall.

* * *

With a yawn, Adeya wandered into the city circle by herself. She wore a loose pair of breeches and a white tunic the same style as Wynne's; all made from thick, coarse cloth, plainly cut and sewn. Her long gold tresses fell loose and clean down her back. She walked, not noticing the men's stares that followed her or the strangely quiet group gathered close around the training area. She yawned again, trying to stifle it with a hand, but it just grew larger.

Entering the common hall, Adeya crossed to the back chamber and pushed aside the mat. She stopped.

The bed lay stripped. Every bandage and bowl had been clear away. The folded blankets sat stacked in the corner.

Adeya paled. Hurrying away, she crossed the common hall to the nearest cook fire. Two Avanna women tended a large cauldron of stew while another worked a cleaver at a chopping block.

"Where's Kyen?" She stopped the woman at the cauldron. The woman shrugged, made to keep on, but Adeya gripped her. "Nella—where's Nella?"

"Hands off! Left to pick a goat for slaughter, I reckon."

Adeya released the woman and trotted out the door. She ran to the herd pens. Standing on tiptoe, she looked over the horned heads and fuzzy backs of brown and white, but only two men and a handful of boys stood in their midst.

"Nella? Have you seen Nella?"

One man shook his head. The other shrugged.

Adeya scanned the circle, biting her lip. The crowd at the training area had dispersed, but Oda and Inen remained. She caught sight of them picking up pieces of poles and ran to them. "Kyen? Where's Kyen?"

Oda and Inen exchanged a look.

"Dead," said Oda. "He gave up the ghost while you were gone."

"What? No..." Her face fell. "He was doing better when I left. How?"

He shrugged. "Dunno. Gennen and the others dragged his body up the slope to bury him, last I saw."

Inen kept a straight face beside Oda, saying nothing.

"Which—which way?" she cried.

"Up the mount, along the path to the baths, but an offshoot will take you to the burial spot." Odallyan pointed.

Adeya took off running even before he'd finished his sentence.

Oda and Inen watched her go. They looked at each other and sniggered.

"Heh! I can't believe she thought I was serious," said Oda. "Poor little chitling!"

"Mainlanders!"

The two swordsmen walked off together chuckling.

Adeya ran halfway back up the path to the bathing pool before she stopped. Gasping for breath, she looked up the mountain. The rims of the valley rose, sheer and steep, golden under the late arclight, with bits of green clinging here or there. Not a shape or shadow could be seen moving further up. She frowned as she searched the still cliffs.

"There is no offshoot," she said to herself. Tears bubbled into her eyes, but she scrunched up her face. Her fists clenched at her sides. Turning, she set off back down the path, running so fast she tripped. She pushed her long hair out of her face and climbed back to her feet.

Everyone had emptied from the city circle when Adeya returned. She ran through the long jagged shadows cast by the ruins up to the common hall. At the doorway, a warm, low murmur smelling of goat stew and fresh bread washed over her. All the campfires blazed, joining the cook fires to fill the expansive hall with yellow. The entire remnant of Avanna sat around in groups, eating, talking, laughing or arguing.

Adeya walked into the hall, still breathing hard. She searched the faces around each fire. Scores of gray eyes and black-haired heads surrounded her, all unfamiliar. Spotting Gennen's white head at the largest cook fire, she pushed through a couple large swordsmen. They jostled her back, casting her to the ground, before passing her by without a second glance. Adeya picked herself up. She hurried into the light of the cook fire.

Inen, Wynne, and Odallyan sat around while Nella stirred a pot of bubbly stew. Next to Gennen, deep in conversation with the old man, sat Kyen.

Chapter 24

Adeya, taking in a shallow, shaky breath, stopped. "Kyen?"

He looked up and smiled a little. "Hello."

A weak giggle escaped her.

His smile faltered.

Tears spilled from Adeya's eyes down her cheeks. Drawing in a gasp, she buried her face in her hands and wailed. Kyen, Gennen, and the others gaped. As her voice rang through the common hall, those at nearby fires stared at Adeya. Her shoulders shook, first with a fit of giggles, then ragged sobs, followed by more giggling. In between she struggled to get enough air to breathe.

"Did she just crack?" whispered Inen.

"Quit fountaining, mainlander!" Wynne scoffed, balancing her empty bowl on a finger. "Pull yourself together and act like a woman!"

Oda sniggered but cleared his throat and composed himself.

Adeya cried harder, sinking to her knees. Fits of choking joined the sobs and giggles.

Kyen started to get up but Nellalain reached Adeya first

with a hanky. She put an arm around her shoulders, measuring out a huffy look to each of them.

"Stop gawking like you've never seen tears. You're all ruffians!" Then to Adeya, "There, there, you poor dear. It's alright. You've been worried sick, haven't you?"

Adeya lifted her face long enough to nod. She buried another wave of sobs in her hands.

"It's all right now. Come have a seat, and I'll make you a cup of tea. Don't listen to those scoundrels." Nella shot Gennen a frown. He hunched under the look and lowered his eyes.

Helping Adeya up, she settled her between Kyen and Oda then busied herself getting the kettle on the fire. Adeya used Nella's hanky to try to wipe her cheeks but hid her face in it instead. Her sobs slackened as she shuddered to draw a breath.

Kyen leaned over. "Are you alright?"

Adeya, taking in a little choking gasp, nodded into the hanky.

"Then why's she crying?" Wynne whispered to Inen.

Inen shrugged and mouthed the word "women."

Wynne—unable to reach his head—smacked him on the arm.

Inen rubbed the spot and shook his head at her.

Oda sniggered again.

A steely look from Gennen settled them down.

"Here we are." Nellalain came with a steaming cup and handed it to Adeya. "This will calm your nerves. Bowls up, all the rest of you. We can't be at the fire all night."

Inen, Oda, and Wynne, all crowded in to get their fill

first.

Ignoring the scuffle and curses, Kyen said to Adeya, "Are you sure you're alright?"

"I'm sorry. Yes." She laughed a little and bit back more tears. "Just—just relieved. And tired."

"She's not slept a wink since you arrived." Nellalain handed Kyen a bowl, and he passed it to Adeya.

"She's not slept since Ennyen wounded you," said Gennen.

"Three nights ago?" Kyen frowned.

"It's alright. In Isea, all the healers are trained to stay awake through the night to care for—" A long yawn cut her off.

"Heh! Blades of Avanna are trained to stay awake for a week!" Wynne held out her already emptied bowl. "More!"

Nella gave her a look as she dished up a bowl for Gennen. Wynne scowled back, but said nothing as she kept her bowl stretched out.

"I'm sorry," said Kyen.

"No. It's alright." Adeya gave him a teary smile. "I'm just glad to see you up."

An uncomfortable silence settled around the fire. Kyen picked up his bowl but didn't eat. Adeya stared into her mug of tea.

Wynne, oblivious, demanded, "Where's my white loaf, Nella? You promised!"

"Here it is." She pulled the bread from the folds of a cloth.

"She gets a white loaf?" cried Oda. "What about the rest of us?"

"If you can keep dirty words off your tongue until sundown tomorrow, I'll make you one, too."

Oda cussed under his breath.

Wynne broke her crusty loaf under the envious stares of the two other swordsmen.

Nellalain came and sat down next to Gennen.

"Now that we're all comfortable," she said. "Gennen has told me that you are Kyen of the House of Crossblade, but I don't believe you know me. My name is Nellalain of Veleda." She held out her hand to him.

Kyen looked up. He set aside his bowl for a moment to take her proffered fingers and bow over them. "Veleda? How did you end up here?" He took a big bite of stew.

"I'm Gennen's wife." She smiled.

Kyen choked so hard he had to put his bowl down again.

All the others shared grins except Gennen. He glowered at Kyen, but he was too busy hacking and coughing to notice.

Odallyan elbowed Adeya, leaned in confidentially, even though he spoke loud enough for the whole camp to hear. "Gennen spent his whole life swearing off marriage with every other sentence!"

"He seh every woman is un'isciplin' and ba' tempereh'," threw in Wynne, talking with her mouth full. "An' he woul' 'ie before he marry one."

"I was speaking strictly of Avanna women," said Gennen with a pointed glance at her.

"You're married?" Kyen managed to croak.

Nellalain, who'd been smiling placidly over the whole

conversation, ladled stew into a bowl for herself. "I kept my poor husband's inn—I was a widow and childless, you see —on the borders of Veleda on the Great Highway. Gennen visited one a night. He said he had business in the area, but he stayed on, and on, and on. He'd make repairs in exchange for room and board. He even drove off a few unscrupulous fellows causing a ruckus one night. Then, one day, after a great speech over how he'd likely die in a fortnight, he asked me to marry him." Nellalain laughed. "I always fancied myself running off on an adventure as a young girl. How I would have laughed knowing adventure would come to me at such an age!" She rubbed Gennen's arm as she leaned against him.

The old man colored and set about stuffing the whole bowl of stew into his face.

Kyen gaped at them both.

"Gennen's like a good loaf of bread." Nellalain's smile took on the smallest hint of mischievousness. "Even if he's a little crusty on the outside, he's soft on the inside."

"I am not *soft*!" Gennen slammed his bowl down.

Sniggers traveled around the campfire.

Oda leaned in next to Adeya with a fiery look in his eyes. "I'm looking for a good woman, myself. What do you say to being mine?"

Adeya, appalled, leaned away from him.

Gennen and Kyen both shot Oda a hard look; their expressions so identical, they looked like father and son for a moment.

Odallyan chuckled nervously and sat back in his own space.

Nella took the empty bowl from Kyen's hands, refilled it, and returned it.

Adeya tried to lift a bite of stew to her mouth, but a large yawn intercepted it.

Gennen, giving Oda a last warning glance, turned his attention to Kyen. Leaning over, he planted the slice of river reed in front of him with a thunk. The firelight caught its ruler-like edge.

"You never answered my question," said the blademaster.

Chapter 25

The circle around the fire fell quiet.

"Dally words with me, Kyen, and I'll thrash you senseless for another three days," said Gennen. "Why did you let Ennyen win?"

Every eye turned on Kyen.

"I didn't let him win," he said.

"Then explain it to me," said the blademaster. "What exactly happened?"

Kyen took a bite of stew.

"How long do you think you can keep running from him?"

He swallowed. "I'm not going to kill Ennyen."

"Do you think because you escaped Ennyen once that you'll be able to escape him again?" asked Gennen. "And again? He's not going to stop until you're dead."

"I will not kill Ennyen."

"I didn't rescue you so you could eat my goats and sleep all day!"

Kyen chewed on the end of his spoon.

Anger tensed through Gennen's frame as he waited and

still received no answer.

Nella put a hand on his arm. "It's late. I'm sure we're all tired. Why not talk about this in the morning?"

Gennen stared down Kyen, but he avoided meeting the blademaster's eye.

Oda scoffed to himself.

Wynne huffed and sat back.

Inen watched with a stony composure.

Adeya sagged, falling against Kyen's shoulder and drawing all their attention. He looked at her in surprise. Her long hair curtained her face as she leaned on him, her eyes closed, her breathing deep and steady. Kyen, careful not to move his shoulder, set his bowl aside.

When he saw the princess slump from exhaustion, Gennen relaxed.

Nella favored him with a smile as she rose. "Let's get the poor dear to bed."

"Adeya?" Kyen shook her gently.

"Huh?" She lifted her head and gazed at him, sleepy and dazed.

"Can you walk to bed? You're falling asleep."

"Oh, did I—" A huge yawn cut her off. "Yes."

Kyen helped her to her feet. When she swayed, he offered her his arm and supported her as they followed after Nella. Outside the mat, Nella took Adeya's arm from him, saying, "I'll see to her from here," and they disappeared inside.

Kyen stared long after the mat flapped into place. His eyes, unseeing, looked forlorn. He was still standing there when Nella came back out.

"Let's find you a pallet for the night," she said.

"Hm?"

"A place to sleep. I'm sure you wouldn't want the floor."

"That's alright. I think I'll stay here for the night." His gaze shifted toward Odallyan still at the fire. He noticed the look and grinned wolfishly back. Looking away, Kyen lowered himself to sit inside the door frame with his back against one side and his leg stretched out to the other.

"Let me get you a blanket then." Nella ducked back into the room only to reappear a moment later.

"Thank you," said Kyen as she draped it over him.

"Good night."

As the fires died, the carousing quieted, and the people of Avanna drifted one by one to their beds. Kyen sat up late. The last embers died away, leaving the common hall in darkness.

* * *

A litter of bedraggled mats and blankets carpeted the common hall. A few women worked the cook fires while a strong, mid-morning arclight streamed through the doorway and the windows. A small huddle of Blades waited for food around the fires. Their low murmur floated to where Kyen slumped asleep in the doorway.

Adeya, pulling back the mat, spotted him on the ground. He woke at the rustle, looking up.

"What are you doing there?" she asked.

He yawned, tried to stretch, and stopped with a wince.

She laughed at him. "We should change your bandages."

"Uh… maybe later."

"Don't 'maybe later' me, Kyen of Avanna," said Adeya, still smiling. "Maybe now."

When he hesitated, she grabbed his arm, yanked him up to his feet, and pulled him behind the grass mat.

"Could we get Nella to do it?" he asked.

"You don't have any reason to be embarrassed." Adeya settled onto her knees and pulled a roll of bandages from her pouch.

Kyen stared at his feet.

"Come on. Sit." She waggled a finger at the spot in front of her.

He obeyed with a sigh.

Adeya tried to get at his tunic laces but he leaned away out of her reach.

"I'll do it." He stripped off his tunic and, red in the face, fixed the wall with a sullen stare.

"It'd help if you relaxed." Adeya began unwrapping his old bandages. As she worked, shouting erupted in the common hall beyond. She paused and Kyen's face fell as they both looked at the mat. The voices rang incomprehensible as angry echoes.

Adeya edged closer to him as she returned her attention to his bandages. When she spoke, she kept her voice to an undertone as she unwounded the strips. "I know they're your people, but… are you sure we can trust them?"

Kyen looked at her with surprise.

"I don't mean to offend."

"You didn't," he said with a weak smile. "I just never considered what mainlanders must think of us—"

The shouting grew louder, interrupting him. His smile faded. "So long as Gennen keeps them in check, they'll be trustworthy enough."

"You trust Gennen, then?"

"Without him, I'd have been gone yesterday."

Adeya pulled the last strip of linen away. The redness around the gashes had faded, and no more dried blood stained the underside of the bandage. "You're healing well."

Kyen made no reply, saying instead after a moment, "Do you know where we are?"

"Further up into the mountains. There was a valley and a lake. A steep climb," said Adeya, wrapping his wounds in fresh linen. "Would these ruins be on the map?"

"Most of the mountains this close to Norgard are uncharted," he said, rubbing his forehead. "My memory's so fuzzy. How many days did Gennen travel before coming here?"

"A day and half. Maybe two."

"We can't be far from the Great Highway, then. We could still make for Bargston, yet, and Eope. I saw the entrance at the foot of the stairs, but it seems a landslide closed it."

"That's the golem," said Adeya. "Gennen has it standing guard."

"Golem?" He looked over his shoulder. "Gennen has a golem?"

"Hold still!"

"Sorry."

They sat in silence for a moment; the shouting in the common hall had quieted down.

"We've got to make for the Great Highway before Ennyen comes," said Kyen.

Before she could respond, the grass mat flapped open. Gennen stepped into the room.

Adeya tied off the last bandage, and Kyen looked up as he loomed over them.

"My scouts tell me," Gennen paused, crossing his arms. "That Ennyen tried to pass the golem last night."

Kyen picked up his tunic. Pulling it over his head, he tugged it on and tightened up the laces at his neck.

"The time has come for you to take up your sword as a Blade of Avanna," said Gennen. "Claim your bladeday, defeat Ennyen, and take your place among your people."

"I gave up on that a long time ago."

"You're more the blockhead for it."

Adeya pursed her lips.

Tying off his tunic laces, he said nothing. He rose, walked past Gennen and out into the common hall. The blademaster followed him with Adeya on their heels.

"You can still earn your sword by passing the Blademaster's Test—my test," he said. "It would fulfill tradition, and nobody would question your place."

"There's no test I can pass that will do that." Kyen quickened his step.

Gennen pursued him as he headed for the door; Adeya half-trotted to keep up.

"Ennyen won't be satisfied without a fight," the blademaster continued. "Train under me. Face the

Blademaster's Test. Become a Blade of Avanna, and you can beat him."

"No, with respect, blademaster."

"If you don't face him, Ennyen will kill you."

"Then, let him kill me. I don't care," said Kyen.

"Ah—" Adeya opened her mouth, looking hurt, but couldn't get a word in.

"You should care!" said Gennen. "Don't you understand what's at stake if Ennyen wins?" Faces turned as he raised his voice, his words echoing through the common hall; eyes followed them as Kyen kept walking towards the door.

"What are you afraid of?" Gennen demanded. "Why not train with me?"

Kyen reached the threshold.

"Face me like a man, Kyen!" he shouted. "Why not?"

He stopped.

"Why not?" said Gennen.

When Kyen looked back, his gray eyes were as hard as granite. His voice carried a quiet edge. "I don't want to talk about this." He walked out.

Gennen growled and clenched his fists. He marched after Kyen. "I've spent the last seven seasons of my life looking for you. Even when every rumor reported you dead. I'm not about to throw it all away by letting you turn your back on me!" His words rang through the city circle drawing more attention: the washerwomen looked up; the training warriors halted their swings; Wynne, Oda, and Inen came up behind them. The people of Avanna crowded the doorway of the common hall to watch.

Kyen strode out onto the city circle without answering.

Gennen stopped, huffing. Adeya hurried up beside him, clutching her amulet.

"You've always had a gentle heart," said the blademaster. "But I'd never expected you'd show yourself a coward."

"He's not a coward!" cried Adeya.

Kyen, lowering his head, sped up as he crossed the city circle, heading for the stairs.

A herd of goats being brought up from the steps crowded the central stair and forced Kyen to a stop. The two shepherds looked up at him, but he averted his eyes and backed away. Turning, he headed for a street opening into the ruins.

Gennen watched him with his pale eyes as cold as white marble. He huffed and, as he watched, his face took on a grim set. He drew in a great breath.

"Hail!" His ringing voice stopped Kyen short; he stood transfixed, tensed, braced as if expecting a blow. Gennen clapped a fist to his chest, knelt down and bowed his head. "Hail! Kyen, son of Odyen, of the House of Crossblade, Crown Prince and King Imminent of Avanna! All Hail!"

Chapter 26

Kyen stood riveted in place with his head hung, his face shadowed.

Throughout the square, from the shepherds to the washerwomen, everyone dropped to their knees and placed a fist to their chest. Inen, Wynne, and Odallyan sneered but reluctantly bowed also.

The only one left standing was Adeya. She stared in wide-eyed shock, gaping.

A deafening silence had replaced the rustle of kneeling bodies.

All at once, Kyen bolted. His footsteps rang out as he fled across the circle and into the ruins.

Gennen returned to his feet and as he did, everyone else in the square rose also. Most returned to their tasks. Many sent uncertain glances down the road after Kyen. Gennen and Adeya exchanged looks; his hard and serious, Adeya's slack with disbelief. Without a word between them, she turned and ran after Kyen.

She reached the street as the flap of his cloak disappeared around the corner. She sprinted after him.

"Kyen! Kyen, wait!"

Running deeper into the ruins, she found herself in a labyrinth of broken towers and tumbled stone. Kyen's footsteps were receding into their stillness; they seemed to echo from every direction at once.

"Kyen!" She dashed further down the street, pausing to glance up the dim alleys. "Kyen?"

Nothing moved. His footsteps became fainter and fainter. The street ended at the sheer rise of the cliff, and when she reached its base, she paused, listening, but the stillness had taken over. Nothing moved.

"Kyen?"

The quiet of the ruins swallowed the echo of her voice.

She put a hand to her mouth to call again but hesitated. She lowered it.

"Kyen," she said, her voice barely a whisper. "Don't leave." With her eyes running up and down the ruins, she turned a slow circle. Her gaze stopped.

A stairway with a cracked balustrade waited at the end of one alley. She gripped her amulet and headed for it. Following it down, she descended into the middle tier of the city. Broken pillars stood tall over crumbled walls, reaching for roofs long since caved in. The outlines of round chambers, their foundations bigger than the common hall in some places, sat low in piles of rubble.

Morning passed to afternoon while Adeya wandered, peering into dark recesses and clambering over ruins. Rounding the curve of an old wall, she found herself at the middle landing of the central staircase. Above, the stairs led to the common hall, below to the golem-guarded entrance. Beside the stair on a pale, weathered block sat Gennen.

With his legs crossed, he puffed on his pipe. His narrow eyes fixed the entrance to the city below.

Adeya started to back away when he looked up at her, and they stared at one another. Little clouds from his pipe drifted to the wind.

"Well?" he said. "Come over. It's not like I have fangs, princess."

She crossed the landing but stopped, keeping an arm's length out of Gennen's reach.

Taking his pipe from his mouth, he tapped it out on the rock and muttered to himself. "Disgusting Veleda habit. I don't know how I picked it up, and I don't know how to put it back down." He twiddled it between his fingers as he eyed Adeya up and down, waiting.

She plucked at the fringe of her sleeve.

"Didn't find him, did you?"

"No." Her shoulders slumped. "Did you?"

"The boy's harder to find than a treejack in a timberland." With a huff, he glared down the stairs. "I'm done chasing him."

"That's why you and the others came looking for him, isn't it? He's to be king of Avanna."

"He never told you, did he?"

"Kyen's not much of one for answering questions." She lowered her eyes.

"That's very like him."

"Are—are you sure there's not been some mistake?"

"Kyen is the eldest son of Odyen, King of Avanna. I've known him since he was first in swaddling clothes. There's no mistaking him." Gennen sighed. When he looked up again, his pale eyes glinted with a ferocity. "And what about you? What are you to him, princess? It breaches honor for a Blade to travel alone with an unmarried woman."

She bristled. "I am a summoner in training, searching for the arcangels. As I had no other escort, Kyen offered to protect me. I'm sure you're aware the summoners of Isea are sworn to celibacy?"

The glint in Gennen's eyes turned into a sparkle as he smiled at her speech. "Kyen's sense of honor has always been as sure as the mountains."

"And you?" she shot back. "You said you're his teacher of some sort—a blademaster?"

"Aye, his blademaster. At least, I tried to be." He chomped on the stem of his pipe. "Kyen quit on me."

"It's not like Kyen to quit," she said.

"It's not." He agreed.

"Then, what happened?"

"As a boy, Kyen failed the Retributioner's Test. Twice," said Gennen. When Adeya kept staring at him, uncomprehending, he continued, "To earn the right to practice with a steel blade, a pupil has to prove he or she can kill a man. Don't worry, princess," he added, seeing her look of horror. "The first was a thief. Students are tested against criminals already sentenced to death. It's the best way to weed out those unfit for the battlefield. No blademaster would accept a student too soft to kill a man."

"But you did?" asked Adeya.

"More the fool I am for it," he growled. "The Council wouldn't agree to my finishing Kyen's training unless he earned his sword first. Schemers for the throne took advantage. Ennyen at their head challenged Kyen's right to become king—a disgrace in itself; no one should challenge a crown prince until after his bladeday—but the Council approved it. If Kyen defeated and killed Ennyen, the Council would grant him his sword. If Ennyen won, Kyen would lose his life, and Ennyen would take the position of crown prince."

"And Kyen lost?"

"Kyen never lost," he said. "He beat Ennyen but refused to kill him, just as he refused to kill the thief. The Council erupted. Kyen came to me afterwards. Told me he'd decided to quit his training as a warrior, and he vanished from Avanna the next day. Then, Avanna fell, taking the Council and its mess with it before anything could be sorted out."

"How could they be that unfair to Kyen?" said Adeya.

Gennen smiled at her. "Does Isea have no injustice?"

She shut her mouth.

"Kyen has no idea what's riding on his shoulders," he said, grinding his teeth on his pipe stem. "Fool, coward boy."

"Kyen's not a coward!" she cried. "You're just afraid that if Ennyen wins, all the remnant of Avanna will follow him."

"The remnant of Avanna can jump off the Brink, for all I care." He growled. "My concern is for Ellunon. I'll not live forever to keep the Blades in check. They need a leader."

"Well, then, who cares if Kyen passes some stupid test?" she said. "He's the best swordsman in Ellunon, even if he's not some Blade of Avanna. He's more right to his sword than you do!"

Gennen looked at her with wide-eyed surprise, taking the pipe from his mouth.

Adeya, drawing herself up, glared back.

He threw back his head and laughed. "I like you, princess. You've got some fire in you."

She deflated with a huff.

"You're right. You're very right," he said, still smiling; but it faded. "You best be off, if you're to tell him that. You've a lot of ground to cover in order to find Kyen before nightfall. He's mastered disappearing, if nothing else."

Adeya, still eyeing him angrily, started down the steps.

Gennen waved her along with the stem of his pipe. He smiled to himself as he watched her go.

Chapter 27

Reaching the bottom of the stairs, Adeya looked back.

Gennen still smiled down from his perch.

She frowned and turned on her heel with a huff. Giving the golem's pile a wide berth, she crossed the entrance circle and entered a side street. The hush descended again as she walked into the bottom tier of the city. Narrow towers rose on either side, their tops broken off, their white edges jagged against a gray sky. The bright afternoon arclight cast pools of shadow at their feet and magnified the contrast of every detail: every blot of turquoise lichen, every vine spreading emerald curls, every black fissure and hole. All of it stood out against the background of white stone, sharp and vivid.

The hush grew so heavy that the smallest noise resounded everywhere. Adeya's footsteps, though soft and hesitant, seemed to announce her presence up and down the street. A blue bird hopped along a hole in a ruined dome, the click of its tiny claws on the stone catching her attention. She stopped to watch it. A single cheep from its beak echoed through the ruins before it fluttered away. A bit of rock dislodged by its flight crackled to the ground.

She watched the bird until it winged out of sight before returning her attention to the hole in the ruin. She stepped back, taking in how the broad, tall dome dominated the surrounding towers. The jagged hole in its side opened like a black mouth in the seamless white masonry. She approached it, clambering over the pile of rubble at its base and peered inside. The back half of the dome had been smashed out allowing the arclight to stream in and touch on a cluster of glass pillars.

With wide eyes, she stepped inside. She stared at the pillars, each cold and clear as crystal. A myriad of cracks ran up and down their depths yet left the surface smooth. Adeya passed between them, running her hand along the surface of the nearest one.

A stone clattered behind her.

"Kyen?" She looked towards the sound.

A shape moved in the shadows.

Her breath froze as a feline figure slinked into the light —a cougar fiend. Its grin grew wider, and its pointed teeth gleamed.

Adeya bolted.

With a chortle, the fiend bound after her. She dashed back out the hole and sprinted onto the street. The fiend loped out after her, skidding on the cobblestone as it tried to turn, then chased after her.

Cutting across the entrance circle, Adeya ran hard.

"Gennen!" she yelled. "Gennen! Fiend!" Hitting the base of the stairs, she looked up. The block where Gennen had been was empty. She glanced back.

The fiend ran into the entrance circle and slid to a halt,

glancing around. The golem shifted to life behind it, but the fiend spotted Adeya first. She bolted up the stairs as it charged her.

Gasping, she climbed the ascent, pushing herself up the stairs with her hands as well as her feet. She passed the block, sprinted the middle landing, and mounted the steps towards the common hall.

Behind her, the fiend chortled. It bound onto the middle platform behind her, closing in rapidly.

Half sobbing for breath, Adeya stumbled the last few steps into the city circle and fell to the ground.

"Help! Fiend!" She cried.

Oda, Wynne, and several warriors in the training area looked over.

"Fiend!" Adeya yelled at them.

Wynne drew her blade and dashed forward; Oda and the other warriors followed suit.

The fiend reached the top of the stairs at Adeya's heels but balked when it saw Wynne charging. Screaming, she slashed its front leg off at the shoulder, bringing it to the ground. Oda and three of the other warriors struck alongside her. The fiend shrieked and went down under their flashing blades.

Whimpering and gasping, Adeya dragged herself away.

Dark smoke rose as they slashed the fiend's body into pieces. Its screaming cut off.

One warrior backed away, then another, and another. Finally, Oda stepped back.

The fiend had been reduced to a black, fist-sized lump on the ground. This Wynne kept stabbing, her teeth bared in a fierce scowl.

Oda grinned at Adeya and propped his blade against his shoulder.

"You ran screaming from one little fiend?" He laughed. "Chitling!"

He and the others turned to leave.

"Leave off, Wynne! You're blunting your blade," said the last warrior as they walked past Adeya.

Wynne stabbed the now marble-sized lump left of the fiend. Sliding her blade underneath it, she flung it with a yell. The tiny bit of black went flying, arcing down to disappear into the ruins.

"Come back from that!" Wynne yelled after it. She turned her glare on Adeya, chest heaving, while Adeya stared back with wide eyes. Wynne flung her spiked braid over her shoulder and stalked past to rejoin the others in the training area. "Keh!"

Rising on shaking legs, Adeya hobbled towards the common hall. She held back a sob by pressing a hand to her mouth.

* * *

As the Arc disappeared behind the mountains, the final sliver of light departed from the cliff-tops above the ruined city. The mountain loomed in orange and black, still holding the Arc's failing rays, but a deepening dimness veiled the valley beneath its slopes. The shadows hung thickest around the canyon and the mound of boulders blocking it when Kyen poked his head out of the ruins.

After surveying the entrance circle, he climbed a nearby wall and looked at the canyon. His eyes sized-up the boulder mound—a jumbled heap of rocks, some the size of Kyen's fist, some larger than he stood tall, and every size in between.

Walking the length of the wall, he approached the pile. His gaze traveled to its pinnacle and beyond, the dark canyon. He hopped from the wall to the nearest boulder of the pile and waited. When nothing moved, he set his foot in a chink, gripped a handhold, and started to pull himself up.

The boulders shifted.

Kyen staggered backwards. Wobbling, he spread his arms to keep his balance as the pile began to rise, including the boulder underneath his feet. It was rising quickly, and he leapt to the ground, landing hard on all fours.

Stone grated on stone while the boulders levitated as if pulled by invisible strings. A gleam shone out as the pile organized itself into a body—a massive, lopsided man-shape with a squat stone atop that housed the diamond-like gem.

Dust rained down as the shifting stilled.

Kyen backed away to look up at the glinting gem.

The two regarded one another for a long moment.

He bolted, running hard for the crevasse opening between the golem's legs.

The golem slammed its foot down in his way. A deep thud shook the ground, and the impact sprayed Kyen with dust and stones. He stumbled backwards, covering his face.

Shaking off the dust, Kyen sprang forward, a different direction this time. He sprinted around the golem, heading for the space that'd opened up when it moved its leg.

The golem swung down with its boulder-fist. Kyen veered. The fist whooshed through the air beside him, forcing him to leap out of the way.

The canyon waited ahead, clear and open, and Kyen ran for it.

The golem, having twisted at the waist with its swipe, kept rotating. Its body spun in a full circle as the golem's other arm came swinging down on Kyen from above.

He skidded to a halt and scrambled backwards.

The golem's fist pummeled the ground in front of him. The awkward line of boulders forming its arm sagged.

Kyen's eyes widened. He turned and fled.

The arm-boulders crashed down on his tail, one after another. Clouds of dust and rock enveloped him.

Coughing, he sprinted free and kept running until he reached the opposite end of the circle. There he stopped, panting, and looked back.

The golem, its arm now laying on the ground, straightened up. The gem winked at Kyen like an eye. The armless half of the golem's body began shifting upwards. The boulders rolled on the ground towards its leg and crowded up into its figure. It formed a bulge which, with much cracking and grinding, crowded up its thigh, traveled through its torso and pushed its chest boulders out to form a new arm. The dust around it settled as the shifting stilled.

Kyen huffed out a sigh as he watched the golem.

Behind it, in the shadows of the canyon, dark shapes moved. Three fiends stalked forward.

The golem's head swiveled, and the gem glinted at the

fiends. With thunderous footsteps, it stomped towards them.

The fiends balked.

Dropping to its knees at the canyon's mouth, the golem toppled forward, and the shape of its body collapsed into a crashing landslide. The fiends turned and fled as the boulders sealed the canyon up again.

A muscle worked in Kyen's jaw as he watched.

Behind him, Inen stood from where he'd been keeping watch in the shadows.

Kyen glanced over when he walked up.

"No one leaves without Gennen's permission," he said, crossing his arms. "You want out, you've got to ask him."

Kyen, turning his back on Inen and the golem, mounted the central staircase.

Chapter 28

Yellow light poured from the windows into the night when Kyen reached the common hall. Keeping his head down, he entered. The normal racket of voices had quieted to peaceful murmurs as the well-fed warriors sprawled about their mats. Edging around the perimeter, he made his way to the fire where Gennen sat with Nella, Oda, Wynne and Inen. Adeya was wrapped in a blanket beside the blademaster, a mug of tea in her hands, staring into the fire.

Nella stood when she saw Kyen enter the light and started to dish him a bowl from the cauldron over the coals. He accepted it with a soft "Thank you," and sat next to Adeya.

Gennen shot him a look but said nothing.

Silence fell between them.

Wynne glared at Kyen with open disgust.

Odallyan yawned.

Inen looked unimpressed.

"A fiend breached the hold today," Gennen said to the fire. "No doubt, sent by Ennyen. It nearly killed Princess Adeya."

Kyen looked up, turned to Adeya, but she kept her eyes fixed on the flames while her tea cooled in her hands.

Gennen leaned across her, saying to him. "Won't you reconsider? Train with me, Kyen!"

He met the blademaster's eyes for a long moment then looked away. "No, with respect, blademaster."

Gennen breathed out a growl but settled back into his seat to glare at the coals.

"Maybe it wouldn't be so bad having Ennyen as king," said Oda, lounging back.

"He's working with fiends, Oda," said Inen.

"Do you think that will matter to the Blades of Avanna?" asked Gennen. "They'll follow anyone who promises them a battle."

Wynne slammed down her bowl so hard it cracked in two. "I won't follow Ennyen. Even if he is king! I hate fiends!"

"That's the third bowl you've broken, Wynne," said Nella.

"I don't care! If Ennyen takes the throne, I will revolt! Even if I'm the only one!"

"Gennen."

Every face around the fire, including Kyen's, turned to Adeya when she spoke. Lifting her eyes from her tea, she met his pale gaze with her aquamarine one. "If Kyen won't finish his training with you, will you train me instead?"

Wynne, Oda, and Inen erupted:

"She's a mainlander!"

"It's against tradition to train a mainlander!"

"Can a mainlander like her even lift a sword?"

"Your forefathers were all mainlanders!" Gennen shouted back. "Blockheads!" He calmed himself to address Adeya. "I'm not sure if you know what you're asking for, princess. Do you know what's required physically, mentally, to be a Blade of Avanna?"

"I don't," she said. "But I'm tired of being chased around. I'm tired of being rescued. I'm tired of feeling powerless against the fiends. When Ennyen comes, I want to be able to defend myself."

"You? Fight Ennyen?" said Oda.

Wynne broke out laughing so hard she fell over backwards.

Inen shook his head in resignation.

Gennen, ignoring them, puffing silently at his pipe, regarded her for a long moment. At last, a wry smile rose to his face. "I will."

"Gennen! You can't!" Wynne whined.

"She'll take all the secrets of Avanna to the mainland," said Inen.

Still ignoring them, he smiled as he said, "Dawn on the training ground, princess. We start tomorrow."

"Heh, heh, this'll be fun to watch," said Oda.

Kyen hung his head over his bowl and kept eating without a word.

Gennen rose with a loud yawn and a stretch while Nella stood up beside him. "Get to bed, you idiots," he told his three warriors before heading off into the dark with his wife.

Growling to herself, Wynne hopped to her feet to leave, Inen joined her, and Oda, yawning, followed them both.

Adeya shrugged the blanket closer around her and

sipped her tea.

Kyen set aside his empty bowl.

A flame wavered over the yellow embers, casting a thin glow.

"Why didn't you ever say anything?" she asked.

He drew in a deep breath and let it out in a sigh.

"After everything we've been through, and you never told me you were born to a royal family?"

"It never seemed worth mentioning," he replied. "A prince without a kingdom isn't of much consequence."

"But the throne of Avanna is yours. All these people, the remnant of Avanna, you're their king!" she cried.

"I'm no king. I'm not even a prince, not anymore."

"But Gennen said you defeated Ennyen."

"He told you about that, did he?"

"How can you not be a prince if you won?"

"When a Blade challenges the throne, it's a duel to the death," he said. "When I didn't kill Ennyen, the throne couldn't be settled on either of us."

"Gennen seems to think you're still the rightful heir," she said.

"It's hard to tell what Gennen thinks," replied Kyen; he glanced at her. "Are you really going to train with him?"

Adeya fingered the lip of her tea mug, sighed, and said, "Yes. Your wounds aren't healed enough yet to be training me. I see no reason why I shouldn't keep learning if I can..."

"Gennen is a good blademaster. You'll do well." Kyen drew up a knee to his chest and propped his chin on it.

An ember in the fire popped, spitting a few sparks into

the darkness.

"Kyen," she began. "Why... why did you fail the Retributioner's Test?"

"I don't know. It was a long time ago, and I don't like to think about it," he said.

"There's more to it, isn't there?" she asked.

"Talking about it won't change it," he said. "And remembering doesn't do me any good."

Adeya huffed.

They both watched the coals wavering, deepening from yellow to orange.

"With the fiend," Kyen spoke up. "Are you alright?"

Adeya's eyebrows rose as she eyed him. Then she lifted her chin, saying, "Talking about it won't change it."

Kyen looked at her, wide-eyed.

She rose to her feet, brushed out her skirts, and settled the blanket on her shoulders as if it were a cape. "And remembering doesn't do us any good."

He stared after her, open-mouthed, as she walked away with her nose in the air. At the grass mat, she paused to look back.

"Good night, Kyen of Avanna," she said, before slapping the mat aside and disappearing into the room behind.

Kyen kept staring as the mat settled back into place. He shut his mouth. With a sigh, he returned his gaze to the fire. There he sat, chin propped on his knee, his stormy gray eyes staring into space. He remained there as the last embers died into darkness.

Chapter 29

A blue dawn rising cast the ruins in shades of black and navy as Kyen walked among them. Cloak pulled close and hood drawn up, he followed the outer edge of the city where the ruins met the wall of the valley. He paused and looked up. The pale cliffs rose straight and sheer without a ledge, a crack, or a bush for several stone's throws. His stormy gray eyes traveled up the ascent, lingering on its pinnacle high above.

Turning away, he wandered deeper into the city. The hush of lingering night softened his steps and stifled his breath into silent, cloudy puffs.

When he came out on the middle landing, he mounted a weathered block and looked down the stairs to the entrance. The canyon split the bowl of the mountain like a black thorn, the boulders of the golem blocking its base. Kyen's gaze rested long on the valley's exit, his expression withdrawn and his eyes distant. The blues of night paled around him, and the first arcbeams of morning broke over the bowl's rim, but he paid no heed.

Still gazing at the boulders, his brows drew down as he frowned. He turned away and, leaping from the block, crossed the street towards a ruined tower. A jagged hole opened at its base, and he walked into it. Within, the tower rose like a silo, a hollow shell; rubble that'd once formed floors and stairs mounded on the floor. Picking his way across the pile, he stopped near the back and kneeled. He shifted the rubble aside this way and that, eyes searching. Rolling away one last rock too heavy to lift, Kyen brushed away the dirt. Five clear gems gleamed out of the dust and pebbles, each containing a dull light. He gathered them up. Wandering back to the road, he turned them over in his hands and examined them.

Each stone glowed with aura: one with a pinprick, several with bead-sized droplets, but the last eclipsed them all. Light filled to the edges of the stone, leaving only a rim of clear glass.

As Kyen stepped out onto the street, he paused. His stormy gray eyes shifted up, hard and serious.

On the rim of the balustrade perched the caladrius fiend. Its mouth leered at Kyen.

He stared back evenly. He lowered his hand with the gems down to his side but made no other move.

The fiend chortled, three descending tones, as if laughing at him.

He turned and fled.

* * *

Covered in bandages and bruises, Adeya sat on a broken wall by the training area. The clacks of striking practice swords and the grunts of warriors walking through drills carried to where she rested. She flexed a wrapped wrist, rubbing it with her other hand, looking at the joint with concern.

"Back for another day of punishment, chitling?" Oda walked up with a scabbarded sword over his shoulder.

"My name is Adeya of Isea." She glared at him. "Sole Heiress to—"

"Yeah. I know. You said that. Listen, you impressed me. I expected you to quit yesterday. So I thought I'd bring you a present." He chucked the sword into her lap, and she fumbled to grab it. "In case you meet another fiend, I figured you ought to have a blade on you." With a grin and a Blade's salute—a fist thumped to his chest—Oda walked away.

Adeya frowned at the sword. Pulling it partway out of the scabbard, she examined it. The steel blade glinted in the arclight. As she examined it, a shadow fell over her and she looked up to see Gennen.

"Come with me, princess." He turned away.

She rose and, tying the sword to her belt, hurried after him. "Gennen, nobody has seen Kyen in three days. Do you think he's alright?"

"The fool coward is hiding in the ruins."

"He's not a coward!"

"My scouts keep an eye on him. Put yourself at ease. You'll need to focus today."

"More training?" Adeya's face sank.

"Training?" Gennen smiled. "You think we've been training? We've been assessing your strengths, princess. To see if you're fit to even begin training. It might begin today, if you can pass the Seer's Test."

"Why do you people have tests for everything?" She asked, but Gennen ignored her.

"Every single man and woman of Avanna must pass the Seer's Test," he said. "If you pass, you're worthy to begin training as a Blade of Avanna."

"And if I don't?"

"Then, you must leave, knowing that if we meet again, princess, I will slay you where you stand."

"Oh." Adeya touched the amulet at her neck.

"Come!"

She hurried up to his heels. Gennen walked to a shed-like building that stood up against the common hall. He pushed aside the grass mat door and entered. Adeya followed after him but stopped on the threshold, staring.

Inside, the round chamber offered empty floors and bare walls but for a wooden stand fashioned like a perch. On it sat a bird with feathers so white, it seemed to glow. About the size of a hawk, it boasted a graceful, swan-like neck and a cascading plume of a tail that reached the floor. It lifted its head out from under its wing when they entered. A hooked beak of gold and large blue eyes as bright as jewels adorned its face.

Seeing Gennen, the bird called out like a ringing bell: three rising notes. He stopped beside it to stroke its downy head. The bird closed its eyes, and happy little chimes sang from its throat.

"A caladrius?" Adeya whispered.

"This is Matherfel," he said. "A fine caladrius, indeed. He's been a relic of Avanna since my great, great grandfather's time. His is the first test you must pass."

She looked a little pale. "What—what do I do?"

"Step forward."

Adeya crept into the room.

"If he looks steadfastly upon you, then you are destined to be a great enemy of the Consuming Dark, and I will train you," said Gennen. "If he looks away from you, the Dark's hold on you is already too strong. You will die a victim and a puppet to its power and a mortal enemy to every Blade in Avanna. You will have one mercy—to leave our hold unharmed and to never come back. One mercy and no more."

She swallowed and inched towards the caladrius on its perch.

Gennen stepped away from stroking the bird's head.

Matherfel opened his bright eyes, and, noticing Adeya, his eyes grew wider. He stared at her for a moment.

Adeya swallowed again. Neither she nor Gennen made a sound, not even to breathe.

Matherfel blinked. He cocked his head first to one side then the other. Blinking again, he fluffed his feathers out and shook himself.

"Did... Did I pass?" Adeya looked at Gennen.

He was frowning, his brows a single bushy line.

Singing another chime, the caladrius looked to the blademaster and seemed to smile.

"I passed, didn't I?" she asked. "Gennen?"

"Caladrius are deep seers; creatures of the Firstwold, dwelling both as mortals and on the plain of the arcangels," he said. "No man can hide before them, but the depths of the soul are laid bare. Matherfel either looks on you or he looks away."

"Well, he didn't look away, did he?"

"Neither did he look fully on you as he ought to..." Gennen turned to Matherfel; the bird sang to him and hopped over to get another scratch. He rubbed the bird's head absently.

"So what does that mean?" she asked.

"I don't know. I know of only one other that Matherfel looked on with uncertainty. The Council decided it sufficient at the time, despite misgivings among them," he said. "I suppose it must be sufficient for you as well. Come. Time to begin your training." Turning on his heel, he marched back out into open air.

Adeya hurried after him. "How could Matherfel doubt me? I'm to be a summoner! I'm of Isea, a people that are the devoted servants of the arcangels!"

"The Consuming Dark has a hold on us all, princess."

"Not on me, it doesn't!"

"You must listen to me seriously if you're to be a Blade of Avanna," he said. "The Dark's hold isn't just in the form of fiend venom or black weapons. It's up here." Gennen tapped his forehead with his pipe; then he looked at his pipe with disgust, knocking it out on his hand and stowing it in his pocket. "Its chains can run deep and strong, and it'll choke the life from you before you even recognize its grip. You must beat the Dark inside, before you'll be fit to fight with a sword. Now hurry along."

"I don't know what Matherfel sees," she said, drawing herself up. "But I think I would know it if the Consuming

Dark had a hold on me."

Gennen only grunted for a reply.

"And," she continued. "You said there was another pupil that Matherfel looked on with uncertainty. Well, whatever became of that student?"

"It's yet to be seen," said Gennen. "He's currently got his head buried in ruins."

"You—you mean Kyen?"

Another grunt.

"How could anyone—or anything—have misgivings about Kyen?" she cried. "I've never met anyone kinder or braver. He's done nothing but help the arcangels fight the Consuming Dark."

"Yet the life is being choked out of him, that's plain enough to see," he replied, then said under his breath. "I'm beginning to wonder if the Council's misgivings weren't all unfounded... HA!" Gennen suddenly stopped, turned on her with a toothy grin, and poked her on the shoulder. "No Council to check my recklessness now, though! We will train you, princess—come disaster of it!"

"But—" She began.

"No buts!" Gennen marched onwards. "We will begin."

"But, Kyen—"

"Put Kyen out of your head, or I'll put him out of your head for you. You're a Bladepupil of Avanna now. You must be as focused as the point of a dagger!"

"But—" She pointed. "It's Kyen!"

Behind them, Kyen was crossing the city circle.

Gennen looked over his shoulder and sighed when he saw him. He met Adeya's gaze again, measuring the plea that shone bright in her eyes.

"Well, go on then!" he snapped. "It's nearly lunch anyway. Come right back and don't dally!" He crossed his arms and watched her hurry away. His pale gaze followed Kyen as he disappeared into the common hall, then Adeya as she disappeared after him.

He took his pipe out of his pocket, put it back when he noticed it in his hand and walked away, growling under his breath.

Chapter 30

Inside the common hall, Adeya hurried to catch up with Kyen. She reached his side as he arrived at the bubbling cauldrons where the cook was handing out bowls and bread.

"Where have you been? Are you alright?" she asked, accepting a bowl and holding it out for soup without noticing.

Kyen looked over at her; his gray eyes alighted on her bandaged wrist, a scratch on her arm, the bruise on her cheek. "Started training, did you?" He put a hunk of bread in his mouth so that his freed hand could accept a second piece. He walked away balancing two bowls. Adeya followed him as he went to sit against a wall.

After arraying his food around him, he tucked in, drinking from his bowl and not bothering with the spoon. Adeya sat down beside him.

Across the hall, a group of warriors sweaty from training crowded through the doorway, bringing their loud echoes and carousing to the cook fires.

"I was beginning to think you left without me." Adeya set her food aside.

Kyen, about to put the bowl to his lips again, paused and lowered it to look at her. "It'd be against my honor to leave you here."

A ruckus from the fires drew their attention. Kyen's eyes fastened on a fistfight breaking out, especially on Oda egging the combatants on from the sidelines. Looking back, he said, "I've been searching the outskirts of the ruins for another way out. But it looks like the only way is past the golem."

"Could Kade get us out?" Adeya asked in a lowered voice.

"As a last resort, maybe. But his aura wouldn't last long against Ennyen and his fiends. I'm sure they're not far, waiting."

They both watched Gennen arrive at the scene of the fight. He twisted the ears of the two brawlers and marched them both outside, ignoring their yelps.

"How's your training going?" Kyen asked.

"I'm a Bladepupil of Avanna now." She sat up a little straighter. "I passed Matherfel's inspection."

Kyen drained the rest of his bowl and, putting a hunk of bread in his mouth, dug into one of his pockets. He pulled out the five gems—their soft glow lit up his hand—and bit off the bread. When Adeya saw them, her eyes widened.

"Arcstones!" she said. "There's still aura in them, too."

"Not much," he said. "Kade already used up one." He pulled aside his collar; the line of a new scar shown pink and fresh where the gash had been.

"He healed you?"

Kyen shifted his collar back in place. Picking out the

brightest of the gems, he held it out to her. "Here. I want you to have this one."

She picked it up with ginger fingers. Clear as glass, whiter than a candle flame, the arcstone's radiance reflected in her aquamarine eyes.

"What am I going to do with it?" She looked at him. "Kade's with you. Don't you need it?"

"Just in case," he said, talking around the mouthful of bread, not meeting her eye.

"Just in case of what?"

He picked up his second bowl of soup to drain it.

"Kyen, just in case of what?"

He watched the line at the cook fires, moving along in order now; the growing group of warriors sat around, shoveled down food and tried to swipe each other's bread. Their jabber filled the common hall.

Adeya stared at Kyen while waiting for a response, but when he lowered his second bowl, he eyed the new longsword at her side.

"Where'd you get that?" he asked.

"Odallyan gave it to me—but I was asking you a question!"

"May I?"

With a huff, she drew it out, and Kyen took the sword to examine it. He held up the blade, shut one eye, and looked down its edge. As he did, his face fell.

"What?" she asked.

"The weak of the blade is bowed and the edge wobbles." He handed it back. "It looks like a blacksmith's apprentice has been practicing. You'd have a hard time cutting anything with this."

Adeya jammed the sword back into its scabbard. She set about untying it from her belt, but the furious jerks from her hands made her fumble at the knot. When she finally loosed herself of the bum blade, she slammed it into the ground.

"I've never been so disrespected in my whole life!" She shouted at Kyen, her voice echoing through the common hall.

He shrank against the wall as those nearby turned to look at them.

She glared at him, huffing, bristling to the bursting point. "I'm *glad* you're not like *that*!" Snatching up her bowl, she began stuffing its contents into her mouth.

Kyen, grabbing his chunk of bread, took a bite and chewed, all the while casting uneasy glances at her. He reached for what remained of his soup bowl when a foot kicked it and spilled it over the ground.

They both looked up.

A Blade of Avanna nearly as big as Inen stood over them with his arms crossed. He wore his black hair in a long ponytail and his flint-gray eyes fixed Kyen with a hard stare. Scars on his arms looked like a criss-cross of sword slashes.

"So you're the king imminent Gennen told us so much about?" he said.

Kyen looked away; he righted the spilled bowl with careful fingers and set it aside.

Adeya glared up at the Blade, but he ignored her.

"You don't look like much." He uncrossed his arms.

"Are you really suited to lead the Blades of Avanna?"

Kyen reached for his second hunk of bread, but the Blade kicked it out of his reach. It tumbled across the floor.

"Maybe we should prove you?" A grin broke out over his face. "There's no reason I couldn't be the king as well as you. Or better!"

Kyen drew up a knee to his chest and folded his hands on top of it.

"Get up!" The warrior kicked his other leg, still outstretched.

"I don't want to fight," he said, still not looking up.

"Get up!" The Blade kicked his leg again, this time harder. "I want to see if you have what it takes to be the King of Avanna."

Kyen drew his other leg under him out of kicking range.

When the Blade reached for his hilt, Adeya jumped to her feet with her fists clenched at her sides. "Leave him alone!"

The Blade looked amused when he turned his flinty gaze on her.

She scowled back, but the Blade shook his head. Drawing his sword free of its scabbard, he addressed Kyen, "What kind of king lets a mainlander—a mainlander and damsel—do his fighting for him? Are you really that soft? Soft and a coward?"

"He's not a coward! I said leave him alone!" Adeya stepped between them.

"This is between Blades, mainlander!" He shoved her out of the way, hard.

With a cry, she stumbled and fell sprawling to the floor.

A fleshy smack mingled with the echo of her voice.

Even before she'd hit the ground, Kyen launched to his feet. He seized the man's sword arm, and, using his own momentum and a nasty wrench, he swung the Blade around and into the wall. The warrior's face hit the bricks with a smack as Adeya landed on the ground.

As she started to prop herself up, Kyen pinned the Blade against the wall. The set to his jaw and the spark in his stormy gaze made her eyes widened.

"Remember your honor." He gave the Blade's arm an extra twist, drawing from him a grunt of pain and pushing his shoulder joint to the brink of dislocation. His sword dropped from his hand. It hit the ground with a clatter.

Kyen slung the Blade to the floor opposite from Adeya but didn't stay to see him go sprawling. He turned and strode away, pausing only long enough to pick up his second hunk of bread. Adeya, climbing to her feet, dashed after him. The Blade watched them leave the common hall while rubbing his shoulder.

Adeya ran in Kyen's wake as he strode across the city circle. He was walking fast.

"Kyen! Kyen, wait!"

At the top of the stairs, he stopped and let her catch up, his back to her.

"They'll never leave you alone if you don't stand up to them," she said, coming up behind him.

"I don't want to kill anyone."

"So you're just going to let them walk all over you?"

"You don't understand!" Kyen whirled on her, every line in him taut and hard. "How many is it going to take before they stop challenging me? Proving the Throne is a duel to the death!'"

She took a step back; her hand rose to the amulet at her neck.

"How many is it going to take?" Kyen repeated. "Three? Five? Ten? Will they ever stop?"

Adeya, tears shining unshed in her eyes, dropped her gaze to the ground.

"I don't want to kill anyone!" he said.

As he watched, a tear spilled down her cheek. She sniffed, still not looking at him. When he saw it, everything about him softened.

"I'm sorry. Don't—don't cry." He reached out as if to put a hand on her arm but stalled halfway.

"It's not right how they treat you." Adeya wiped at her tear, but another spilled down to take its place. "You're the hero of Ellunon."

"I'm not even a Blade of Avanna, Adeya," he said. "I'm not anyone. It's better if I disappear."

She sniffed again.

"The sooner I find a way out of here, the better." With a sigh, he started down the stairs.

"Kyen?" She walked to the edge of the step he just left.

He paused to look over his shoulder at her.

"Don't—" She wiped at her face. "Don't disappear without me. Please?"

"I won't." He looked sad as he said it. "Keep your things packed. I won't be far."

Chapter 31

Adeya wiped sweat from her forehead. Bits of her hair had escaped her ponytail, and stuck to the damp on her face and neck. She sat on the rim of the sparring square, looking towards the central stair. She sighed.

Behind her the Blades of Avanna, all with wooden swords in hand and spaced out in a grid, took a breather under the mid-afternoon arclight. Their guffaws and chatter filled the air as a cold breeze coming off the mountain gave Adeya a shiver.

"Well done on your drills, princess," said Gennen as he approached.

She started to smile.

"You almost kept up and fumbled only fifteen of the forms," called Odallyan from the ranks. Wynne, Inen, and several others chuckled.

Her smile vanished though she pretended to ignore them.

"Gennen?" She looked up at the little man. "I saw Kyen do a disarm once. He said he'd teach me how to do it, but I was wondering if you would?"

"A disarm?" Gennen's eyebrows rose. His pipe puffed

like a miniature chimney.

"He somehow traded places with the man attacking him, just by grabbing his arm."

He waved his own pipe smoke out of his face. "No, that's too advanced for you. Not yet. Come!"

"But—"

"Come!"

Adeya stood as he entered the sparring square.

"Drills mean nothing if you can't use them in combat," he said. "Today, you begin sparring—practice fighting, princess!"

She stepped over the rim. "Will I spar…Oh." Her question died when Inen entered from the opposite side. He stood easily two heads taller than the princess and twice as wide. The muscles on his forceps and biceps bulged when he crossed his arms, waggling the wooden sword. It looked like switching cane in his massive hands.

"You will spar Inen." Gennen sat himself on a block.

Adeya paled. "But Inen is so—Couldn't I spar someone else? Like Wynne?"

Gennen chuckled and took his pipe from his mouth. "Inen is the only Blade I trust to go easy on you."

She looked back at Inen, and he stared her down. Hints of blue lightened his pewter-colored eyes, but his face seemed a stern mask with the nasty scars across his cheek and forehead.

"Go easy?" She swallowed. Raising her wooden sword, she crouched on guard. Inen moved in kind, a giant mirror of the princess, all in muscle.

"Get to it, princess. We don't have all day," said

Gennen.

Drawing in an unsteady breath, she tightened her grip on her sword, dug in her toes and charged. She swung at him, but he blocked it and attacked back with three rapid strikes. Adeya cried out and stumbled backwards, struggling to catch the blows with her wooden sword. The first two she deflected, but the third caught her in the hip. She staggered sideways and landed in a heap outside the sparring ring.

Adeya lifted her head from the dust.

Chuckles from Wynne, Oda, and the other Blades floated over.

"Get to work!" Gennen snapped at them.

The noise of wood swords clacking together answered him.

Inen, without lowering his sword, backed away to his starting place.

"Again, princess," said Gennen. "And stop swinging wide! You're leaving yourself vulnerable!"

Gripping her practice sword, she pushed herself up and stepped back into the sparring square.

Again, Inen waited. Again, Adeya made the first move. She thrusted. Inen turned it aside with his weapon then sliced up. She winced sideways as the sword whistled past her. Staggering a little, she tried to regain her balance but Inen was already on her, stabbing for her gut. She lifted her sword to deflect it. But Inen's move was a feint. His blade whipped in from the side without warning and smacked her across the upper arm. The blow landed hard enough to throw her around and send her stumbling face-first into the dirt.

"Hold!" cried Gennen.

Inen stood down as the blademaster hopped off his block.

Wincing and holding her shoulder, Adeya struggled back to her feet to meet him. Her sword dangled limp in her hand.

"You're bouncing around like a hunted snow hare." Gennen growled around the stem of his pipe. "Look at yourself."

She gazed down her arms, bruised, dust sticking to her sweaty face along with her hair.

"You're not seeing! Look at yourself!" He snapped.

Adeya held up her hands, one open-palmed, the other gripping the practice sword. Her brows furrowed together. Her fingers were trembling. Her breathing—shallow little gasps—quivered through her body.

"The battle isn't just out here." Gennen swept out a hand that included Inen and the sparring ring. Turning, he popped his palm against Adeya's forehead hard enough to make her flinch. "It's in here."

She rubbed the spot with her fingers, frowning.

"If you can't calm the battle in there, no amount of skill will save you from the battle out here," he said. Then stepping back, he cried, "Try again!"

Adeya gripped the hilt of her practice sword with both hands. Closing her eyes, she drew in a deep breath and let it out slowly. As she did, the tremble running through her calmed. She opened her eyes and launched herself at Inen, this time with a slash aimed for his legs. He stepped out of range only to lunge back in with a forehead strike. She sidestepped, slashing out for his shoulder, but he flicked the sweep of her sword aside and whipped his around to strike.

She grabbed his sword wrist. Wrenching his arm, she tried to take a step around him, tried to force him forward. Inen's shoulder jerked out, but Adeya's move lacked leverage. He dropped his weight under her twist, swung around and slammed his hilt into Adeya's face. She crumpled to the dirt.

"Hold!" Gennen hopped off his block again.

Inen backed away, flexing his shoulder a little.

Adeya sat up holding her head.

"Better," Gennen glowered. "For a wool-eared blockhead! Didn't you hear what I said? That disarm is too advanced for you. I thought you listened better than that, princess!"

Adeya shook her head and looked at him struggling a little to focus. That didn't diminish her scowl. "I want to know how to disarm, Gennen."

The blademaster puffed at his pipe; his pale-eyed gaze bored into her.

Struggling upright, she staggered backwards a few steps but caught herself. She met his pale gaze with her bright, aquamarine one. "The disarm, Gennen, please?"

He snatched her sword arm by the wrist. "Grip like this. When you twist, throw your whole body into it. Duck under his arm, not around it."

Adeya nodded.

"Practice on Inen. Inen? Where—come here, Inen!"

The giant warrior hung back, still rubbing his shoulder.

Adeya stepped forward when a distant wailing made the three of them look up. The other Blades paused their practicing.

"Fiends!" shouted Wynne.

Chapter 32

The wailing grew in pitch and number until a howling chorus echoed between the towers.

Gennen leapt the sparing square and sprinted towards the central stair. Adeya ran after him, but Inen, Oda and Wynne all passed her and reached the steps with Gennen first. She arrived beside them, and, together, they looked down the staircase, down the lower three levels of the ruins, toward the canyon's entrance.

Cougar fiends, a horde of them like dark ants, swarmed out of the canyon into the entrance circle. The golem stood formed up, swinging its massive arms like clubs and stomping, but the horde flooded around its feet, too many to stop. The wailing reached a frenzy as they breached the foot of the steps.

"Blades to the front!" yelled Gennen.

The Blades of Avanna—those in the sparring square, those tending goats, those at the cook fires and laundry lines —all grabbed their weapons and came running. Even youths with barely ten seasons joined them, swelling their ranks to nearly fifty swords. Little, black-haired toddlers tried to waddle up, waving play swords, but a handful of older swordsmen scooped them up. They carried the children away into the common hall where Nella waited in the doorway. She watched Gennen for a moment, concern plain on her face, before she disappeared with them inside.

Perched on the top step, Wynne peered down at the horde; at least fifty strong streamed up the stairs towards them. "Keh! Is that all?"

"Go shelter in the common hall, princess," Gennen told Adeya.

"No! I can fight," she replied.

Gennen eyed her for a moment. Turning to a nearby Blade, he sized up the three extra longswords that he carried on his back. He snatched one from him. The Blade opened his mouth, but Gennen cut him off.

"She's borrowing this." He thrust the longsword at Adeya.

She took it and tied it to her belt.

"Circle up!" Gennen yelled.

The Blades backed away from the stairs as one. They assembled themselves in a semi-circle around it with their thickest ranks standing between the fiends and the common hall. Adeya, getting shuffled around, ended up on the east arm of the group with the ruins at their back.

The wailing of the fiends reverberated in the air, nearing.

Gennen took hold of his sword and drew it. Its silvery blade glinted white in the arclight. Steel sang as all the other Blades unsheathed their swords with him. Adeya drew her sword last of all and gripped the hilt tightly with both hands.

Like a black wave breaking over rock, the horde of fiends crested the top of the stairs. As one, the Blades charged. The roar and thunder of war cries from mortal throats drowned out their unearthly wails. Those at the front of the horde balked as the onslaught of warriors collided with them. Adeya rushed in with them, and, even though she couldn't keep pace, she attacked the first fiend that broke through their initial sweep. She slashed its leg out from under it and took off its head with a couple lobs. While its body flopped and struggled, she rounded on the next one.

The fiend lunged at her, ready for her attack, but she dodged sideways and slung her blade straight into its snapping mouth. The steel sank half-way into its head. Undaunted, the fiend clamped its jaws on the blade and wrenched, ripping the hilt from Adeya's hand.

It slung her blade aside. She watched it skitter over the cobblestones.

The fiend stalked forward. Two more who'd broken through the lines joined it. Their toothy grins broadened as they closed in.

Adeya put her hand on the hilt of her dagger.

From out of the ruins, Kyen vaulted into the city circle. He landed at a roll, came up at a crouch to snatch up Adeya's fallen blade, and launched himself into the three fiends. He slit the first in half, whirled to take off the third's head, and he bashed repeatedly into the middle fiend's midsection. Adeya stared at Kyen, moving between the three fiends like blur, the black haze of their disintegrating limbs rising around him. They cowed before his flashing blade, limping and stumbling to escape its deadly edge.

Another fiend, stalking up from the side, sprang at Adeya. She noticed it at the last moment and ran.

"Sword!" she yelled as it chased her.

Kyen flipped the blade backhand and threw it.

Though running hard, arms outstretched to catch it, Adeya didn't reach the sword before it hit the cobblestones. The fiend snapped at her heels. She made a dive, catching up the hilt. She rolled onto her back as the fiend leapt on her.

She slashed.

The blade sliced off its front claws, and the fiend landed hard on top of her, floundering, crushing the breath from her. Gasping, she tried to pull herself out from underneath it as it wiggled and struggled upright. Getting up on its nub-legs, it snapped for her throat.

The teeth cracked shut inches from her as Kyen pummeled into its side. The fiend stumbled sideways, and Adeya scrambled free.

Still struggling to breath, she rose to her hands and knees and brought down the sword with a yell. It took two blows, but she sliced off the fiend's head before it could rise. Its body jerked away and fell, evaporating into smoke.

"Sword!" cried Kyen.

She passed the hilt up to him.

He whirled on a fiend that'd been sneaking up on their backs. It lunged to bite as he swung, and he split the fiend through its mouth all the way into its chest. Whipping the sword free, he bashed it twice more until it backed off.

Adeya, rising to her feet, saw another fiend loping towards them. She backed away as fast as she could while Kyen beat off the fiend behind her. She didn't see the second fiend creeping up on her from the side.

"Sword!" cried Adeya.

Kyen flipped the blade back hand and, whirling around, flung it hard like a spear. It flashed past her.

Adeya jumped as the sword impaled the second fiend in the head. Its open jaws halted a span from her arm. The fiend whined and sank, but not before Adeya grabbed the hilt. She wrenched the blade loose in time to sling it around and slice into the fiend about to pounce her from the front. She hacked at it until it balked from her and tried to drag its wounded body out of range.

Adeya left off, backing away. She bumped into Kyen, whirled with the sword upraised, but froze when she saw it was him. "Oh! Just you."

"You alright?" he asked, not taking his eyes from the fiends.

"Y-yes," said Adeya breathlessly. "You?"

"For the moment."

They stood together, back to back, Adeya still clutching the sword and Kyen unarmed. The wounded fiends around them dragged and limped away, wailing feebly. Throughout the city circle, fiends missing legs, heads, hindquarters, all hobbled a retreat towards the stairs. Some twitched and thrashed on the ground without enough of a body left to move. The circle of Blades held strong around them, constricting, pushing the thinned, injured horde off the city circle. They crowded at the top of the stairs, stumbling over one another in the rush to escape.

Above their shrieking and the yelling warriors, a call pierced the air and brought everyone to a halt. Three descending chimes.

Chapter 33

Kyen and Adeya looked to the sky in alarm.

A dark shape shot up the stairs and into the air over the city circle. The fiend caladrius. It flipped in the air, flinging out a dark miasma, and plummeted into the battle like a smoking meteor. It slammed into Inen claws-first, flattening him with its impact.

"Oda!" Gennen yelled over the mayhem. "Matherfel!"

The swordsman gave a curt nod and dashed out of the skirmishes still waging around him, slashing his way through a fiend that barred his path.

Several Blades rushed in to rescue Inen.

The caladrius fiend, pinning Inen with a claw to the neck, bent its grinning face towards them. It puffed its feathers out and chortled. The dark miasma radiating off its body thickened. Black, misty tendrils reached out to meet the charging warriors.

They stopped up short. The nearest sliced a tendril, but the blade passed through the miasma as if it were vapor. It came away smeared by the darkness which began spreading, eating through the steel. The Blade threw the sword down and backed away.

Inen yelled, trying to twist out of the fiend's grip to crawl away, but the caladrius fiend turned its grin on him. It struck like a snake, sinking its fangs into his neck. He screamed.

Kyen darted away from Adeya. Dashing between the Blades, he lifted an arm, and a ribbon of light materialized in the air beside him. He slung it out as he reached Inen; the ribbon snapped forward like a whip crack. It sliced the fiend's body in half, slamming it off Inen's chest and into the ground. One wing, one leg, and a wedge of body evaporated into smoke. What remained of the caladrius floundered, flopping around to face Kyen.

Another ribbon of light joined the first, and both shot out towards the fiend as Kyen threw his hands forward.

The caladrius fiend chortled. The tendrils of miasma dissipated into a mist that reformed, becoming a vortex of swirling black fire.

The ribbons snapped taut, snagged by the vortex as it sucked them in.

The caladrius's body, leg, and wing regrew, and it rose to its feet.

Crossing his arms over his face, Kyen gritted his teeth and leaned backward. The taut ribbons, anchored in the air around him, strained thin. His heels began sliding over the ground, inch by inch.

The miasma swirled faster, pulling in the ribbons length by length.

The black caladrius stalked towards Kyen, grinning, bringing its vortex closer.

He tried to take a step back, but his feet slid forward

another stretch. Sweat stood out of his face.

With a cry, Adeya charged in from behind. As soon as she entered the miasma, her amulet flashed out. The light burned the air clear, and the fiend flinched as if struck. The ribbons snapped in the middle, and the halves nearest Kyen whipped back to disintegrate into sparks. As they did, he stumbled backwards and fell.

Adeya came at the fiend, swinging. It ducked the swiping blade and hissed at her.

A throaty yell distracted them both. Gennen charged in to join her, his silver sword gleaming. He struck down on the black caladrius, but it squawked and gave an awkward flapping leap backwards to avoid being hit. With a great spread of its wings and a burst of air from its feathers, the bird launched into the air. It winged away out of their reach.

Another call, three rising chimes, resounded, and a white shape streaked out of the sky. It pummeled into the fiend with a spray of black feathers. Matherfel tumbled through the air, gripping the black fiend with claws, beak ripping, wings flapping. The fiend wailed and wrestled. Feathers flew. Before they hit the ground, the two detached.

The fiend banked away.

Matherfel flapped, stationary in the air, its song rising like ringing bells.

The dark caladrius wheeled and dove down the stairs. Beneath it, the fiends still able to move turned to flee. They ran down the staircase back towards the canyon.

Matherfel sang again as he turned to fly a circuit around the city circle. The cheers of the Blades joined in. They pointed their swords towards the sky, whooping and yelling.

Oda and a few others were jumping up and down.

Kyen, Adeya, and Gennen all looked at one another. She smiled, but neither swordsmen returned it.

As the cheers faded, the moaning and screaming began.

Chapter 34

Several Blades lay writhing on the pavement. From claw scrapes and fiend bites, an inky substance crept over limbs and faces. Inen curled up on himself, convulsing and groaning. Fiend venom, already spreading from the bite in his neck, had sealed one of his eyes shut and was working its way over his mouth. His other eye stared, crazed and unseeing.

He started to rise, but three Blades rushed forwards to pin his arms, holding him down. He tried to punch one and struggled to throw off the other. He screamed at them, a strange wailing tenor warping his human voice.

Adeya grimaced at the sound.

Gennen looked grim, gripping the hilt of his blade with white knuckles.

Another scream joined Inen's. Wynne's voice—yelling profanity. She wrestled with two Blades trying to restrain her from chasing the fiends down the stairs. She yanked herself this way and that in their grip, her voice ragged and hoarse in its curses.

Hefting his white blade, Gennen started towards Inen, but Adeya put a hand on his arm to stop him.

Kyen was already moving forward.

With a shove, Inen sent one of the three Blades sprawling. The other two threw their entire weight on his arms to keep him down. He roared at Kyen when he stopped beside him. The darkness had covered more than half his face.

Taking an arcstone from his pocket, Kyen held it up on his palm. He closed his eyes. Six wings of white fire suddenly blazed into life around him. All the Blades gasped and backed away. Those holding Inen stared up, open-mouthed. Gennen's eyes widened. The wings spread, the lowest pair brushing over Inen, the highest pair rising to point their wingtips towards the sky, the middle enfolding and shrouding Kyen. With a flash, they transformed into ribbons and leapt out. One ribbon dove towards each of the downed warriors.

The men holding Inen jumped back as the nearest ribbon pierced the bite wound on his neck. He jolted as it struck. The five others also spasmed as the ribbons slammed into the fiend-poison seeping through their bodies.

The ribbons pulled taut and, as they did, tendrils of darkness ripped from all the wounded Blades. Some cried out, some convulsed, some beat a fist against the ground. All but Inen.

He arched his back and screamed when the ribbon piercing him jerked. But it didn't come free. Again, it snapped upwards, harder. Out with it dragged a shred of darkness like a bit of tattered cloth. Inen collapsed back, huffing, clear-eyed, restored skin and limb and face. Seeing Kyen standing above him, his eyes grew wide. He dragged himself away.

The six ribbons floated together, pulling the dark swatches with them. All the shreds latched together into a mass that exploded. It blasted the ribbons of light to pieces and burst out into a thousand dark tendrils. All of them stabbed for Kyen.

His brows furrowed, and he bowed his head.

A flash of light bounced the tendrils off the air in front of him. The ribbons reformed and lashed around them. They looped and swirled until the dark, seething mass disappeared into its white knot.

All six ribbons jerked tight in different directions. The knot constricted. With one last yank, they crushed the mass out of existence then came apart. A faint shimmer like white sparks faded in the air where the mass had been. The ribbons dematerialized into a haze, disintegrating backwards along their length to disappear at the point where they'd been anchored in Kyen.

He lifted his head, taking in a sharp gasp like a man who'd been underwater too long. The hand holding the arcstone dropped limp to his side. The crystal crumbled from his loose fingers like crushed glass.

In the silence that followed, every Blade stared at Kyen. Inen checked his hand forward and backward then rubbed his cheek—the one that'd been covered in the dark poison. He accepted an arm from a nearby Blade who pulled him to his feet. They both stepped away.

"Kyen?" Adeya approached.

He swayed a little, looking out of it.

Gennen lingered behind her, his brows furrowed, an

intense glint in his pale eyes.

"Are you alright?" she asked.

His gray gaze shifted towards her, but no recognition broke through his dazed expression. He looked pale.

"Kyen?" She put a hand on his shoulder.

With another breath, sharp and deep, his eyes suddenly refocused on her. "I'm—I'm alright."

Turning, he wandered away. The Blades parted around him, giving him a wide berth, eyeing him with suspicion. Even fear.

Adeya watched as he walked slowly towards the ruins. Gennen came up beside her; he wore a deep scowl on his face as they watched Kyen together.

"Was that what I think it was?"

"An arcangel," Adeya told him. "Kyen's been hiding it. That's why the fiends attacked."

"How long?"

"Since before the Black War. I'm not sure how long before that," she said.

Matherfel swooped over their heads. He veered to Gennen, and alighted on the arm he offered.

"Gennen!" Oda ran up. "Gennen, the golem is gone!"

"Don't be an idiot," he said. "The golem is bound by oath to that spot."

"But it is," said Oda. "Go look, if you don't believe me."

With a frown, Gennen marched away towards the steps. Adeya followed him. From the top of the stairs, they both looked down towards the canyon. Its dark mouth, where the golem usually piled itself, yawned open and empty

Gennen's scowl deepened. "Set double guards, Oda. Go on, get!'"

"Okay, okay!"

"I have a bad feeling about this," he muttered under his breath.

Chapter 35

Adeya bit her lip, brows drawn together in focus, while Wynne loomed beside her. Arms crossed, the swordswoman's sharp eyes, gray like slate, followed her every move as she dabbed tincture over the bite wound in Inen's neck. Not a trace of the inky venom remained, but bloody toothmarks punctured matching crescents across his neck and shoulder.

"If Kyen has an arcangel," said Wynne. "Why didn't he just heal Inen up completely?"

"Kade isn't some wish-granting water jynn from Nalayni." Adeya corked the tincture bottle and put it in the healer's pouch that lay open beside her. "He only has so much aura. He has to conserve it."

"Are you sure this is necessary?" Inen shifted as if to stand.

Wynne's glare pinned him in place, and he lowered his eyes to the ground.

"What about Matherfel? Can't I see him instead?" he asked.

"He left to hunt," said Wynne. "He'll heal you up when he gets back. So sit still!"

"There's no shame in being bandaged. Why must you Blades of Avanna always play so tough?" Adeya unrolled a strip of linen. She held it first one way then the next, as if trying to decide the best angle to wrap the bite.

Raucous laughter rang through the common hall catching their attention. Three massive bonfires blazed high despite the strong afternoon arclight streaming through the windows. Warriors crowded the fires where several circles of dancers spun in rings. Instead of holding hands, they held one another's swords to form the circle: one hand grasping a hilt, the other gripping the flat of a blade. So linked, they skipped and bobbed round and round, they looped underneath one another or wove together into a tighter circle. All their swords crossed to form a star, flashed between the dancing bodies, or expanded back into a circle. Even weaving in and out amongst each other, no one let go of hilt or sword, all the while keeping the circle whole and spinning round. Those crowded to watch clapped, stamped, laughed, and shoved each other.

"How you not cut yourselves, I'll never know." Adeya, with a shake of her head, returned her attention to bandaging Inen.

"Dance with me and I'd show you how." Oda sauntered up.

"No, thank you." Adeya tugged the bandage's knot tight. She bent for her pouch, but Oda stooped and snatched it first.

"Ooo, what's this?" He poked a hand inside.

"Give that back," she said. "You might break something!"

222

"Oh, ho!" His eyebrows rose as he looked at her. His hand drew out the bottle of tincture.

"Don't you dare—"

"Oops!" He opened his fingers with a smile. The bottle of tincture dropped and shattered on the floor, splattering everywhere.

"Oh, go away, Oda," said Wynne.

"You're an idiot, Odallyan," said Inen.

He chuckled and pulled a face in response.

Adeya, swelling like a balloon, balled her fists at her sides. She popped to her feet and stomped up to Oda.

"I have had ENOUGH of you!" She snatched her healer's pouch away from him. "You torment me! You play tricks on me! You call me names! I am a Princess of Isea, and I will be respected!" Adeya drew her longsword and brandished it at Oda.

Wynne and Inen stared as Oda's eyebrows rose even higher. He laid a casual hand on his hilt.

"Are you challenging me to a contest?" he asked.

"Do I have any other choice? Words don't seem to work on you!"

"I accept," said Odallyan. "Name your terms, little chitling."

"Terms?" Adeya lowered her sword.

"What do you want if you win?"

"If I win, you must treat me with respect." She pointed her sword at him again. "You shall answer honestly, conduct yourself humbly, and never even think of another mean trick against me again!"

Oda smiled so broadly he looked to be on the brink of

laughing.

"And!" She continued. "You will address me by my name—as 'my lady, Adeya.' From now until you die."

"I accept your terms," he said. "If I win, I will take you as my warslave."

Wynne's and Inen's eyes grew wide.

"I accept," said Adeya.

"Oda, she's only a bladepupil," said Inen.

"She can't participate in a contest unless she has her blademaster's consent!" said Wynne. "This isn't valid!"

"No problem." He shrugged. "Go find Gennen, chitling. Then meet me in the training square."

"Fine!" Turning on her heel, she marched away.

Inen and Wynne exchanged glances, and Wynne hurried after her.

"You don't know what you're doing, mainlander!" She said as Adeya strode through the common hall. "You'll be Oda's warslave!"

"It can't be worse than how he treats me now," she replied.

"Oh, it's worse. It's bondage! You'll have to serve Oda's house the rest of your life. Catering to his every whim and desire. You'd have to lick his feet if he asked you!"

"Since when did you care?" Adeya shot at her. "I'm just a mainlander, remember?"

Wynne growled. "Gennen's a fool if he lets you throw your life away."

Adeya crossed the hall towards the cook fires with Wynne keeping on her heels. She found Gennen seated with Kyen while Nella watched a giant soup cauldron on the fire.

The three looked at her, each noting the bare blade in her hand, when she marched up.

"Gennen, tell me how to beat Odallyan," said Adeya.

Gennen set his bowl aside, and Kyen frowned.

"She challenged him to a contest," said Wynne. "They're to meet in the training square, if you give your permission."

"Did you wager anything?" asked Gennen.

"That he treat me with respect and use my name," said Adeya. "If I lose, I am to be his warslave. So you have to tell me how to beat him."

At the word "warslave," Gennen's eyebrows drew together.

Kyen's frown deepened, and everything about him grew still.

"She's barely a pupil, Gennen. Oda is stronger, faster, a fully trained Blade! She doesn't stand a chance against him," said Wynne. "You can't allow this!"

Gennen thought a long moment before saying, "I will witness." He rose.

"Gennen," said Kyen.

The blademaster shot him a hard look. "What? You have something to say?"

"I won't allow this."

"By what authority?" He smirked. "Are you the prince or aren't you?"

"Keep out of this, Kyen!" Adeya shot at him. "I'm tired of being bullied. If steel is the only language you dunderheads are capable of understanding, then I will speak it! I refuse to be walked on like this!"

A muscle in Kyen's jaw worked, but he said nothing.

"Come with me, princess." Gennen, taking her by the elbow, led her off. "We shall see how the knife falls."

Kyen with a hard expression followed them beside Wynne. They left behind Oda jostling shoulders and calling to the crowd. "Come watch me put the mainlander in her place! She thinks she can be one of us? Ha! Mainlanders only have one place among us—as warslaves!"

Leaving the common hall, the four walked out into the afternoon light slanting through the city circle.

"You have to tell me how to beat him, Gennen," said Adeya, in a lowered voice.

"You understand the wager, don't you?" he said.

"Just tell me how to beat him," she said. "You think I can, don't you?"

"Oda is stronger, heavier, more skilled," he replied. "You don't stand a chance."

Adeya's stopped short.

"Keep up, princess!" He snapped back at her. After she hurried back in step with him, he continued, "That's why you don't engage him, strength on strength or skill on skill. You will lose."

"Then what do I do?" She gripped her amulet as they neared the sparring ring.

"No amount of training, strength, or experience can completely eliminate one thing, princess—error. But you must be patient, and you must be calm. Fear makes you hasty. Clouds judgment. Oda will make a mistake. Strike when that happens, and then it won't matter if you're weaker, stupider, or smaller." Gennen stopped at the stones which ringed the sparring area.

Adeya, drawing herself up, clenched the hilt of her sword. Gennen nodded her in. She entered the ring to wait for Oda. He was still exiting the common hall, escorted by a large crowd of warriors.

Wynne and Kyen stopped on either side of Gennen.

"With respect, blademaster," said Kyen in an undertone. "How can this even be a contest?"

"I learned the hard way to have more faith in my bladepupils," said Gennen. "Don't make my mistake."

Kyen glanced at him as if struck, but the blademaster folded his arms and fixed his pale gaze on the sparring ring.

"Besides," he continued. "Odallyan needs to be humbled. Adeya's already better at blades in ways Oda can only dream about. Watch her, boy. She may teach you a thing or two."

Kyen observed Gennen for another moment as if trying to read him, but as the Blades arrived with Oda he put his attention on the sparring ring. His gray eyes grew steely as he watched Oda hop into the ring. Around him, murmurs passed back and forth, the Blades all grinning and elbowing each other.

Oda drew out his sword and bobbed from one foot to the other. He gave the blade a flourish, swirling it first on one side, then the other, the arclight catching along its edge.

"Wait, we're not going to use practice swords?" Adeya looked at Gennen.

"A contest is no fun without a little danger, chitling," said Oda. "You can declare mercy early, if you're scared."

She bristled. Settling into a fighting stance, Adeya

pointed her sword at him.

"No? Then we start now!" He lunged at her.

Adeya cried out, wincing as his blow slammed into her block. She staggered backwards.

"Oda!" Gennen snapped.

The swordsman grinned back.

"Only the witnessing blademaster has the authority to give the start," said Gennen. "Get back to your place!"

"Well, then, hurry up!" Oda capered back into position. He cracked his neck and rolled his shoulders.

Gennen waited for Adeya to regain her original spot and stance before saying, "You will fight until one declares mercy. No other limitations. Understood? You may start!"

Chapter 36

Oda, grinning from ear to ear, circled Adeya. She moved with him, keeping her sword pointed at him. He swept his blade in fancy arcs and twirls so that the edge sung as it whipped through the air. Without warning, he charged.

Adeya dodged sideways as he slashed. She blocked another slash then turned aside a thrust. At his third slash, she leapt away. Oda's sword sliced the air where she'd just been standing. Grinning, he hung for a moment with his blade outstretched behind him at the end of its arc. He straightened as she edged around him.

Leaping forward, Adeya stabbed at his face, but Oda casually leaned out of the way. She twisted the thrust into a swipe, but Oda blocked it. Their blades locked together.

Oda pushed his weight against Adeya, but when she held firm, he grabbed her by the hair and wrenched. She gasped in pain. He pulled harder, forcing her head to crook at an awkward angle, and shoved at the same time. Adeya gritted her teeth and dug her feet in, fighting to keep her balance. Slinging Oda's sword aside, she kneed him in the groin—hard. He released her with a yelp.

Adeya backed out of reach.

Oda, doubled over, staggered out of range, muttering curses under his breath. He struggled to straighten up as he walked a few steps, glaring at Adeya.

Chuckles ran through the crowd.

The side of Gennen's face twitched as if with a smile, Wynne snorted, but Kyen looked grimmer than ever.

Adeya shook out her golden locks. Glaring back at Oda, she lifted her sword. She attacked before Oda could straighten up but he still managed to parry her blow. His blade flashed towards her face, and snicked her hair as she leaned away. He slashed again, but instead of aiming for Adeya, he connected their blades. Winding the two together in a rapid circle, he twisted Adeya's hilt from her grip and sent the sword flying. It landed in the dust with a thud.

She started after it, but he ducked in her way.

From the sidelines Gennen watched with narrowed eyes as Oda stalked Adeya into the corner. Kyen stood still beside him but for a muscle working in his jaw. Wynne glanced at them both, uneasy.

"Time to surrender, chitling." Oda grinned; he flourished his blade. "You wouldn't want me to put a scar on that pretty face, would you?"

Adeya, even swordless, fell back into a fighting stance.

"Suit yourself." He launched himself at her, still lobbing with a one-handed grip on his sword. Adeya dodged him. He swung hard, and with each swoop his blade flew wider and wider. She ducked then sidestepped then backed away. Her heel hit stone—the rim of the square. Oda slung out again with such force, the arc of the swing took his blade clear behind his back.

Adeya jumped into the opening. She grabbed his sword wrist, ducked under his arm, and threw all her momentum into the twist.

Oda gasped in pain. His body snapped taut as the wrench in his shoulder pushed it to the brink of dislocation. He tried to shift off the angle of tension, but Adeya, standing behind him with both hands gripping his wrist, twisted harder.

"Ow-ow-ow-ow-ow!" Oda's blade dropped from his fingers as he danced on tiptoes.

"Don't you *ever* dare touch my pretty face!" Adeya shoved him forward and snatched up his dropped sword. As Oda staggered to catch his balance, she ran and grabbed her fallen sword, too. She pointed both blades at him.

Oda, holding his shoulder, straightened. A shocked disbelief filled his face as he stared at her.

"Do you declare mercy?" she asked.

His disbelief morphed into anger. He started to charge her, but Adeya jabbed at his stomach with both blades, forcing him back. She backed him up to the rim of the sparring ring.

"Do you declare mercy?" she repeated.

Oda relaxed out of his fighting stance. A fidgety smile struggled to mask his anger.

"This is stupid," he said. "You're just a mainlander. Contests are only binding between Blades. Everyone knows that."

Throughout the crowd faces fell and scowls rose. Oda turned to leave the ring, but the warriors pressed forward to block his way. Voices rose from the crowd.

"There's no reason the tradition shouldn't hold."

"She is a bladepupil."

"Declare mercy or keep fighting!"

"You're honor-bound."

Many voices took up the echo of this last phrase.

"Do you declare mercy?" Adeya asked again, still pointing the swords at him.

Oda laughed, sweat standing out on his face. "What are you all even doing here?" he addressed the crowd. "You didn't really believe me, did you? This is just a farce. A practice run to benefit the mainlander. None of you believed this to be a serious contest, did you?"

The frowning faces in the crowd grew into glares.

"Either declare mercy or continue the contest, Odallyan," said Gennen with a smug smile. "Or your oath will carry no weight henceforth. You are honor-bound to the terms of the contest."

Growling under his breath, Oda turned to face Adeya. He stood straight and tall with a placidity that loosely veiled his mortification.

"Mercy."

"Really?" Adeya's face lit up. "I won? I won!" She beamed at Gennen and Kyen.

The blademaster gave her an approving nod, but Kyen looked disconcerted. Wynne leapt in the air with a shriek then bound over the stones to rush Adeya.

Adeya's eyes widened. She blocked with the swords and flinched away as if expecting an attack but Wynne pummeled her with a giant hug.

"You did it, mainlander! You did! You stuck it to Oda! I can't believe it!"

"Th-thank you?"

The tension melted out of the air. All the Blades began crossing the rim to join them, crowding and jostling past Oda. A sea of hands clapped Adeya on the back, pumped the air at her side, or ruffled her hair. She laughed and smiled like breaking dawn under all the rough attention. Wynne clutched Adeya with an arm around her shoulders, but even her high-pitched chatter went unheard in the babble.

"Can you believe it? A mainlander!"

"And only a bladepupil too!"

"Odallyan's so annoying. High time someone rubbed his face in it!"

"You'll not be a half-bad Blade! For a mainlander."

"You can keep my longsword, if you'd like, Lady Adeya."

"Three cheers for the Lady Adeya!"

"Huzzah!"

While the huzzahs continued, Oda stood apart from them with his arms crossed. He watched the throng around Adeya with a sour look.

"If I didn't know you to be an idiot, I'd say you threw the match." Inen stepped up beside him.

Oda scoffed in disgust. "How was I supposed to know to take her seriously? She's a mainlander—a mainlander!— a bladepupil, a chitling."

Inen turned narrowed eyes on Oda and stared until he bobbled uncomfortably on his heels.

"I mean, my lady Adeya." He growled out the words.

Inen smiled approvingly.

"Still," said Oda. "It wasn't a fair match. I was just toying with her. It doesn't mean anything."

"Your decisions in battle are yours," said Inen. "You'd be a better swordsman if you owned them."

"Whatever."

The huzzahs, which had continued far past three, grew louder. Adeya attempted to excuse herself and push through the throng but found herself hoisted up and carried on the shoulders of two large warriors. Laughing and smiling, she clung to them as they marched her out of the sparring area. She beamed down on Gennen and Kyen as she passed.

Gennen, looking supremely pleased, followed.

Kyen lingered behind. He smiled a little, but it didn't reach his eyes.

"No! Wait! Please, put me down!" Adeya laughed as they carried her towards the common hall. The crowd of Blades trailed after them. In the sparring square, Avanna children hurried over the rim to begin re-enacting the battle with wooden swords.

No one noticed when a figure crested the central stair and entered the city circle. Nobody noticed until his booming voice resounded in the air and killed the hubbub.

"Kyen, son of Odyen, of the House of Crossblade. I challenge the throne!"

All the Blades—Wynne, Oda, Inen, Gennen, Adeya, Kyen—all turned.

With a hand on his hilt, Ennyen stood, his dark eyes fixed on Kyen. The fiend caladrius swooped up the stairs behind him, a shadow flitting across the afternoon sky.

Chapter 37

Kyen seemed to sink where he stood.

Adeya paled. With a pat, she directed the warriors to lower her to the ground.

Gennen's bushy eyebrows drew tight together.

The fiend caladrius winged a circle to alight on a ruined wall. It settled itself, grinning down on them.

In the silence that fell, Ennyen walked to the middle of the circle.

"Blademaster Gennen, you will witness?" he said, his eyes not leaving Kyen.

"I will witness," said Gennen.

Adeya started forward, but Inen and Wynne barred her way with their arms.

"Don't interfere," said Wynne. "These are matters of Avanna. Our kingdom, not yours."

She gripped her amulet with both hands and watched, her aquamarine eyes bright. All the Blades behind them looked on.

Kyen, with a slump in his shoulders, with his head hung, walked out to meet Ennyen with every eye on him. He stopped just out of blade range.

"If you want the throne, you can have it," he said.

"The throne cannot be given, only taken. The Blades of Avanna will respect nothing less," replied Ennyen, drawing his sword. "Avanna is only honor-bound to the Blade who slays the heir."

"I will not fight you, Ennyen."

"Then, you will die." He flashed forward, closing the space between them in a blink, but Kyen only watched. The black blade glinted moments before it plunged into his body. It stabbed through Kyen's rib cage and punched out through his back.

Adeya covered a cry that escaped her mouth.

Kyen, jolting back a step, steadied himself, his jaw clenched tight.

Ennyen's frown deepened as he stared Kyen in the eyes. He whipped the blade free, flinging Kyen face-first into the cobblestones. His body hit the ground with a smack.

"Kyen!" Adeya started for him, but Wynne grabbed her wrist and yanked her back. She struggled against the swordswoman's hold. "Kyen!"

Gennen wore a grim set to his jaw, the light having left his eyes.

Kyen's arm slid along the ground for a moment as if he meant to get up. But then it fell still, and he moved no more.

After observing him for a moment longer, Ennyen stepped back and rose from his fighting stance. He whipped Kyen's blood from his blade with a flourish. Taking the edge of his cloak, he cleaned off what specks remained with great attention.

"Kyen." Adeya choked over a sob. Tears rose to her eyes and spilled down her cheeks. She collapsed against Wynne's arms crying.

Ennyen stepped over Kyen's body. Sheathing his sword, he addressed them, "Are you witness, blademaster?"

"I am witness," Gennen sighed. Without feeling, he proclaimed, "All hail Ennyen, son of Madiryen of the House of Dearthart, the King of Avanna."

"All hail, the King of Avanna." The Blades echoed him.

Gennen clapped a fist to his chest and moved to kneel, but before he could lower a knee, a moan drew everyone's attention.

Ennyen looked back.

Kyen's arm shifted again on the ground, drawing underneath him.

"No," he whimpered, curling up on his hands and knees. "Don't... Stop it!"

Gennen's eyes grew wide, and Adeya looked up from her tears.

Ennyen's dark gaze narrowed.

Kyen's body jolted as if struck. He gasped and tensed, nearly thrown flat to the cobblestones. With trembling arms, he raised himself up on his hands. All at once the tension left him, and he gasped. He hung his head. His back rose and fell with huffs that slowed and steadied until at last he drew in one deep breath. His fingers curled into a fist. Slamming it against the cobblestones, he screamed. Facedown into the pavement, his whole body contorted as the sound tore through him. His voice turned ragged as it echoed through the ruins.

Adeya turned the color of paper, her grip on the amulet as white as her face.

Kyen's breath ran out. His voice died into silence. It left him hunched over himself. His fist flattened out into fingers that pressed against the ground.

All at once, he shoved himself up to his feet. Staggering backwards a few steps, he caught his balance. Kyen faced them, his own blood staining the front of his tunic, his fists clenched at his sides. A haunted glare in Kyen's stormy gray eyes searched the circle until it found Ennyen. His face darkened.

Ennyen hefted his blade as if thinking.

Kyen coughed, gagged, spat out blood. He wiped his mouth on the back of his hand.

"I see I'll have to try that again," said Ennyen, unlatching his cloak. "My hand must slay you for the throne to be mine, but if your arcangel pulls a healing trick like that again, I will let Jezeru have his way with you both." He tilted his head towards the fiend caladrius.

Its grin widened as its faceless nub turned towards Kyen.

Kyen's trembling stilled. His face hardened into an black expression unfamiliar to him. His eyes never left Ennyen.

Ennyen slung his cloak aside. All at once he launched forward. A blur of dark limbs and flurry of black steel slammed into Kyen before the cloak could flutter to the ground. Not a single blow landed. The blade whooshed past Kyen on every side, pushing him backwards, but he ducked and dodged and sidestepped and danced around it. Avoiding the blade like the wind, he dashed backwards. Kyen suddenly slipped by Ennyen, tripping him with a kick to the ankle, sending him stumbling, almost falling, face-first to the pavement. He sprinted for the laundry area, and Ennyen whipped around.

Kyen veered amongst the cauldrons, heading for the common hall and yanking clothes lines down behind him. The posts and racks toppled into Ennyen's way, but he slashed them aside as they fell and leapt through, not slowed for a moment.

He turned to face Ennyen, still hurrying backwards as the swordsman chased him onto the portico. He slashed out, but Kyen dodged behind a pillar. Ennyen feinted first one way then another, Kyen jerking back and forth trying to anticipate him.

With a yell, Ennyen hacked into the pillar with a hard swing. The black blade bounced off the rock with a clang, and splinters burst up through the pillar. Kyen bolted, and Ennyen chased him as the pillar crumbled. A section of the portico roof collapsed in a spray of stone at their heels.

Pelting back towards the middle of the circle, Kyen headed for Ennyen's fallen cloak. Ennyen launched at him again, but Kyen slid to a stop, snatched up the cloak and lunged into Ennyen's attack, the blade grazing past him. Surprise registered for an instant on Ennyen's face. Kyen, whipping the cloak over Ennyen's blade, wrapped it in the crook of his arm, grabbed the crossguard, and slammed the palm of his hand into Ennyen's face. He tried to lean out of the way, but Kyen's hand still glanced off his cheek, unbalancing him. Kyen grabbed the side of his head and slung Ennyen sideways into the ground. Whipping the black blade out of the cloak, he flipped, grabbed it with both hands and raised it high over Ennyen. With a yell he stabbed down the moment Ennyen rolled to his back.

His eyes widened.

The blade froze a finger's breadth from his neck.

The two swordsman stared at one another: Kyen, panting hard, the black blade in both hands, pinning Ennyen to the ground with a knee on his chest; Ennyen, taking a few deep breaths, lay immobilized. The cloak fluttered to the ground behind them.

Kyen glared down at Ennyen for a long moment. His hands twisted on the hilt of the dark sword, every muscle in him taut.

Ennyen waited, but when nothing happened a small smile rose to his face.

The point of the dark blade began to tremble in Kyen's grip.

"Still can't do it, can you?" said Ennyen.

Kyen staggered backwards to his feet as if struck.

Hopping up to a crouch, Ennyen rose slowly.

"I won't kill you," said Kyen, still breathing hard. "There are few enough true Blades of Avanna left without your death, Ennyen. Our people need you, they need your sword. Stop this."

"Excuses," he replied. "You'll never be more than a spineless throwback."

He lunged. Kyen slashed out to force him backwards.

The strike lacked power, lacked speed, and Ennyen sidestepped easily. He ducked in as a black flash, entering under Kyen's guard for a fraction of a second. Kyen barely swung the sword free of his grasping hand and stumbled backwards.

Ennyen stalked around him.

"I will not kill you," said Kyen.

"Will not?" A dark smile rose to Ennyen's face. "Or can not?"

Every muscle in Kyen's body tensed up. He lowered his head, his hand clenching and unclenching on the sword hilt.

"You couldn't kill the thief either. What use is a Blade that cannot kill?"

With a yell, Kyen hefted the sword. Ennyen tensed and made to back away but Kyen hurled it as hard as he could. It skittered across the cobblestones and disappeared over the steps. The ring of it clattering down filled the air as they glared at one another.

The smile vanished from Ennyen's face.

"If you want the throne, take it. But I will not fight you any more," said Kyen.

Ennyen straightened up from his fighting stance.

"The Blades will escort you to the entrance," said Kyen. "Don't come back." He turned and strode away.

The Blades of Avanna watched, breathless and still. None of them moved.

"Who's going to follow you?" Ennyen's smile returned. "Kyen of Crossblade?"

The warriors stood by and watched Kyen walk past.

Halting, he faced them with eyes as hard and sharp as steel. "Do as I say!"

The Blades all looked at one another; no one moved.

"Do as he says," Gennen growled. "Escort Ennyen out of the hold."

Inen stepped forward. Oda and a few other Blades joined him. They surrounded Ennyen and ushered him towards the steps. Ennyen cast one last dark smile at Kyen before he allowed himself to be led away.

Chapter 38

Kyen distanced himself from the group of Blades. He stood, his whole body stark with tension, at the edge of the sparring ring. He stared into it with unseeing eyes. His fingers traced the thin gray scar showing through the bloody slice in his tunic. It was all that remained where the black blade had pierced his chest.

Gennen stopped behind him. Anger seethed beneath his hard expression and pale eyes. "Why didn't you kill Ennyen?"

Kyen's head drooped.

Adeya came up behind them both, her hands still gripping her amulet. The Blades of Avanna gathered to watch at a distance.

"You had him. You could have put an end to all this foolishness. Why didn't you?" said Gennen. When he received no answer, he growled. "Are you such a coward?"

Kyen's fingers left his chest as his arm dropped back to his side.

"Answer me!" The blademaster shouted.

"What does it matter?" Kyen said softly.

"What does it matter?" he snapped. "You're ready to hand Ennyen the throne—you'd put your people into his grip—and you say 'what does it matter'?"

He kept quiet.

"Where's your honor, boy?" said Gennen. "You used to have honor, but I'm not so sure anymore."

"With respect, blademaster." Kyen bowed his head towards the blademaster without looking at him and moved to walk away.

Gennen leapt in front of him. Drawing his sword, he brandished the point at Kyen, forcing him to stop.

"You will not walk away from me." The blademaster said, his voice low, threatening. "I should slay you where you stand. You've shamed me, you've shamed your people, you have shamed yourself, worse than any other prince in the history of Avanna!"

Kyen looked on him, his face impassive, his gray eyes dull.

"You don't deserve the throne," Gennen continued. "Only a spineless coward surrenders his people into the clutches of someone like Ennyen. Adeya would make a better prince than you. In fact, if something ever happens to me, I'm leaving her in charge!" He shouted the last bit aloud, sweeping his glare over the crowd. "Better her than you."

"Yes, blademaster," said Kyen, without heart.

This made Gennen begin growling under his breath. He suddenly slashed out at Kyen, striking him with the flat of his sword, sending him stumbling sideways.

"Gennen!" Adeya started forward.

"Stay out of this!" He shouted at her.

The harshness of his tone pinned her in place.

"I've had enough of your blockheadedness, boy!" he yelled. "I've tried words—oh, I've tried, but you are deaf. You are blind. And you're an idiot. Must I beat sense into you?"

Gennen launched an onslaught of swings at Kyen, but he dodged sideways to snatch up a river reed. Using it like a sword, he deflected and blocked Gennen's blows, but the white sword carved the pole down bit by bit with each strike.

Kyen, diving forwards, slung out with the reed and cracked the blademaster across the jaw. As he staggered, Kyen seized the white sword's hilt and ripped it out of his grasp. Gennen caught his balance to find himself at his own sword point.

Growling, he charged Kyen.

The white blade flashed in arclight.

The sword's point caught the blademaster across the face, and he staggered to the side. Looking up, he pressed a hand to his cheek and checked it. Blood emerged from a cut underneath his eye, oozing in a rivulet down his cheek.

Kyen, breathing hard and holding the white sword hilt-to-cheek, stared Gennen down. An edge of indifference—a hopeless, uncaring indifference—left a half-crazed light in his stormy gray eyes.

"Stand down," he said softly. "With respect, blademaster."

Gennen hesitated then slowly backed away.

Kyen lowered the sword.

"All you ever do is run," said Gennen. "Since you failed your Retributioner's Test—since you failed to finish Ennyen as duty, honor, and tradition all called you to. You quit on me. Now you run away with your tail between your legs like a beaten dog."

Kyen let the white sword fall to his side as he straightened, pain cracking through his indifference. "I'm not the only one who quit, with respect, blademaster."

Gennen's face fell, and all the anger sagged out of him. A weight of regret suddenly hung heavy from his shoulders.

"I didn't leave Avanna because of you," he said; with his next sentence, his voice raised to a shout. "I left because of them!" He pointed at the Blades of Avanna behind Adeya. They frowned or looked stunned. Wynne's eyes grew bright and her jaw worked.

"Because when you, Kyen, gave up," he continued. "That's all I had left to me. A rabble of honorless, bloodthirsty, selfish Blades with no idea who the real enemy even is anymore!" In a softer tone, he said, "At least I had the guts to come back, to take a stand, to try again at molding these Blades into warriors of honor. All I'm asking is that you do the same. Come back, Kyen. Finish your training."

Kyen's eyebrows furrowed for a moment, only to be lost in a rising exhaustion that stole the light from his eyes.

"There's no point anymore," he said. "Not with me."

For a long moment they looked at each other: Kyen motionless and slack; Gennen frowning and baffled.

"You're right about one thing, boy," he said. "You will never, *ever* be a Blade of Avanna."

Without a word, Kyen threw down the white sword. It hit the ground with a resounding clang. He turned and walked away, heading towards the ruins.

With a huff, Gennen marched to retrieve his blade then whirled around. Adeya moved aside and the Blades parted as he stomped off between them. The warriors drifted back to the common hall in his wake.

Adeya looked after Kyen. Down the street, he'd stopped, leaned against the wall with a hand. His other hand covered his eyes. She was about to start after him, but he turned the corner and vanished.

Tears rose to her eyes. Alone, she sat on the edge of the sparring ring, buried her face in her hands, and cried.

Chapter 39

Adeya's eyes were red and swollen from crying as she alighted on the middle landing of the staircase.

The Arc had sunk behind the mountains, leaving the ruined city in the dimness of twilight. Gennen sat on his block. He breathed out long clouds of smoke from his pipe and pressed a blood-spotted handkerchief to his face, all the while staring at where the golem once stood. A dozen Blades like toy figures camped in a semicircle around the canyon now. At the sound of Adeya's footsteps, he looked up.

"Can't find him, can you?"

"Wasn't looking," she said.

"Come. Have a seat." He scooched over and patted the block next to him.

She wandered over and slumped down beside him with a sigh.

Gennen took away the cloth from his cheek to examine the blood on it; the cut Kyen had given him stood out as a pink line beneath his eye.

"Would you like something for that?" Adeya asked.

"Nah." He smiled fondly on the bloody handkerchief. "It'll match the first one. Do you see it?"

She leaned in to look.

He ran his finger along a hairline scar, below his eye but above the new cut. "Kyen gave me this one, too. He was fourteen. First time with a steel blade. And I pushed him too hard." Gennen smiled a little. "He missed on purpose. Any other bladepupil would have taken out my eye. To this day, I'm a blazer if I know how he got under my guard." Taking a long draw from his pipe, he breathed out a *whuff* of smoke.

"He... he is the best swordsman in all Ellunon," said Adeya.

"Mm, could be," he answered. "If anyone can ever get through that blockhead of his..."

"Kyen's just not like you." She said. "He's not like any of you."

"Of course he's not!" The blademaster grunted and chomped on his pipestem for another draw. "He's a throwback. It makes him a nightmare to train."

"Why does everyone call him that?" She frowned at him.

"Because his blood remembers." Gennen drew in a long breath and let out a whirl of smoke. "All the people of Avanna are descendants from the greatest warriors of the Firstwold: Avannai and her brother, Tavai. But every few generations, a Blade is born who is unlike the rest of us. It's as if they've stepped out of the past, out of a time before the Breaking. As if they've come from the Firstwold itself. I've been called a throwback at times myself, and in my great grandfather's days, throwbacks were held in honor in Avanna. Now, though, most believe it makes you unfit to be a Blade. Makes you weak-hearted and soft."

"Is that what you think, too?"

"Me? I don't know what to think anymore. I took it upon myself to train Kyen, but now I doubt I'll ever finish." He sighed. "All his skill means nothing if he's too coward to strike."

"Kyen's not a coward..." she said weakly.

"Other Blades wouldn't hesitate to fell Ennyen if they could," he said. "But Kyen? He'll never be a Blade of Avanna at this rate. He'll never become anything if he keeps closing himself off. His sister, Kilyenne, knew how to talk to him. But since she died in the fall of Avanna, nobody can seem to reach him anymore." Gennen eyed her. "Well, almost nobody."

"Don't look at me. Kyen won't open up to me either," said Adeya.

"But he watches you."

She hugged her knees to her chest. "What good will that do? Ennyen will be back, won't he?"

"He will. And you'd better not meddle in their battle when he does. Ennyen isn't an idiot like Oda. You really wouldn't stand a chance." Gennen tapped out his pipe, stashed it in his coat, and sat back. "But, perhaps..."

"Perhaps what?"

"Perhaps, you can show Kyen what it means to have courage."

"But Kyen can't be a coward..." she said. "He's the Hero of Ellunon."

"Everyone is afraid of something, princess. But come!" Gennen rose to his feet. "I will do what I can for you, sworddaughter."

"More training?" Her face fell.

Gennen hopped off the block. "Time's short. The Blades and I depart tomorrow. And I'd like to leave you with a last lesson."

"But I'm sick of fighting! Hasn't there been enough for one day?" said Adeya, sidling off the block after him.

"No whining, princess!"

She sighed and lagged behind as the spry old man bounded up the stairs.

* * *

Adeya sat with Inen and Wynne on the portico surrounded by a chaos of goats, bundles, and blades. The people of Avanna slung packs on the larger livestock and strapped children to their backs. They hefted their burdens and tightened their boot laces. Bleating, crying, yelling and cussing filled the air while Adeya wrapped a fresh bandage around Inen's wounded neck. Wynne sat behind her, weaving her long golden tresses into a braid.

"You won't come with us, Lady Adeya?" asked Inen.

"No." She tied the bandage off. "Kyen and I are headed to Eope. You'll need these." She passed two rolls of bandage into his large paw of a hand. "Have Wynne change them out tomorrow and the next day, won't you?"

He nodded.

Wynne, a frown creasing her forehead, colored and

bent deeper over the last weaves of the braid. Adeya sat back, waiting for her to finish. She surveyed the milling crowd. Gennen approached Nella to take the pack from her shoulders with his usual scowl. The Blade who'd harassed Kyen tried to hold on to the lead lines of five goats pulling him in every direction at once. Little black-haired children dashed around or brandished wooden swords at the adults trying to scoop them up.

Adeya sighed.

"Are you well, Lady Adeya?" asked Inen.

"I am…" She looked over at him. "I was just wondering where you'll go."

"Who knows?" said Wynne. "Anywhere and everywhere!"

"We are nomads now, like the highlanders of Bishire," said Inen.

"Why not find a place to settle in Isea? The cities emptied after the arcangels fell silent," said Adeya. "If you speak to my father and offer him your service in exchange, I think he'd allow it."

"Keh! That sounds boring." Wynne tied off the tail of her braid. "There! Finished!" She seized Adeya by the shoulders and held her at arm's length to look at her. The elaborate braid started high on her head, weaving her hair into a golden coil that reached her waist.

Adeya patted at it. "Maybe now it'll stay out of my face! Is it beautiful?"

"Beautiful? You are a bladesister now—you're only as beautiful as you are deadly!" Wynne shook her by the shoulders, fixing her with an intense stare.

"If you say so." Adeya laughed.

Oda, shoving his way out of the throng, jogged up to them. "Are you done yet? Gennen said he wanted us on the vanguard an arcquarter ago!"

Inen rose to his feet.

Adeya moved to stand but Wynne seized her in a brief hug. "You're one of us now. Don't dishonor the name of Avanna, bladesister." She shoved herself away and, with a sniff, hurried off into the crowd.

Adeya, looking both ruffled and touched, stared after her in surprise.

"She likes you," said Inen.

"Goodness knows why! I thought she hated me." Coming to her feet, Adeya brushed out her skirts, stooped to sling her pack over her shoulder, and adjusted the longsword at her hip. She looked from Oda to Inen. "I don't suppose—you haven't seen Kyen have you?"

"No, my lady," replied Inen.

"Still hiding is he? Coward!" Oda scoffed.

Adeya sighed as she looked over the heads of the Blades and into the ruins. "I'm going to go look for him."

"You'd do well. There's a storm fixing to come down off the mountains." Inen shielded his eyes to look up towards the peak, and Adeya joined him. The head of the mountain, though always ringed by wisps, now hid its head in a thick swirl of cloud that was slowly spreading across the sky even as they watched.

"We should be alright," said Adeya. "Farewell, if I'm not there to bid you goodbye."

"May we meet again, my lady Adeya." Oda grinned

wolfishly; Inen elbowed him. "What?"

"May your blade always find its mark!" The larger swordsman put a fist to his heart and bowed.

"Thank you."

With a parting wave, Adeya set off through the crowd. She pushed through the throng—several of the Blades paused to stand aside for her—and she shimmied through a herd of goats. Exiting the crowd, she headed for the central stair. As she crossed the city circle, a dark, reddish splotch staining the paving stones caught her eye. Old blood. She paused for a moment to gaze on it. With a shudder, she hurried on. Descending the stairs, she passed from the top tier of the city down to the middle landing.

Gennen's block sat off to the side.

Empty.

She glanced at it. With a rueful smile, she started towards the steps and the bottom tier of the city.

A dozen Blades, leaning against the wall or sitting cross-legged on rubble, guarded the entrance to the canyon. They all looked at her as she reached the bottom pavement.

"You've not seen Kyen, have you?" she asked them.

The warriors waggled their heads.

Adeya sighed. She wandered away into the ruins. The Blades and the canyon disappeared behind high walls and broken-topped towers. A silence fell as she walked. She paused to look into the recesses of a dome, having to blink and peer hard into the darkness. Finding it empty, she moved on. She wandered down the street, towers rising high on either side. Ahead, the road ended at the sheer wall of the cliff.

Adeya huffed another sigh as she stopped in the middle of the street. She turned a slow circle, shielding her eyes and squinting up at the white ruins glaring under the afternoon Arc.

One of the towers, standing a floor higher than the others, lifted a cleaved side to the sunlight. A diagonal slice had severed the tower in times past, leaving only a lip of the topmost floor, half of the next, and a gape in the wall of the third. Over the rim of the middle floor dangled a boot.

Chapter 40

When Adeya's eyes found the boot, she smiled in relief. She approached the ruin and called up.

"Kyen?"

The hush descended around the dying echoes of her voice.

The foot hung limp.

Picking up her skirts, she clambered over the rubble of a fallen wall into the remains of the tower. Within, she met a stone stairwell, running back and forth into the dimness above. She climbed it, and after passing a couple empty floors, met the fourth floor where arclight flooded through a gash in the ceiling. She kept going one more floor. As her head emerged from the stairwell, she paused. Her skirts slipped from her hands, and her eyes grew bright.

Half the room had been cleaved off and arclight streamed, falling over Kyen's leg but leaving the rest of him hunched in the shadows. The one foot dangled over the edge, the other was drawn up to his chest. His black hair, beginning to grow shaggy, hung in his face and obscured his expression.

Adeya fingered her amulet. She mounted the last few

steps and stood looking at him.

He sat unmoving. A breeze from the mountaintop brought in chill whirls of breath that toyed with his bangs.

She approached him, trailing a hand on the wall, and lowered herself down next to him. She tucked her skirts beneath her legs against the wind.

In front of them, the absent wall allowed a visage of broken ruins, and beyond, the expanse of the mountains descending, and beyond that, the foothills until the haze of distance swallowed them.

Adeya glanced at him.

His chest slowly rose and fell beneath his bloodstained tunic. In the shadows of his face, his stormy gray eyes stared, empty, listless, unseeing at the floor. He didn't seem to notice her presence as she watched him.

Scooting up to where the floor ended, Adeya let her legs dangle over the edge. She leaned forward to peered down at the street. Her eyes widened at the drop, and she tensed. She popped up, straight-backed, hands gripping the stone, and stared fixedly at the distant landscape. Taking in a great breath, she sighed it out, sinking a little.

A cold wind swept across the ruined towers, singing softly through the crags and spires.

Adeya brushed a hand over her braided hair, patting for any stray bits that escaped, though none had.

Next to her, Kyen's gray gaze drifted towards her. He lifted his head to look at her, staring out of a languid daze. His eyes stopped on her hair. He watched as Adeya pulled the braid over her shoulder and stroked the long golden coil as she looked out over the distance. All at once, his gaze sharpened, his eyes widened for the briefest moment. He looked away.

Adeya caught the movement and glanced at him. She smiled.

He kept his eyes fixed on the ground; a muscle worked in his jaw.

Her smile faltered, but she tried to rally it when she said, "The Blades of Avanna are leaving. Won't you say goodbye?"

He leaned his head against the wall, staring over the drop off.

Her smile faded without a return. She smoothed a wrinkle from her skirt for a moment, before saying, "With the Blades and the golem gone, will we leave for Eope now?"

"I guess so…" said Kyen without looking at her.

Adeya sighed. She swung her legs back and forth a little bit. The cold wind swept over the tower, trying to catch at her skirt. She tucked it further underneath her.

Kyen's gray gaze inched sideways to fix her braid with a pained stare. "Did Wynne teach you that?"

"Oh, the braid? Yes." Adeya fondled her hair. "Wynne said it's the traditional hairstyle for swordswomen of Avanna, to keep hair out of the way in battle. Do you like it?" She smiled at him.

Kyen met her gaze evenly but didn't smile back.

Her face fell. She bristled and looked back over the distant landscape with an arch lift to her head.

Down below, the people of Avanna came into view. They milled around the entrance circle and the Blades standing guard merged into the crowd. Adeya watched them, swinging her legs while Kyen stared off into the distance again. A tremor ran through the crowd and they ebbed away from the canyon's entrance. A cascade of boulders pushed through the opening, spilling out into the pavement.

"Looks like the golem's returned," said Adeya.

Kyen started upright. He stared down as the boulder pile grew into a mound that blocked the canyon. His brows drew together.

Jumping to his feet, he bolted for the stairs and leapt down them, three steps at a time.

"Kyen? Kyen, wait!" She scrambled up after him.

He burst out on the street, sprinting hard. Adeya capered out behind him and ran after him, but he quickly outstripped her. He reached the entrance circle a full stone's throw before her, stopping at the edge.

The Blades of Avanna were still backing away from the canyon mouth. The mound of boulders began rising, crashing and clunking, as the golem formed up its body. It straightened, dragging the last few boulders from the crevasse. The rock serving for a head settled on its shoulders. The golem bent down swinging towards Kyen. In the place of a jewel's sparkle, a spread of grinning teeth glinted from a blacked gem.

Adeya, stopping behind him, squeaked when she saw it.

He started backing away, pushing her behind him.

From behind the golem's heels, a mass of dark bodies surged through the canyon. A horde of cougar fiends spilled into the square with a chorus of wails and chortles. The fiend caladrius swooped down from overhead.

The Blades of Avanna yelled. Drawing swords they charged, but Gennen's shouts cut above the war cries.

"BACK! Protect the women and children! Blades back!"

They stopped. As one they drew away into the ruins opposite Kyen. The children and elders followed Gennen's shouts into a half-ruined dome beside the circle. Fiends flooded after them, hedging them in, herding them inside. The golem, still crouched, lifted a foot above the black horde and reached out an arm after Kyen.

Seizing Adeya's hand, he whirled around and fled.

The fiend caladrius came swooping over the golem's shoulders and winged after them. Its shriek rang through the ruins, followed by the golem's earth-shaking footfalls.

Kyen sprinted down the street between the towers, Adeya struggling to keep up. Their arms stretched out, but he dragged her along without slowing.

A bam and a crash rumbled from behind them. The golem, plodding after them, had smashed an arm through one of the towers. The whole ruin thundered down in a mess of stone and rubble that cascaded around the golem's feet.

The caladrius fiend, bursting out in black fire, winged its way over their heads as they ran.

Ahead, the sheer wall of the cliff reared up. Veering sideways, Kyen slung Adeya into one of the side alleys. She ran up against the wall, rebounded off, and stumbled to keep her feet.

"RUN!" Kyen yelled, not looking back as he sprinted hard down the street.

Chapter 41

Thud after thud of the golem's footsteps shuddered up the ruined walls.

As Kyen ran, he reached into his pocket and pulled out the arcstones—only two left. He picked one that shone with a droplet of light like a bead. Up ahead, the sheer cliff of the valley cut off the road: a dead end. Reaching it, he stopped and whirled around.

The golem's foot slammed into the road, crunching the pavestones. One thunderous step after another, it loomed. Over its shoulder, the fiend caladrius flapped stationary in mid-air. Its faceless nub swiveled from him, to the alley where Adeya turned tail and ran, and back to him. Pulling in its wings, it dive-bombed after Adeya.

Kyen's jaw clenched as he saw it, but he had no time to react; the golem's towering body blocked his view. Gripping the arcstone, he slung out his arm as if throwing a javelin. A white shaft exploded into existence beside him and shot like a arrow at the golem's face. Its fist swung up to block. The ribbon struck the fist, bursting it to shards that reabsorbed into the golem's chest before they could hit the ground. It lowered its arm, its dark gem grinning down at

263

him. Another footstep shook the ground. The golem rose over him, its stones crushing and grinding ceaselessly.

Kyen looked at the arcstone. The shining bead had shrunk.

Suddenly, a chorus of war cries made him jump and reach for his sword.

Wynne, Oda, Inen, and Gennen vaulted out the ruins from his right. Swords drawn, the trio ran between Kyen and the oncoming golem, and Gennen stopped at his side.

"Save your aura, boy!" he said, hefting his white sword with a grin. "I've got a better idea."

"The fiend caladrius is after Adeya, blademaster," said Kyen.

Gennen's grin faltered. "Wynne, Inen, Oda, help the princess!" he snapped. "Leave the golem to Kyen and I."

"But—"

"Do as I say!"

The golem thudded to a stop, towering over them and raining pebbles.

"Got it!" Oda bolted away, calling over his shoulder. "Leaving you the easy one!"

With a growl, Wynne chased after him, and Inen jogged on her tail.

The golem lifted an arm of boulders over their heads.

"Think you can climb it?" Gennen grinned without taking his eyes off it.

"With or without being crushed?" asked Kyen.

"Heh! You scared, boy?"

The golem's fist hurtled down.

They darted sideways.

The fist smashed into the ground behind them with a spray of rocks and dust.

Gennen dashed around the golem's heels with Kyen trailing behind, both covering their heads against the raining stones. The golem's torso shifted to follow them.

"It's after me, Gennen," said Kyen. "All the fiends are!"

"Exactly, boy!" cried the blademaster. "Get it close to that tower!" He pointed down the road—to a tower with its ruined top exposed to the sky. He put on an extra burst of speed, running ahead, his voice carrying behind, "Tell your arcangel to slow it down when it gets near!"

"What? Ah!" Kyen ducked sideways as the golem's fist sailed down. He hit the ground at a roll, came up at a crouch, but not far enough. The boulder-fist smashed down on him. A flash of light cracked out to meet it, splitting a fissure up its center. The fist hit the ground in pieces, leaving Kyen unharmed in the middle.

He leapt up and scrambled through the rubble.

The golem pulled its arm back up, and all around Kyen the rocks and rubble began moving. He slipped and stumbled, clawing his way over them. The rising boulders caught him as they rejoined the golem's body. They began to squeeze together around him, but he shimmied himself free moments before they crushed tight. He leapt for the ground, landed hard on all fours, and shoved himself up to a run.

Behind, the golem's body shifted within itself, absorbing the broken shards of its old fist and bringing out from its chest a new fist—one twice as large as the first. Another footfall shook the street as the golem pursued him.

Sprinting hard, Kyen glanced back.

The golem swung at him.

He ran harder.

Its fist whooshed past his heels, smashed into the ground, and plowed across the street, ripping free dirt and cobblestones. The end of its swing crashed into a stand of broken pillars, toppling them all.

"Kyen!" Gennen waved his arm from the roof of the tower.

Gritting his teeth, he pushed himself faster.

The golem's footsteps thudded behind. One giant foot slammed down in front of him a little off to the side. Its next leg, grinding and groaning, rose right over his head. He veered sideways towards the tower.

The golem's leg smashed down in his wake like an avalanche of rocks from the sky.

Kyen tripped from the shock wave of its impact, but, catching himself on his hands, he push himself faster.

He slammed into the wall of the tower and turned, pressing himself flat against it as the golem neared. He panted hard for breath and swallowed.

"Closer!" Gennen yelled from above.

The golem loomed over Kyen as it stopped in front of the tower. It began raising its fist.

"Not close enough! I can't jump that far!" came Gennen's shout from above.

Kyen closed his eyes for a moment. When he opened them again, they blazed a brilliant gold. He looked up towards the golem.

The ground underneath its feet burst into vegetation.

Massive vines as thick as trees sprayed paving stones as they shot upwards. They weaved and entwined up the golem's legs, wrapped around its torso, and seized up its arm aloft in the air. The golem groaned to a halt, its joints jammed up with the leafy verdure. The vines spouted off tendrils and reached out to entwine the tower.

Kyen's gray eyes returned with a blink. He bolted, throwing away the spent arcstone in a shower of glass.

The vines enswathing the tower and golem alike suddenly constricted.

The golem slammed up against it. Its head bashed into the wall below the roof.

Yelling a war cry, Gennen took a running head start and leapt onto the golem's shoulders. It writhed when he landed, but he clung to the vines still curling over its body. He clambered across them until he reached the stone with the black gem. The teeth gritted and gnashed. Lifting his white blade high, Gennen stabbed down with both hands and a yell.

The blade glanced off the gem. A crack split the surface. The gem disintegrated into white sparks.

The moving and grinding of the golem's body slowed to a halt.

Kyen, backing away, craned his neck to look up as the golem stilled.

Golem and tower alike, lashed together, sagged against one another. Boulders began to fall as their forms started to collapse.

"Gennen!" Kyen yelled.

The blademaster turned back towards the tower but the

shoulders of the golem dropped out from under him. The lip of the roof soared upwards out of reach. Stones dropped and crashed, and the tower teetered, tipping over the sinking golem. They began to fall apart from the ground up, showering the street with rubble as they disintegrated. Gennen, half-clambering shifting stone, half-climbing through the verdure, made a grab for a vine and hung on. The golem's body lost all shape as its boulders toppled to the ground in a gnarly mass. The leaning tower crumpled as the boulders pulverized its base. In the landslide, Gennen's vine snapped. His white head disappeared into the rubble of the tower falling over the golem's remains. It hit the ground with a thud that blasted dust up and down the street. Every nearby ruin trembled.

"Gennen!" Kyen dashed into the cloud. The last boulder rolled to a standstill as he reached the pile. Mounting it, he frantically began ripping, dragging, and pulling rubble away.

Gennen's hand, still clutching his white sword, appeared underneath.

Kyen wrenched away a vine, then throwing his weight against a huge rock, shoved it aside. It toppled from the mound.

Underneath, Gennen coughed. He lay half-buried, with blood streaming from a knock on his forehead and from his nose.

"Blademaster!" Kyen knelt beside him.

Gennen, wincing at him through one eye, shoved him away.

"Leave off, boy! Go get the others to safety."

Kyen backed away. He frowned down on Gennen as the old swordsman struggled to pull himself free.

"I'm not some frail old grandpa!" He snapped. "Now go!"

Turning, Kyen ran. He headed for the alleyway where Adeya had disappeared. He paused at the entrance to glance back.

Gennen, dragging his leg loose, stumbled out of the pile. He glared at Kyen from across the street.

"GO!" he yelled. "You're wasting time!"

Kyen sped away down the alley.

Chapter 42

The golem's booming footsteps shook down bits of rock while Adeya pelted between the alley walls. Gasping for breath, she stole a glance over her shoulder.

The golem, towering over the ruins, had passed the alley. It lifted an arm high in the air.

The fiend caladrius swooped between them and grinned down at her.

Adeya paled and ran harder.

Overhead, the fiend drifted back and forth, following her from above as she ran. It outstripped her with a flap of its wings then circled back.

The alley opened into a street and, across it, a small staircase ascended to the middle tier of the city. Sprinting to it, Adeya scampered up the steps. An earth-quaking thud and crash from the golem sent her stumbling. She caught herself on the balustrade and half-pulled herself to the top of the stairs. She drew her blade and whirled around.

The fiend caladrius, bursting into black fire, dived at her. Princess and fiend collided—Adeya's sword swinging, fiend's claws outstretched—with a flash of blue light. The flash extinguished the fiend's aura. The sword struck and lodged in the fiend's body as it pummeled her into the ground.

Adeya landed hard on her back with a cry. The fiend struggled and flopped about on top of her, beating its wings and shrieking. Her sword, stuck in its body, wrenched back and forth, but she hung tight to the hilt, tugging to get it loose. Blacks feather whipped back and forth on either side of her. Half-sobbing, she wrested the sword sideways. It jerked free.

The slash left in the fiend's body by the blade sealed itself up. It regained its footing, trying to pin Adeya down. It poised its neck back, opened its jaws to strike, but several shouts made its head snap to the side.

Wynne, Oda, and Inen charged in with swords flashing.

While the fiend was distracted, Adeya lobbed at it. The strike, made awkward by close range, fell too slow. The fiend ducked and hopped backwards. With a shriek, it winged into the air. The Blades' swords arced high to catch it but the fiend flapped out of their reach.

Wynne seized Adeya under the arm and hauled her upright.

"Are you alright?" She glared at her.

"Yes—"

"Watch out!"

The fiend, circling overhead, roared into another ball of black flames. It dived.

All three Blades shied away, but Adeya stepped forward, hefting her sword.

The fiend squawked and tried to bank to the side, but Adeya's amulet flashed out again. Its light incinerated the dark aura. The fiend swung back out of reach and flapped above them. It gave off a shrill, shrieking wail as it frowned down on them.

"This way!" Wynne grabbed her arm, and the four of them fled. They followed the street as it skirted the rim of the middle terrace.

The fiend flew after them, swooping back and forth to keep pace.

"How did you stop its miasma?" asked Oda.

"My summoner's amulet shields me against fiends," said Adeya.

"Is that why it's after you? I thought the fiends were after Kyen!"

"Your guess is as good as mine!" cried Adeya. She squeaked and ducked her head as the fiend dive-bombed. Its claws just missed her hair.

But it didn't miss Inen behind her. He stood waiting, sword upraised. With a deft swing, he carved the bird out of the air, and its body smacked into the wall behind them as two pieces. Still, the fiend fluttered and shrieked and fumbled after them.

They sprinted away. Together they ran out onto the middle landing of the central stair. A crashing thud from lower in the city trembled the ground and brought Adeya to a stop. She looked back.

Over the tops of the ruins, the golem stood vine-bound to a tower on the bottom tier. As she watched, the golem's body lost shape, and the tower fell with a rumbling crash that echoed back and forth through the city. Her eyes widened.

"Kyen!" She started forward, but Wynne grabbed her arm to stop her.

"You're no help to him dead!" She nodded down at the canyon entrance.

The horde of fiends crowded and blackened the entrance circle below. A group pulled away from the main body to bound up the stairs towards them.

"Go!" Wynne shoved her forward.

Adeya ran after Oda and Inen as they crossed the platform. A ruined dome with half a roof rose to meet the lip of the middle tier. The warriors of Avanna crowded inside, blocking the entrance, fending off the pressing line of fiends.

Oda and Inen ran between a break in the balustrade and leap through the hole in the roof.

"Wait! Wait!" Adeya cried, but Wynne grabbed her wrist. She jumped, dragging Adeya with her, right into the front lines.

Wynne hit the ground at a crouch and sprang up to slash the nearest fiend; but the impact threw Adeya to her hands and knees. Oda and Inen slashed and hacked at fiends on either side of her.

"Back! Get back behind the line!" Wynne screamed at her.

Stumbling to her feet, Adeya cried out as a fiend lunged at her. She slashed it down, and Wynne whirled to help hack it to the ground. Leaving her to finish it, Adeya fled to the back of the dome, dodging and ducking through the battle. She reached the huddle of elders and children sheltered under the remaining roof. Despite their age, the oldest Blades stood at the ready with swords drawn. Adeya looked over the bulk of their force that crowded the dome's entrance, attempting to block the push of fiends. But even as she watched, the fighting milled deeper and deeper inside.

Movement from above caught Adeya's eyes. She looked up.

On the second tier, Kyen bounded up to the balustrade. His gaze swept the hordes of fiends, the Blades losing ground, the elders and children huddled in the back. His eyes found Adeya.

Chapter 43

"Kyen!" Adeya smiled and started towards him.

He held her eyes.

She stopped in her tracks as she took in the look on his face. Her smile faded. "Kyen?"

For one moment longer, his gaze fixed her in place; his expression hardened.

Adeya's eyes grew wide. "Kyen, no! Don't—!"

He took off running.

Down the stairs.

Straight for the fiends.

"Kyen!" She ran after him, but the crowd of the battle blocked her.

Outside Kyen neared the bottom of the steps. The fiends nearest turned their grinning teeth at the oncoming warrior. Their smiles spread wider, and they hunched down, tails whipping. He slung out both hands, and two ribbons of light exploded from the air over his head. They shot down the middle of the horde.

Kyen swung his arms wide.

The two ribbons slammed the horde apart, slicing limbs,

throwing bodies, and crushing them into the ruins. The fiends pressing the Blades all gave pause. Their grins fell, and together they turned on him, abandoning the fight against the Blades. They chased Kyen as he took off running straight through their ranks, pelting for the canyon. All around, the injured pounced on one another or bit into rubble to regenerate. Clambering to restored limbs and bodies, they sped after him as one. Their wailing and shrieking hit a higher pitch. Kyen vanished into the darkness of the canyon, and the black horde emptied the circle in pursuit of him.

The Blades inside the dome lowered their swords, watched the last of the fiends disappearing, and looked at each other in confusion.

Adeya took off running, shoving her way through them. "Kyen!"

"Stop!" Wynne grabbed her arm as she exited the dome.

"Let me go!"

"Chit—I mean—my lady Adeya! Wait!" Oda grabbed her other arm.

"But Kyen!" Adeya looked on them, her aquamarine eyes bright.

"Don't you see? He's drawing them off," said Wynne.

"Now's our chance to escape!"

"But Kyen!" She looked towards the canyon. The last fiend vanished into its mouth. Their ringing wails receded into echoes among the rocks.

"Sworddaughter."

The weak, throaty voice drew their attention.

Gennen, using his sword as a crutch, hobbled out of the ruins. Blood ran from his temple and his nose.

"Gennen!" cried Nella, pushing her way free of the Blades.

"Blademaster!"

They hurried to his side. Before they reached him, he dropped to a crouch, breathing hard. Nella fell to her knees beside him in time to catch him before he toppled to the ground. Oda and Wynne knelt at his side as Adeya helped her lower the blademaster to the ground.

"Stop fussing" —Gennen wheezed and coughed— "and listen to me." He thrust the white sword at Adeya. "Take it. Give it to Kyen."

"But—"

"Take it!" He snapped.

Adeya accepted it and hugged it to her chest.

He gripped her shoulder with a bloodied hand as he struggled to focus on her face. "It's up to you now, princess. His training—finish it."

"Me?! But—Gennen!"

The old man dropped back, limp and unconscious.

"Gennen!" cried Nella.

"Is he dead?" asked Wynne.

"No, but his wounds need attention," said Adeya. "But —but I can't—" Rising to her feet, she gripped the sword. She took a step towards the canyon.

"But, my lady Adeya!"

"Adeya, wait!"

She looked back.

"What do we do?" asked Wynne.

"Gennen left you in charge," said Inen.

"What?" Adeya's mouth dropped open.

"He said, if anything happened to him, we're to take orders from you," said Wynne.

"He said that in jest!" She cried with an edge of hysteria.

Oda, gathering Gennen's limp form onto his back, rose. He joined with Nella, Wynne and Inen as they looked to her. The rest of the Blades of Avanna began to gather around. The men, the women, the children: all looked at her. Adeya's aquamarine gaze took in all the dirty faces, the gray eyes, the black-haired heads. She drew herself up.

"As Crown Princess and Sole Heir to the Throne of Isea, hear my order," she said, her voice ringing through the circle. "Go to Isea Palace. Seek audience with the king. Tell him you've been sent by the Princess Adeya, seeking a new hold in exchange for the service of your blades."

"You won't come with us?" asked Wynne.

"No," said Adeya. "I have to help Kyen. But I leave you in charge."

"Me?" repeated Wynne.

"You, Odallyan, and Inen, all equally," said Adeya. "That means nobody is bound to obey you unless the three of you are all in agreement. Do you understand?"

"What?" Wynne flinched as if struck.

Inen looked as if he were struggling to understand.

"Right away, my lady Adeya," Oda saluted with a cheeky grin.

"Go! Before the fiends return!" she said. "Don't waste any more time!"

With that, Adeya whirled around and sprinted into the canyon.

Chapter 44

Kyen flew from the mouth of the canyon. His feet skidded as he hit the dirt of the path and bolted.

Fiends exploded out of the crevasse behind him. Shrieking and seething, the horde flooded onto the mountainside like a wave of black bodies.

Arms pumping at his sides, legs flashing over ground, Kyen glanced back. The forerunning fiends spread out. Their mouths leered as they gained on him, closing in from either side.

Kyen picked up speed. He reached the turn where the path descended along the top of the ridge. His feet pounded around the bend, slipping once in the gravel, but he caught himself on a hand and pushed himself faster. The fore-running fiends pounded at his heels.

The nearest lunged.

A spike of rock burst from the ground between, impaling the fiend midair. It shrieked and writhed, but several other fiends flashed past.

Kyen pulled the last arcstone from his pocket; its bead of power was the size of a droplet. Clenching his jaw, he gripped it and looked over his shoulder. The bulk of the horde overflowed the path behind him, gaining fast. His eyes flickered gold for a moment.

The path exploded into a mine-field of spikes. They jutted into the air, stabbing fiends off their feet, breaking up the surge of the horde and slowing them for a moment. The remaining fiends streamed around their impaled counterparts, two taking the place of every one that'd been impaled.

Kyen sprinted hard down the rest of the ridge. Ahead, the path met the cliff before diving down its face as the staircase. As he ran, he stole a glance at the arcstone. Only a pinprick of light remained in the center. With a grim set to his jaw, he put on an extra burst of speed. Pebbles flew as he ran for the stairs, but the fiends outstripped him on either side, pelting to reach the cliff first. He slid to a stop at the staircase and lunged down, bounding and scrambling down every zig and zag.

Fiends surged to the cliff top, colliding with the forerunners and knocking a few of them off the edge. Others leapt down headlong, their bodies dropping on either side of Kyen. He left the stairs at the bottom to find grinning fiends blocking the path. He veered off onto the ledge that spanned the breadth of the cliff.

The fiends growled and loped after him.

Extending a hand, Kyen dragged two fingers across the rock wall next to him as he ran. Light flashed from the line he marked. A deep thud through the rock followed. Fiends, running along overhead and outstripping him, leapt down to block the ledge's exit.

Kyen stopped, whipping his fingers away from the wall.

As he did, the arcstone flew out of his hand in a shower of glass dust.

Fiends crowded the cliff top, and several clambered down to join the growing crowd on either side of the ledge.

Breathing hard, Kyen sized up the fiends closing in from either side. The fiends in front leered at him and stalked closer. Those crowding the precipice overhead grinned down. Those behind watched him with lolling tongues. He backed to the center of the ledge.

A deep crack resounded from deep inside the cliff. Its top spat out a puff of dust in a long line, startling several of the fiends back. One ran forward anyway and leapt at Kyen from above. It pummeled into his back. They both tumbled to the ground and fell from the ledge. Kyen twisted to catch the lip, but the fiend dropped into open space. With a shriek, it plummeted.

Dangling from his arms, Kyen planted his feet against the cliff face. He started to hoist himself up but froze halfway.

A dozen grinning fiends crowded forward to meet him.

He glanced down.

The fiend thrown into the air hit the ground—a spray of giant boulders, sharp rocks and shale. A ragged tree stuck out an angle from the cliff side.

With a final look at the fiends, Kyen let go. He shoved off the cliff-face with his feet, propelling himself into the open air. He twisted around and free fell for the tree. His body hit the trunk, but the spindly tree bowed and snapped. He plummeted the rest of the way to the base of the cliff. He landed on the talus slope, toppling through the shale, and rolled up to a crouch amidst a small landslide. Winded and clutching his ribs, he pushed himself into a run. The fallen fiend charged out of the rocks after him.

The horde on the ledge let off a chorus of angry wails as it scrambled after him. They jostled their own over the edge in their haste. None heeded the bits of stone clattering down from the cliff top or the cascades of dust streaming down its sides.

When the horde swept onto the slope, it broke amongst the rocky, boulder-studded ground like black water over river pebbles.

Kyen fled ahead of them, weaving between the rocks. At the base of the slope, he vaulted up a house-sized boulder and clambered to the top to look back.

The entire horde filled the talus slope. Their wails rang back and forth through the valley.

Kyen's stormy gray eyes tracked along their approaching ranks to rest on the cliff face.

Another deep crack resounded through the earth. The ledge of the cliff suddenly exploded as the face of the cliff split away from the mountain. A sheer slab, it tipped forward. Its bottom splintered and the cliff sank into itself, crumbling as it collapsed.

Kyen turned and, leaping from the boulder, entered the trees.

An earth-shaking thud threw him off his feet and grew into a thunder of crashing stone that roared over the wailing of the horde.

He scrambled back into a run, stealing one glance back.

The cliff face had disintegrated into a landslide.

Boulders careened ahead of an avalanche of rock and dust. A great slab rode the center of it, pulverizing everything on the talus slope as if it were made of clay. The horde's shrieking changed to wails of terror as the landslide bit into its rear flanks. They tried to escape off either side of the slope but the mass of crashing stone engulfed them.

Kyen pelted through the trees; trunks flashed past. The ground quivered under his feet, and the roar intensified to a deafening pitch. A handful of fiends reached the forest behind him, escaping as the landslide swallowed up the others and slowed at the base of the hill.

The trees parted, and Kyen burst out onto the sands of the glittering lake. He stopped at the edge of the water and looked back.

The remaining fiends burst out of the trees in pursuit. They stopped when they saw him, their grins stretching wide.

Several boulders, the last of the landslide, crunched into the grove behind them, shaking and toppling trees. In their wake, the largest of all—a great slab-like tower—collided with the boulder at the bottom of the slope. The boulder splintered to bits, and the slab catapulted upright, crumbling as it cleared the treetops.

The fiends poised to pounce.

Kyen watched them with a grim set to his jaw.

A shadow fell over them all.

Like a falling pillar, the slab slammed down on Kyen and the fiends. Its furthest rocks hit the surface of the lake, throwing out a spray of water. A tidal wave of dust, brought down by the landslide, engulfed everything.

Chapter 45

The clack and clatter of the last falling stones filled the dusty air. The slab lay like a broken obelisk across the beach, still and silent.

In the quiet that followed, the dust settled. The Arc, deepening from yellow to orange, hung low between the stormy mountain peaks. Its light shimmered weakly on the water, overtaken only by the distant flash of lightning in the roiling clouds above.

Between the largest crack in the obelisk, rocks shifted and tumbled loose. Kyen clambered out, pushing free of the broken stone. He staggering down to the sand and dropped to his hands and knees. He sat, head hung, his breath coming in and out as great gasps. Slowly, his breathing steadied, and, after a moment, he slouched back and looked up at the sky. Exhaustion lined his face.

"Still running?"

The exhaustion in Kyen's face deepened as he lolled his head over to look.

Ennyen stood a stone's throw down the beach. The remains of a low campfire burned in a little shelter of trees behind him. He smiled, crossing his arms, but it didn't change the grim look of satisfaction in his dark eyes.

Still trying to recover his breath, Kyen sank where he sat and looked away.

Ennyen approached, drawing his dark blade. He stopped within easy slashing distance, but Kyen made no move. His hand lay limp next to his side, next to his empty belt—the spot where his sword used to be tied.

"You'll never be one of us," said Ennyen. "Your father should have cast you back to the Arc before you ruined us all—throwback!"

Kyen lifted his face as Ennyen pointed the black blade at his throat. He watched, unmoving, his gray eyes tired.

A yell from the trees caused Ennyen to snap his blade towards the sound.

Adeya charged out, swinging Gennen's white blade.

Kyen's eyes widened.

Ennyen lunged to meet her.

Kyen bolted up to stop them, but Ennyen struck like black lightning first. She cried out, struggling as she caught the first few strikes, and stumbled backwards. His blade flashed out a third time, but Kyen tackled him from behind. Leaping onto his back, he seized Ennyen in a headlock and wrenched him away from Adeya. The two swordsmen staggered backwards together.

Ennyen grabbed Kyen's arm. Ducking down, he threw Kyen over his shoulder and flipped him into the ground. He hit the sand flat on his back. Ennyen stabbed down, but Adeya lunged in and slashed at him, forcing him to change his stab to deflect the white blade.

Ennyen launched himself under her guard.

Kyen rolled and grabbed his ankle.

He jerked to a stop, his blade slicing a finger's breadth from Adeya's throat. She cried out and staggered backwards. Gripping the white sword, she thrusted for his stomach.

Ennyen kicked Kyen in the face and turned aside her blade at the same time.

Kyen dropped back to the sand.

Ennyen swung at her, and Adeya, backing away, tried to block, but he'd aimed the force of his blow at her sword. It knocked her blade wide. He flashed forward, grabbing the base of her sword with his bare hand. With his other, he stabbed. Adeya ducked backwards to avoid it, but Ennyen yanked at the same time. He plucked the blade from her grasp like a toy from a child.

With a face impassive, he hefted the white sword and threw it into the lake. It vanished into the shallows with a splash. He strode towards Adeya, blade pointed at her. She backed up as fast as she could without turning to run.

Kyen, nose bloody and groaning, rolled onto his hands, facedown in the sand. He was struggling to get up, holding his head, and failing.

"I warned you, maiden," said Ennyen, pointing his longsword at her one-handed.

Adeya clenched her trembling fingers, trying to take in a couple deep breaths. Then, she charged him.

Ennyen eyed her coolly. When she neared, he struck down on her, his blade flying from above like a black bolt out of the heavens. Adeya grabbed him by the wrist, ducked underneath his arm, wrenching his sword-hand as she went. His eyes narrowed; he shifted his weight and twisted around with her to keep her from getting leverage. He whipped his sword-hand out of her grasp, swung back, and stabbed.

The blade plunged into her belly.

She jolted and gasped.

Kyen, still on the ground, froze where he lay in the sand.

The bloody tip of the black blade protruded out of Adeya's back.

"I warned you," Ennyen told her.

Lightning cracked and rumbled overhead.

He shoved Adeya off the blade, and she dropped. Falling to the sand, she gasped, clutched at her stomach, and writhed on the ground. A bloodstain was spreading over her shirt.

Both hands under him, Kyen lifted his gaze from Adeya to Ennyen. His expression hardened; his stormy gray eyes blazed to life. He shoved himself to his feet and dashed for the lakeside.

Ennyen, returning his attention to Kyen, darted after him. He hefted his dark sword in both hands, preparing to strike.

Kyen dove for shallows. He hit the water with a splash, rolled, came up with the white blade in hand and lunged at Ennyen. Water sprayed everywhere. The white blade became a flashing blur, whipping and singing around Ennyen. Loud clangs of steel on steel reverberated out over the lake. The flurry pushed Ennyen back first one step then another across the shallows.

In the next moment, Kyen yelled and beat on Ennyen's defending sword. Ennyen dodged first one direction then the next, all the time giving ground as Kyen's onslaught pushed him through the shallows of the lake.

Ennyen suddenly ducked in. He flashed past Kyen and their swords blurred together with a clang.

A line of blood spattered the water as a cut opened on Kyen's thigh. He dropped to one knee with a splash. Ennyen, having dove past Kyen, whirled to strike down on his exposed back. Kyen leapt sideways, the black sword slicing through the water behind him. He came up to meet Ennyen bashing down on him, blocking and parrying. Trying to avoid an overhead slash by Ennyen, he staggered backwards to his feet. But the slash was a feint. Ennyen swept his sword wide only to whip it back in at close range. He cracked his hilt across Kyen's jaw.

Kyen fell face-first into the shallows. He caught himself on his hands, pushing himself away, as the black blade flashed down and just missed him. He stumbled upright and limped backwards out of range.

The two swordsmen stood looking at one another, panting. Kyen's leg bled. Ennyen's breast-plate hung dented and askew. A long cut opened under his eye; it loosed a drop of blood that slid down his cheek.

Ennyen eyed Kyen, his expression menacing.

Kyen glared back, undaunted.

Adeya whimpered from where she lay curled up, bleeding on the sand.

Lightning flickered overhead, but no thunder followed.

"The Prince of Avanna," said Ennyen. "Blademaster

Gennen's prodigy. The legendary Hero of the Black War. Now, the last summoner. So many names, but all you've ever been is a spineless throwback."

Kyen wiped blood from his lip with the back of his hand, his fierce gray gaze never leaving Ennyen.

"You know, Kyen, you could never hide it from me. How much you hated all the rest of us." Ennyen, hefting his blade, stared him down as he approached again, splashing through the shallows. "I know you had the arcangel with you. The night Avanna fell, they say you stood at the Longbridge. Watching."

"You don't understand anything," said Kyen; he shifted his stance to raise his blade high, hilt-to-cheek.

"You could have done anything with that arcangel, but instead you stood there. Did you enjoy it?" Ennyen smiled mirthlessly. "Standing on the Brink and listening to them scream? Your father? The Councilmen? How about Ludyen of Silvertalon? He used to beat you and leave you in the alleyway behind the training hall. Did you smile as you watched it all come to ruin?"

Chest heaving for breath, Kyen said nothing.

"Our people must have been trying to flee across the bridge as Avanna was sinking. Did you smile to see the terror on their faces? Heh! Did you cut them down one by one?"

"Don't say anymore." Kyen's fist clenched his hilt till it turned white.

"You could have saved them. You, the last summoner, Crown Prince of Avanna, could have saved them all." Ennyen's smile faded as his eyes narrowed. "But you. Just.

Watched."

Kyen grew very still; the ferocity on his face deepened.

Ennyen charged him with a yell. He collided into Kyen with a glint of steel.

Kyen flashed past Ennyen's blade, darted under his guard. His steely gray eyes glared; Ennyen had a fraction of a second for the surprise to register on his face.

Blood spattered.

The white blade split Ennyen from forehead to chest.

Yelling raggedly, Kyen whipped his sword free, slinging Ennyen's body into the shallows.

Chapter 46

Kyen stood over the body, breathing hard, shuddering from head to toe. Droplets of blood had spattered up his face. It dripped down the length of the white blade. It oozed like ink into the water around his knees. He staggered backwards, splashing away from the floating corpse.

He limped back to the beach but when he reached the dry sand, Kyen sagged to his knees. Burying his face in both hands, he hunched. Silent sobs wracked through his bowed form. Breathing raggedly, Kyen lifted his head. He struggled back to his feet and hobbled over to Adeya.

She lay on the ground, pressing a wad of her cloak up against the bleeding wound in her stomach. She tried to rise as Kyen approached but she collapsed back with a cry of pain. Curled on her side, she whimpered as tears started streaming down her cheeks.

Inside the glove of trees, a fiend appeared—a shadow among the shadows. The storm clouds had thickened overhead, churning, blocking out the Arc. The fiend lifted its head back and sent an unearthly wail up to where the lightning flickered. As the sound resonated through the valley, the fiend sat down as if to watch, grinning, while

Kyen struggled towards Adeya. His wounded leg crumpled underneath him before he reached her. Dropping the white sword, he crawled the last span to her side.

"I'm sorry," he said. Bowing his head, he gathered Adeya into his arms and onto his knees, propping her up. She tensed and gave a little cry as he moved her.

"I'm so sorry," Kyen said.

"Kyen—" Adeya whimpered and choked, struggling to breathe. Her aquamarine eyes stared into his, bright with pain and fear.

Kyen took her face in his bloody hand and leaned in close.

"Go to Finn at Castle Veleda, Adeya," he said quietly; Kyen's stormy gray eyes fixed hers in earnest concern. "Do you understand? Go to Finn at Veleda."

Adeya frowned a little but nodded, struggling to choke in another breath.

More howls rose in the distance. Several more fiends arrived to sit with the first. They waited with their toothy grins turned towards them, but they made no move to approach.

Kyen reached for Adeya's stomach. He gently moved her hand that was pressing her cloak into the wound. Closing his eyes, he placed his fingers over the bloody pool in her gut.

He drew in one deep breath and let it out slowly.

Adeya gasped. She tensed up on herself. She gripped his tunic hard as several sobs of pain escaped her. All at once she relaxed, breathing hard with sweat standing out on her face.

Kyen opened his eyes. He took his hand away, and when he did, only whole skin—still blood smeared, but whole—remained.

She lifted her wide eyes to Kyen, searching his face, and feeling where the wound had been with her hand.

Kyen looked on her sadly. He pressed his palm to her forehead and closed his eyes.

Adeya's eyes flew wide. "Kyen... No... Don't—" Her grip on his tunic slipped loose. Her eyes rolled back into her head, and she fell limp in his arms.

"I'm sorry." Kyen gripped her more firmly to keep her from falling. She dangled, breathing, unharmed, but fainted clean away. He lowered her down and laid her on the ground.

Reaching over, he unlatched her healer's pouch and took out the last arcstone from inside it. It shone like a light in the dimness, filled to the brim with aura. Then, he stretched to grab the white sword and dragged it over.

The voices of the fiends rose again, this time from all around, howling in a frenzy. They continued to emerge from the trees to join the growing ranks, their shapes hard to distinguish under the storm's darkening.

Kyen, taking up the corner of his cloak, slowly wiped Ennyen's blood off the white blade. He put the sword back in its sheath and laid it at Adeya's side. Then he unlatched his cloak and covered both with it. For a moment, he watched Adeya, curled up on the ground as if in sleep, breathing easily. Then, he tugged up the cloak to cover her face.

Lightning flickered again as he stood.

Turning away, he looked to the lines of fiends waiting in the trees, all watching him. Pocketing the arcstone, he stood. He limped towards them, leaving Adeya behind, lying unconscious on the sand. He walked with a hobble. With every slow step, the barest amount of weight made his leg buckle, but he kept going.

Lightning flickered—blazing white cracks splitting the stormy sky. The flashes illuminated for a moment the line of dark forms and their with grinning, glinting teeth. Waiting.

Kyen looked at them with his gray eyes, with a grim set to his jaw. Drawing a deep breath, he bowed his head and limped on to meet them.

Again, fissures of lightning crawled through the clouds. Its final flash exposed the horde of fiends and, in their midst, a woman's dark silhouette waited with the caladrius fiend perched on her shoulder.

Epilogue

"Aaargh!!!"

Finn's scream echoed through the rafters of the feasting hall at Castle Veleda. He slumped back in his chair, rubbing a hand through his flaming red hair.

Beuwell, the royal counselor, stared over the grain report in his hands. He started to open his mouth, but Finn's hand shot up.

"No—more—numbers," he said through clenched teeth. "Please!"

"Yes, prince." Beuwell rolled up the parchment.

"I'm sorry." He huffed a sigh. "Come back in an arcquarter. We'll finish, then, yes?"

"Yes, prince." The counselor bowed and moved to leave.

Finn watched him go, propping his chin on his fist with a sigh. "I wish Kyen were here. I need to get out of this place…"

As Beuwell reached the for door, it banged open. He started back, and Finn straightened in his seat as a guard hurried inside.

"S-sire? Pardon the intrusion, but—but—"

Finn frowned.

From behind the guard, a young woman shoved her way into the hall. She staggered a little as her haunted eyes searched the space. Dried mud and blood smeared her slashed blouse. Twigs and pine needles stuck out of her ragged golden braid. Clean streaks ran from her eyes where the dirt on her face had been cried away. She clutched a white sword to her chest as she swayed.

The guard put out a hand as if ready to catch her.

Her aquamarine eyes came to rest on Finn. Tears bubbled to their surface.

Finn started out of his chair as she staggered toward him. The woman collapsed and fell sprawling to the floor stones before he could reach her. The sword slid out of her arms with a clatter.

Finn dropped to his knees beside her.

"Get the apothecary!" he snapped at the guard. "Quickly!"

* * *

Finn leaned against the doorway where his ten sisters clustered and watched. The young woman who'd collapsed had been taken to the bed chambers of Clarissa, next oldest to Finn. Cleaned and clothed in a white night shirt, she lay unconscious beneath the covers with her gold hair spilling over the pillow. The apothecary sat at her bedside mixing herbs while a maidservant bathed her brow. Finn crossed his arms, frowning as his sisters whispered in the doorway.

"Who is she?"

"She's so beautiful! Is she a princess?"

"She looks like she's been in trouble."

"Is she dying?"

"She's just exhausted," said Finn.

"Where do you think she came from?"

"Are you going to marry her, Finn?"

"No."

"You should kiss her. That cures all the princesses in the fairytales."

"Are you sure you're not going to marry her?"

"That's it! Out! All of you! Go!" Finn, turning bright red, waved at his sisters.

The girls scattered, tittering to themselves and sending secretive smiles over their shoulders.

Finn stood in the doorway, huffing and blushing, and growled after them. An older man with a thick red beard came up, chuckling.

"Don't mind them, son," he said. "How is our guest?"

They both looked in through the doorway.

"She's not wounded in any way, my king," said the apothecary. "Just fainted away, probably from exhaustion."

"The guard said she was carrying this. He picked it up from the floor." The king held out the pale sword.

Finn took it and unsheathed it partway. His eyes grew wide as he examined the keen silvery-white blade, the supple gray leather of the hilt, the elegant swoop up to the pommel.

"Wow." He resheathed it. "Enchanted, do you think?"

"It wouldn't surprise me."

"Sires?"

Both the king and Finn looked back through the doorway.

"She's stirring," said the apothecary.

The woman's eyes fluttered and opened. She gazed, unseeing at the far side of the room for a long moment. Then she bolted upright, scaring the maidservant into toppling her bowl and the apothecary to fumble his herbs. She looked from them, to the king, to Finn, and burst out crying.

"Easy, my lady, easy." The maid dabbed at her head, but the woman only waved her away, crying too hard to speak.

"Leave us," said the king.

The nurse and the apothecary rose and exited the room, shutting the door behind them. Finn took the apothecary's vacated seat. He and the king watched with concern as she cried, her hands twisting and untwisting the sheets. With an effort, she tried to swallow her sobs and looked up with puffy red eyes first at the king, then to Finn.

"Did I make it?" she asked. "Is this Veleda?"

"Yes," said the king. "You're safe here."

"I made it..." The tension melted off her shoulders. "I'm Adeya, Crown Princess and Sole Heiress to the Throne of Isea."

"I thought you seemed familiar," said Finn. "I saw you with Kyen at Isea?"

At the mention of Kyen, heavy tears welled into her eyes. "Oh, you have to help me rescue him! He tricked them with an arcstone and—and—" She curled up on herself, crying into her own lap with her face buried in her hands.

"What happened?" Finn scooched to the edge of his seat, looking at her earnestly, but she only sobbed harder, her voice muffled by the sheets. He exchanged a concerned look with his father. "Where's Kyen? Did something happen to him?"

Adeya nodded into the sheets, sobbing.

"That's not good. The fiends were after—after—you know. You don't think..." Finn and his father shared a silent look of understanding. "They couldn't have gotten *him*, do you think?"

"Arc help us if they did," said the king.

"I know." said Adeya, her muffled voice.

Finn and the king looked at her.

Her sobs began to calm. Her hands unclenched the sheet. She sat up, still giving little sobs and gasps. "I know. You don't have to tell me. I know!" She sniffed, her eyes a little unfocused.

The king cocked an eyebrow, and Finn frowned.

"Princess?" He edged towards the bed.

"Huh?" She looked up at him and blinked.

"Princess, where's Kyen's arcangel?" Finn asked.

The question made tears rise again to her eyes as she said, "Kade's with me."

Don't Miss the Continuation in Book 3!

Illeth's Keep

(Join the Mailing List at arclegends.com!)

If you enjoyed *The Prince of the Fallen Kingdom*, please support Arc Legends by leaving a review on Goodreads or your favorite book retailer!
Thank you!

About the Author

C. A. Doehrmann, an avid writer of sword and sorcery fantasy, loves strong characters, deep adventures, and smash-down, drag-out fights. You can find her writing at arclegends.com where she shares bonus chapters, side-quests, sneak previews, and announcements.

Connect

Website: arclegends.com
Twitter: twitter.com/thearclegends
Email: thearclegends@gmail.com

Made in the USA
Columbia, SC
02 September 2022

66562711R00170